MISS *you* LOVE *you* HATE *you* BYE

ABBY SHER

SQUARE FISH

FARRAR STRAUS GIROUX · NEW YORK

SQUARE
FISH

An imprint of Macmillan Publishing Group, LLC
120 Broadway, New York, NY 10271
fiercereads.com

Square Fish and the Square Fish logo are trademarks of Macmillan and
are used by Farrar Straus Giroux under license from Macmillan.

Our books may be purchased in bulk for promotional, educational, or
business use. Please contact your local bookseller or the Macmillan Corporate
and Premium Sales Department at (800) 221-7945 ext. 5442 or by email
at MacmillanSpecialMarkets@macmillan.com.

Library of Congress Control Number: 2018057872
ISBN 978-1-250-76285-6 (paperback)
ISBN 978-0-374-30702-8 (ebook)

Originally published in the United States by Farrar Straus Giroux
First Square Fish edition, 2021
Book designed by Elizabeth H. Clark
Square Fish logo designed by Filomena Tuosto

1   3   5   7   9   10   8   6   4   2

For Grano
you're an amazing friend
thank you for putting me in my place

and when we speak we are afraid
our words will not be heard
nor welcomed
but when we are silent
we are still afraid

So it is better to speak
remembering
we were never meant to survive.
—AUDRE LORDE

TABLE OF CONTENTS

October something.
All I know is it's Tuesday.
And I know that because it smells like tacos
even though it's only 8:30 in the morning.
Yum ☹

My dearest Hank,

Greetings from the loony bin!
   Wish you were here!
   Just came back from the shuffleboard court and have but moments to spare before my personal masseuse visits me. Did I mention that each morning I'm greeted by a chorus of delicate sparrows, I've learned how to windsurf on a rainbow, and everyone here is heavily sedated on stiff doses of antipsychotics?
   Yeah.
   I know it's been a while and we never really got to say goodbye properly. I also know you're the reason why I'm stuck here and I'm feeling all sorts of ways about that.

   Just to be clear, I will always love you.
   But more than that,

   my dearest Hank,
   I HATE you.

CHAPTER 1
pepe le meowsers

I STILL DON'T CONSIDER MYSELF A CRUEL PERSON. BUT I DID HAVE a moment—or really, several—when I was ready to strangle that cat.

Zoe says that Pepe le Meowsers *chose* her. Her mom joined some mega-gym-spa that had just landed in our town. Zoe went for a tour and on the bulletin board she saw a note about a litter of newborn kittens that were available for adoption. It said if they didn't find homes soon, they'd most likely be put to sleep. By the end of one fateful Zumba class, Zoe was caught in a herd of women, all doing cool-down squats around a plastic crate with five squirming tabbies. As she said, maybe it was just from over-exertion, but when she saw how tiny and fuzzy and malleable these small creatures were, she felt faint. She literally *swooned*.

"I mean, what the what? I'm not even a cat person," she reported to me twenty-four hours later as I sat in her basement. Actually, Zoe wasn't talking just to me. She was declaring her newfound feline love to the world—perched on a metal stool in front of a sky-blue fitted sheet. I was holding her phone, filming her testimonial and trying desperately to stifle a sneeze.

"There was just something so *primal* and yet indescribable connecting us in that moment," Zoe recounted. "I don't know. All of a sudden, I was lying on my back and the whole gym was sort of turning this peachy-sunset color and fading away. And then . . ."

It was as if Pepe knew she was in distress. Apparently, he leaped over the side of the crate and risked his life tripping on a StairMaster machine, then scrambled up Zoe's arm, gumming her face, pawing at her eyes. She still had the tiny pink scratches to prove it. Three jagged lines etched into her left cheek. She also had a splotch of blush on her nose and whiskers drawn on her face in what looked like navy eyeliner.

Zoe Grace Hammer and I had been best friends since our moms bumped into each other while pushing us in strollers. Or at least that's how Zoe always relayed our past. She also claimed that we hid in the bathroom at nursery school and ate blue Play-Doh, but I have no recollection of that. I think that was either told to her or she made it up. Which I guess is the definition of anyone's history, really.

I do not remember how Zoe and I met. Only that she was there, with her sparkling green eyes, already laughing. Waving her hands at me from across the room as the morning bell rang on our first day of kindergarten. She had already dumped out all the wooden blocks onto the carpet for circle time and was using the empty toy bin as a boat. Her first-day-of-school dress was a patchwork pattern of every color in the rainbow. It was also tiny enough to fit a doll.

"Come here!" Zoe beckoned. "I'll save you from the storm!"

Even though I had no idea what she was talking about, I heeded her call.

Our friendship didn't grow or evolve. It was instantaneous. While the rest of our kindergarten class made their introductions, Zoe nested me in her lap, trying to tame my curly hair into a semidecent braid. Two hours later, she presented me with a pact of undying bestfriendhood. Of course, I said yes.

I learned how to sing from Zoe.

I learned how to do a cartwheel from Zoe.

I learned how to melt broken crayons and sneak jelly beans in the sides of my cheeks from Zoe.

All vital skills that made my life feel more colorful and vibrant than ever before.

When Zoe came to play at my house, my mom liked to say that she "brought the party with her." She always had matching Froot Loops necklaces or glitter tattoos that we had to put on right away. She would kick off her shoes and twirl me around and before I knew it, we were mixing ingredients for slime or having a naked dance party in my room or both at the same time. Zoe was pure electricity—darting and leaping everywhere, because walking was too predictable and slow.

To be honest, I preferred going to Zoe's house—with a drawer just for Fruit Roll-Ups and framed Disney pictures everywhere. Her bedroom had so many pillows and ruffles, I felt like we would both float away on a unicorn sneeze or tumble into a vat of cotton candy. Everything was enchanted. Especially Zoe. She was an Irish firecracker, with stick-straight ebony hair that shimmered and huge eyes that took in everything. Her nose was barely bigger than a thimble. As an infant, she'd been the cherubic face of BabyFresh Ultra Diapers and made a buttload of money in some car commercial about antilock brakes. Also, she got to sing the jingle for IPopUPop microwave popcorn and traveled to fifteen states with the national touring company of *Annie 2*.

There was a whole photo album of her commercial work in her living room, but Zoe didn't like to talk about it much. She once told me that the day she met me was the day she decided she was done running off to auditions and memorizing tap dance routines. She just wanted to stay home and be *a plain ol' kid, like you*.

Which I chose to take as a compliment.

I'd always wanted to be Zoe's twin, though I was far from it. Zoe came up to my shoulder—if I was slouching. Where she was petite and wiry, I was a mess of loose limbs. If I had to describe myself, I'd say I was mildly awkward with grand intentions. Mud-brown hair to my chin that was somewhere between wavy and unmanageable, a nose that took up too much face real estate, and a unibrow that was hazardous. I did like that my eyes were the same sea-glass turquoise as my mom's. Also, that I wore mismatched socks on purpose. I was an avid recycler, and one of my teachers called my punctuation "exemplary!?,;"

But I longed to be more like Zoe. From the moment I met her, I did basically anything Zoe told me to do—sit, stand, lie down, roll over. At night, I tried to train my nose to slope up like hers at the very end. I practiced walking with my feet turned out to match her ballet strides and joined the track team briefly to literally chase after her. When we had sleepovers, I memorized the stripy patterns in her mint-green wallpaper, as if they could lead me closer inside. She started calling me *Hank* instead of Hannah, because she said it gave me more personality. I had to agree. Zoe was the sun, and I would gladly orbit her in whichever direction she chose.

Here's a pathetic secret that I have no interest in holding on to anymore: In seventh grade, when I was developing faster than Zoe, I even shaved my lady parts, so we'd look the same *down there*. Which turned out to be the itchiest, most unrewarding experience ever.

Until maybe this moment.

It was the day before our first day of junior year at Meadowlake High. I hadn't seen Zoe in practically two months. And now I'd walked into some situation that felt a little bit like cat porn. Zoe had on a loose gray tank top and what looked like the hot-pink polka-dotted short shorts that she wore for our first-grade ballet recital. Once upon a pirouette, I had matching ones too. (Just to clarify—I wasn't in the recital, because it was by audition and I sucked at ballet. But my mom knew how much I wanted to be like Zoe and sewed me some facsimile short shorts out of retired bedsheets.)

"I just felt so alone and misunderstood until I met you, sweet Pepe," Zoe declared now. "I really didn't know how or if I'd even make it through this horror. You are my *hero*."

Zoe tipped her head back and started kissing the animal all over his body. He squirmed and wriggled, and his hind legs looked as if he were trying to run a marathon. Then she cradled him like a baby and hummed a lullaby until his ears sagged. "Ooh, you see? He loves me too. He really does," she cooed.

I know it wasn't the cat's fault. That thing was probably just as stunned as I was by all this smoochy-faced madness. I just felt allergic to everything inside this basement—the dander, the drama, the long watery gaze that Zoe fixed on this multicolored hairball.

To be fair, Zoe had a lot going on. She had been away basically all summer. First, she spent a month by the Jersey Shore with her grandparents, who were awesome, but they ate dinner at 5:00 P.M. and didn't have a great Internet connection. While Zoe was wandering the coastline, her dad, Travis, moved out of their family house. I didn't know much about his new place, other than it was twenty minutes away and next to a car wash. Zoe described it as "a beige coffin." Then she went to performing arts camp, where she was cast as the scarecrow in *The Wiz* and made out with three different Munchkins. Alli (her mom) picked Zoe up on the last day of camp—the night after an "epic" cast party—and took her straight to a weeklong mother-daughter self-empowerment retreat in the Catskills that involved a lot of sage and a ginger juice cleanse that was "energizing, but in an angry way."

I only knew all this because Zoe posted pics on a special secret Tumblr called Zoozoo4u. She was documenting all of her feelings about life, her parents' separation, and those sexy Munchkins. It was supposed to be password protected so Alli and Travis couldn't see it. Only, the password was zoozoo4u too, so that wasn't much protection.

Zoe loved putting it all out there on social media. She'd even made an Insta account for the two of us called ZoenHank, where she put up pictures of us cheek to cheek or trying on granny glasses at the drugstore. I loved that she did this for us, but I never got into it as much as she did. Maybe I'd watched one too many scary movies about private eyes or online trolls. Something ooked me out about dumping all my thoughts into the ether for some interweb audience to behold. Yes, I was the last holdout from my grade, or my hemisphere really. And the only teenager I knew who owned a dollhouse. But still.

Even though we were less than an hour apart for most of the summer, Zoe and I had communicated mainly through photo captions and hashtags. She said talking would be "too intense," and I wanted to respect that. Also, I didn't have much to report from the home front. I'd been home doing my usual summer job for the past six weeks: arts and crafts counselor at the Y. The most excitement I had was one day when a camper almost choked on some googly eyes. Also, I went to the pool, and learned how to finger knit, which is just slightly less thrilling than it sounds.

Yeah, it was a typical boring summer until I got a text message from Zoe a half hour ago that said:

we're home! wanna come by and meet my new lover?

The first thing I saw when I came over was a hulking green dumpster in the driveway and a lopsided stack of cardboard boxes next to it. Someone had scrawled TRAVIS on the sides of each box in brazen red Sharpie. The *T*s looked so ferocious, as if they might eat all the other letters. Alli was humming while bent over a milk crate of cassette tapes, and I knew I should say *Hi* and *How ya doing* but I didn't have all the words ready yet, so I stole into the basement through the side door.

All I could see was what was missing. The gray beat-up couch where we'd made forts was gone. So was the wooden coffee table where we'd spilled nail polish remover and taken off a blob of finish. And the red easel where I'd painted such childhood masterpieces as *Upside-Down Rainbow*, *Upside-Down Rainbow 2*, and *Today, with Rainbow*.

Of course, Zoe was the only one with any real talent in drawing. She drew me these hilarious stick figures with huge eyes, saying silly things like, *Welcome to planet Marzoompf, may I take your coat?* or *Hey! You look like a fish I once dated*. Together, we had plans to start an art gallery that also served potato pancakes. Or else we were going to write a book called *Have You Seen My Nosehair Named Larry?* (based on a true story). I was in charge of the writing and I still had all the pages in a purple folder in the top drawer of my desk at home. Zoe was in charge of the illustrations. Which—from the looks of it—were now in a dumpster.

Everything that had been in here was gone. There were no plastic bins of markers, Play-Doh, and decapitated Barbies. There was no Leaning Tower of Board Games on the shelves above the washing machine. What I missed most of all was the Powerpuff Girls drum kit and the disco ball . . . catching those last slips of streetlamp light when we convinced her parents to let us stay up just one more hour.

"What happened to the—?" I started to ask.

"I know, right?" Zoe said. "It's just too sad."

"Did he take everything with him?"

"Who? Travis? Ha!" Zoe coughed out a bitter laugh. "No. He has nothing in his new place." She looked around the shadowy basement with a frown. "This is just Alli's whole purging idea. *Start over with simplicity* or whatever that decluttering self-help guru she bought into on that retreat said."

I felt like I'd just been purged of most of my vocabulary.

"Wow," I said again. "That sounds . . ." I didn't want to end my sentence with *dismal*, *horrible*, or *scarring*. But those were the only adjectives I could dig up at the moment.

"Ooh! But I did save one thing for you!" Zoe said. She ran to the basement stairs and brought back a lavender-colored journal with a glittery unicorn on the cover.

"My nana actually gave this to me a while ago, but you're the real writer, so . . ." She pushed it into my hands. I felt bad that I hadn't brought her anything.

"Thank you. I tried to make you one of those tie-dyed head-bands, but it came out supersplotchy. But maybe we could . . . I mean, would it help if you stayed at my place for a few nights?" I offered.

"Oh, you're the bestest, Hank. No, that wouldn't help anything." My face must have registered as insulted because she followed that up quickly with, "I mean, thank you. It would *help*, but there's just too much going on here right now, including—bah!"

Apparently, Pepe had plenty to say. He was purring and batting at Zoe's dark bangs like they were catnip. It looked like a horrible game to me, but Zoe had now transformed from sullen back into camera-ready pep. "I'm sorry," she gushed. "I really do want to catch up about everything and hear about your summer, but can you just press PLAY while he's letting me hold him? I mean, can you even believe the cuteness happening right this very second?"

She held up Pepe in front of me, so I could see his terrified, unextraordinary face. He yelped wildly, clawing at the wisp of air between us. "I mean, the stripes and the whiskers," she explained.

"Yup," I got out before sneezing three times in rapid succession. Zoe tucked the cat back into her chest and wrapped her arms around him protectively. "I swear I'd breastfeed him if I could. Did you know hundreds of thousands of animals go starving every day?"

I shook my head and rubbed my eyes.

"It's so sad. The woman who brought the litter in is from the

Ukraine and she was telling us these horror stories about how cats are abused there and left to roam . . . and while she was telling us all this, Pepe was just clinging to me, yowling. Like he could hear what she was saying. It was just so *tragic*." Zoe's eyes puddled.

"Got it," I said with a cough. Not that I didn't care. I just felt too short of breath and displaced. Zoe knew I couldn't stand to be around cats. We'd even once promised that if we didn't find respectable partners by the time we turned thirty, we'd move in together and adopt a Labradoodle, a ferret, or a baby—really anything but a cat. I guess that deal meant a lot more to me than to her.

"Ugh, you really are allergic." She sighed. More annoyed than remorseful though. "Okay, we'll be quick. Are you ready for your close-up, Monsieur Meowsers?"

Zoe backed herself up onto the stool and shook out her dark mane while I wiped my drippy nose on the bottom of my T-shirt. Pepe got busy climbing up her neck and gnawing on her nose. Then draping himself around her milky-white throat and tickling her with his fur until she shook with giggles.

"Are you getting all this?" Zoe squealed. "Come closer! Make sure you can see his tiny tongue. It's just beyond."

"Uh-huh," I wheezed.

"I really feel like this amazing little creature *chose* me," she began. As she mused, I shut my eyes tight. Partly because they were burning and partly because I thought if I could just listen I'd hear my old friend. My sister-from-another-mother. My rock.

13

Zoe's voice was always so husky and clipped. She said what she meant and she meant what she said. She dared me to be bigger and wilder too. That's why I'd admired and adored her for most of our lives.

But even her voice sounded false now. It dipped and swirled as if she were following some melody I'd never heard before.

"Pepe le Meowsers," she serenaded. "In a world full of pain and uncertainty, will you be my *pussyyyyy* . . . *cat?*"

Pepe loved this line. He meowed on cue.

"Meeeooow!" Zoe chimed in, cackling with glee. The two of them sang over each other, louder and louder. As the cat licked Zoe's mouth, her nostrils, her dark silky hair. The cat was perfectly in tune with her too. Something I could never pull off when we sang together.

Which is why maybe I might have sort of fantasized about wrapping my itchy palms around that feline neck and squeezing until it all just stopped.

Now it's 9:55.
(Cuz, of course, had to stop writing for
"Morning Musings" Group.)

Okay, maybe <u>hate</u> is too harsh a word.

<u>Despise</u>? <u>Abhor</u>? <u>Fiercely repelled by</u>?

(I know, a preposition at the end of the sentence is a no-no, right?
You were always the greater grammarian, Hanky-Panky.)

Speaking of your superior brain . . .

Pop quiz!

When did you decide to abandon me like that?

> a. Yesterday.
>
> b. Today, with a side of tomorrow.
>
> c. It's been so long I don't remember.
>
> d. I still love you more than life itself.
>
> e. Sorry, I think you have the wrong Hank.

But seriously, betrayal takes a long time to plan. Was it a gradual realization or more of a sudden epiphany?

Speaking of epiphanies, there are three girls on my floor here who blacked out from starvation. Lucky ducks.

Coulda.

Woulda.

Shoulda.

I know that sounds horrific to you, but the way they describe it sounds absolutely dreamy to me. They are pitifully small and covered

15

in that malnourished-person body fur and here's the honest truth (even though you don't deserve truth from me): I'm so freaken jealous.

They hit that glorious rock-bottom moment.
That clear and definitive sign in the road that says
DO NOT ENTER.

That's all I wanted, really. I just wanted to faint or qualify as a crisis in some way. I really still fantasize about all the lights going out and maybe some thick straps pinning me down by the wrists.
Especially in the middle of a BodybyBernardo class.
With all those ladies clucking and sweating around me. Alli would probably shit herself.
Ha!

But you couldn't even let me have that moment, Hank.
You just _had_ to step in and "save the day," huh?

None of this is pretty, Hank.
You are not pretty.
I am not pretty.
Fuck _pretty_.
Even the word sounds airbrushed and unattainable. Isn't it hilarious that right by the checkout counter with all the hangry impulse-buy candy bars, you can get those tabloids with the horrifying pictures of

Lady Gaga's boobs falling or some Moroccan princess caught on film in a bikini with <u>stretch marks</u>?

Because it's so scandalous and unacceptable to grow.

I didn't do all this to be pretty, by the way.

It was never about being pretty.

<u>Well, then what was it about?</u> you ask.

A fine question, my fair ex-friend. And one that every doctor, nurse, and counselor keeps lining up to ask. If I ever have an answer, I'll let you know.

Actually, that's another lie. I don't feel like I'll be telling you anything anytime soon.

But if you have something to say to me—maybe something that rhymes with

<u>I'm florry</u>, or

<u>I'm snorry</u> . . . ?

Well, you know where I'll be for the next eon.

Seriously, they don't even let us know how many pounds we have to gain or how many self-affirmations we have to chant before we can get out.

This place SUCKS MY NOT-EVEN-THAT-SKINNY WHITE ASSSSSSS.

Yours till the kitchen sinks!

Xoxo,

Zoe

CHAPTER 2
most blustiferous, indeed

"ALLI! STOP TRASHING HIS STUFF!" ZOE BELLOWED, KICKING OPEN the back door. "You know you're gonna regret it." As I trailed behind her, she turned around and winked to make sure I was listening. Which I always was. There was something magnetic and terrifying about the way Zoe spoke to her mom. Always calling her by her first name and treating her like she was going to get detention. Alli looked thrilled to see us though.

"Oh, hello, girls!" she sang. *"Hello, hello! To the girls I love so!"*

Alli didn't know how to just talk. She was constantly veering into a new tune or making sure her every word rhymed. She simply couldn't help it—she'd been in musical theater for such a long time. That's how she and Zoe's dad had met—on some tour of the Midwest where she played Belle the Beauty and he was the baddest Beast in town. They fell in love the first day of rehearsals. Travis had a young wife back in Michigan, so it took a little while for him to disentangle from that. (Alli had told me a few times that she "refused to be the other woman.") By closing night of their show together, Alli was pregnant with Zoe. She moved back to New Jersey to be near her parents and soon secured her Beast a job with her daddy's insurance company. Travis put a ring on her finger exactly a week before Zoe popped out, and they all lived happily ever after.

Sort of.

Alli had a lot of bright memories of being on the road and hearing standing ovations that eclipsed her humdrum today. She often referenced an agent who wanted her to spread her wings and some trip to LA that was forever being postponed. She always ended that story with her favorite self-composed ditty:

"Cuz I traded in my dreams for a minivaaaan."

Today she was filling up that minivan with what looked like the last decade of her life. Milk crates filled with vases and frames. An espresso machine that looked powerful enough to launch a rocket.

"Oh, Hannah, what a mess, right? I mean, I cannot believe this, can you?"

I actually did believe it. I had spent most of the past decade over at Zoe's house. I knew when to stay in Zoe's bedroom because Alli and Travis were clinking glasses and hooting in the den. I also knew when to get under Zoe's bed and turn up her stereo because

Alli and Travis were fighting about money and being responsible and the price of being a true artist. It was a little like going to the zoo—sickly fascinating and yet I always felt like they were both trapped in either an epic battle or a game of kissy-face tag. Over the years, I'd heard a few vicious phrases repeatedly, like:

You're pathetic.
You act like you're the only one sacrificing around here.

And even:

You think everything is a musical, don't you?!

Which seemed to be the biggest insult possible in their house.

"I mean, you plan, and you dream, and you believe in *looooove* . . . ," Alli warbled now, though it devolved into more of a moan than a melody. She was stunning, even in distress. Her blond hair had been chopped into a defiant pixie style and she was decked out in a lavender Lycra workout ensemble that had lots of straps. The smudge of dirt on her brow looked possibly preplanned.

"Hello?" Alli asked me and Zoe. We'd both been too busy looking at the packed-up belongings to give her the attention she needed. I felt a little embarrassed for her as she let two sparkling tears tip over the edge of her bottom lids without so much as a blink. I almost thought she was daring me to wipe them away for her. When I didn't, she opened her arms and pulled me into a dank hug.

"I mean, I guess the silver lining is, it can't get any worse, right?" Again, I knew silence would be the best response I could give. And five more sneezes, since her size-two stretch pants were coated in cat hairs.

"Alli," Zoe interrupted. "I need you to take Pepe inside. I don't trust him all alone, and we need some fresh air. Hank's allergic."

"No!" yelped Alli. "Is that true?" She broke away from me and searched my itchy eyes for an answer. It was pretty obvious that I wasn't lying, so I just coughed.

"It's all good though," Zoe assured her. "Looks like you could use a break. Plus, I need some one-on-one time with my girl and you have to feed this sweet little beast." She mushed her nose into the kitten's, ringed his face with kisses, and then slung him around her neck as if he were a calico stole.

Alli made a grimace. "Please do not call him Beast," she said in a woeful grumble.

"Oops, sorry," said Zoe, shoving the cat into her mom's arms.

Then, although she was only a few steps away, Zoe took a running start before hurtling herself at me, wrapping her arms around my neck and dangling like a medallion. She'd always been ridiculously small and buoyant. I picked up her ropy legs and she locked them swiftly around my waist. I marveled at how Zoe could propel herself into my arms and know she'd be caught. Sometimes she came out of nowhere and I only knew to prepare as she appeared midair. I prided myself on the fact that I had only dropped her once. (We were in a bouncy house at the time.)

"Hanky-Panky Puddin' Pie!
I love you so, and do you know why?"

Zoe had come up with this routine probably in first grade, and even though I protested, she knew I still adored it.

"Cuz you're kind and you're bright.
You dance like a sprite.
You're musical. You have no fear.
I especially love the freckle on the side of your ear!"

She tried to switch up my winning attributes each time, punctuating every phrase with a smacky kiss on my lips.

"Well, you are—" I began.

But Zoe cut me off. "Hup!" She clamped a warm palm over my mouth to shut me up. "Just let me love you, pleeeeease?" Nestling her head onto my shoulder. I closed my eyes to imprint this moment into my memory-scape. I really had missed Zoe these past two months. Whenever she was in my arms and I could smell her hot, sugar-free-Bubblemint breath, the whole world felt easier to me.

"You girls are too much," I heard Alli say sadly. "I wish I had friends like that."

Zoe slid off me and spun around to face her mom. "Listen! Enough with the pity parade. You're gorgeous. You're vibrant. And you currently teach two very popular Pilates classes. Now, I haven't seen Hank all summer, so give us some space, would you please?"

"I'm sorry. You're right," Alli said with her head bowed. "But does that mean you're going off and leaving me all alone?" she whined.

"You're a big girl," Zoe replied. "And we'll just be out here in the backyard. Now go play with Pepe so I can tell Hank how you and Dad ruined my life."

Alli gasped.

"Kidding!" Zoe shouted. "Oh! And I posted the video to You-Tube, Insta, and catlife dot whatever, but if you want to put it on Meowser's account, go ahead."

Alli looked like she was going to tear up again. "I'm from the last century, remember? I don't know how to download videos. Or is it upload? You see?" She turned to me for backup.

"If it makes you feel any better, I don't know how to do most of that stuff either," I told her.

"Forget it. I'll do it for you in a few minutes," said Zoe, waving her mom away. "Just let me talk to Hank, will ya?"

Zoe and I stayed facing each other—eyes locked—until we heard the screen door open and clatter shut.

"Ladies and gentlepeople, that was the ever-daring, ever-emotive thespian Allison Sinclair!" Zoe griped. She spread her arms wide and faked the roar of a crowd. I started to laugh with her but got distracted by three more raw-looking scratches, these ones inside Zoe's pasty biceps. Plus, now that we were standing without a cat between us, I could tell that those were definitely her polka-dotted short shorts from first grade. There was a chocolate stain on the edge from when we went out for peanut butter parfaits after the recital. And almost a decade later, she not only fit into them but her tiny legs looked like Popsicle sticks below.

Zoe caught me staring and stuck her tongue out at me.

"What are you looking at?" she asked.

"You. What are you looking at?" I wanted to sound confident, but I knew I didn't.

"*You.*" She smirked. "Plus, the sun turning this ferocious pink-purple-orange rainbow-sherbet color. It's like a crazy halo around your head, lighting you up like some magical Medusa. Only, it also makes me see how the days are getting shorter and the nights are getting longer, the summer is ending, and we're never gonna be kids again even if we invented a time machine, which we can't, so we won't, so yeah. That's what I'm looking at."

This was another reason I was in awe of Zoe. She could name and mash together all these images and emotions into one rollicking, run-on sentence. She was never at a loss for words or clogged up and confused like me. I often wished I'd thought to record Zoe's random bits of poetry because she could never repeat them or even admit that what she said was in some way remarkable.

In fact, by the time I repeated, "Magical Medusa?" she was scrambling up her old jungle gym. Of course I followed, though I had to fold myself like an accordion to get onto the pirate ship platform on top.

"Aaaargh," she growled. "'Tis a blustery blustoon out there, matey."

"Most blustiferous, indeed, Captain," I replied.

24

"Yet fear not!" Zoe turned to me and took my face in her hands. "Though the waters may blust, we will prevail!"

"Prevail we must!"

"We must increase our blust!"

She honked one of my boobs and slipped down the slide.

"Did you get my letters?" I asked when she climbed up to the platform again.

I had sent her five handwritten letters and a batch of home-made peanut butter cookies. Even though she had warned me that she probably wouldn't write back—she hated writing, especially when we were out of school.

"Aye, aye!" Zoe barked.

"And did you get to go to the Crab Shanty?" That was her grandpa's favorite spot for dinner, and every time I visited, we went there for fried clams.

"But of course!" Zoe said. "Almost every night."

I sucked in a deep inhale before trying my not-so-subtle segue. "Did you . . . eat?" I asked. "Because you look super-skinnimous to me."

"Ugh, really?" Zoe snorted. Her eye roll was audible. I knew this was never the way to get an honest reaction from her, but I had to ask. Last year, while her parents were caught up in the cyclone known as themselves, Zoe had lost all this weight. She'd sworn to me repeatedly that she wouldn't become one of those girls who only ate lettuce leaves and air. Sauntering by the public pool in their size-zero bikinis and snapping at each other han-grily. But this summer had obviously been a game changer.

She looked like a pocket-size version of her former self.

"Thanks a lot, Hank," she said. "You know, this has been the absolute worst summer of my life and I need you to just be my BFF . . ."

She lost track of where she was, so I picked it up. "AETI."

Which stood for Best Friends Forever And Ever To Infinity. We had a pact of BFFAETI-hood that we'd composed and decorated with smelly stickers soon after meeting. It was buried under the footpath leading to We Make Happy Dry Cleaners in town.

"Yeah," Zoe said. "Probably need to dumb it down for Miss Dumbass over here."

"You're not dumb," I told her.

"But I do have ADHD," she replied. "The results are in! Alli made me go to another therapist out on the shore and they put me on some new attention-enhancing pill, which I swear makes me bloated, and I still can't get through *The Great Gatsby*. So if you really think I'm skinnier, you need glasses."

Then she bugged her eyes out at me and started to nibble on my shoulder through my T-shirt sleeve.

"Ow!" I blurted.

"Really?" she said, before slipping down the slide again and kicking a deflated soccer ball.

"Just . . . surprised me is all," I said, scooting down the slide. I didn't need glasses. I just needed my best friend back. I felt like my skin was stinging. Like everything about Zoe was too manic. It wasn't just the whiskers and revealing outfit. It was the whole package. As if she'd rearranged her five nose freckles or taken out all her teeth and put in new, sharper ones. Even her cobalt eyeliner looked darker and more extreme.

Zoe began scaling up the slide, vaulting herself onto a plastic swing, then dribbling the crushed soccer ball around the yard. It wouldn't go very far though, so most of her kicks just made muddy pockmarks.

"Good thing Alli's calling in a landscaper, huh? You know, she wants to redo the kitchen and then sell this place for a bazillion dollars so we can move to LA and she can do a one-woman show about her wrecked marriage."

"Wait—what?"

"Don't worry. It'll never happen."

"But why?"

Zoe chuckled bitterly. Then she blew a bubble with her gum and chomped into it with a snap.

"Well, children," she said in a clipped tone. "When a husband and wife decide that they can no longer cohabitate, communicate, or stop screwing their *creative headhunter* Roxanne—"

"Are you sure it was—"

"They often proceed to a little place called Divorce Court. Divorce Court costs a lot of money. More money than even a new dolly. Isn't that sad?" She paused just long enough to droop her face into an exaggerated frown before continuing. "It's really sad. Especially because Roxanne has fake boobs and a whiny voice and Travis forgot to put his savings in the piggy bank. Which makes him the biggest dickwad in the history of dickwads."

"Wait—that can't be right. Did he tell you? Did he say . . ." I

27

didn't know how to finish this sentence. Zoe just let me peter out. I'd never heard Zoe talk like this about her dad before. I knew he was a little too charming with the ladies. We all did. It was part of his persona. Zoe and I usually laughed it off—even when we heard him and Alli arguing about how long he looked at a waitress or why he loved his female dentist so much. Sometimes I felt like he was even flirting with *me*. Especially when he pulled out his guitar for us and sang these low, mournful tunes about losses too sad to remember. His lyrics melted into one another and typically involved a speck of stardust or a bottle of Jack.

I never thought Travis would actually do anything to break up his marriage though. I thought he loved his little family too much. Or at least his darling Zoe.

"Pretty amazing, huh?" Zoe scoffed. Her voice was so low and raspy, she sounded like she'd seen it all.

I stood there earning the award for New Heights of Awkwardness before summoning up the balls to say, "Sorry."

"It's fine," she said through a tight smile. "I mean, it's not fine at all. It's ridonkulous and horrible and Alli has some crazy idea that she's gonna sweep out this place and then we can remake our reality in a decluttered geodesic dome or something. I mean, that's our second dumpster already. I swear. We've been home for four days and all we've been doing is cleaning."

"You've been home for four days?" I gulped. I knew it wasn't big in the grand scheme of things—famine, nuclear war, the return of high-waisted jeans. But I faked a sneeze, just to have something to do instead of pity myself.

Again, Zoe read my mind. "Please don't make this into some-thing, Hank. I was gonna go straight to your house, I swear. But Alli was a wreck and Travis was texting nonstop and then she wanted us to join this gym and you were calling and I just *couldn't*. I mean, that's why this cat was like this miracle. Because he just gives unconditional love and snuggles, you know?"

I nodded, even though I couldn't say I actually knew. Zoe leaned into me and kissed my shoulder. "Do you know I love you more than anyone on this whole stupid planet?" she asked.

I nodded faster, blinking back my simmering jealousy.

"Do you?" Zoe poked me in the ribs this time.

"I do," I answered. "And I love—"

"Nope!" She cut me off. "I said it first!" Then she licked my cheek and sprinted up the big rock at the edge of her backyard. Or at least it used to be big. When we were little, we called it Mount Snooji and whenever it snowed we slid down it until our tailbones were bruised and the neighbors told us to go home. It took me a minute to catch up to her. By the time I did, she was hopping up and down with her cell phone, chanting, "No freaken way! No freak-*en* way!"

"No freaken way what?"

"I cannot believe this." She was panting and giggling now, her head still tucked into her phone. "Did I tell you about the account we started for Pepe le Meowsers?" she said without looking up.

"We?" I asked.

"Me and Alli. It's kind of like a video diary of how our lives have changed since we brought him home."

29

I watched as she swiped through roughly two thousand pictures of Pepe le Meowsers. Pepe sleeping, Pepe licking his paw, Pepe stretching on a towel, even Pepe taking a dump. There was a whole series of Zoe smiling and nuzzling Pepe too. Then there was a video of Zoe walking by the duck pond behind Dunkin' Donuts, singing to her furry companion.

"So stupid, right?" said Zoe. "I think it was this one of him in the basket that got the most attention. Look how many people started following us after that!"

"Wow," I said. Only I wasn't looking at the pictures anymore. I was too fixated on another cluster of angry scratches, this time on the inside of Zoe's left wrist. They were carved so neatly in three lines. Almost identical to the ones I'd seen on her upper arm. "Maybe he should be declawed though, huh?" I added.

"What?" Zoe followed my gaze and then balled up her hand into a fist so quickly that for a split second I thought she was going to punch me. "Aw, crazy cat," she said, and shook her head just as her phone buzzed yet again.

The kitchen door banged open and Alli came running out. "Zoo!" she yelled. "Zoo, did you see?!"

Zoe's "Will you be my *pussyyyyy . . . cat?*" video was now trending on Instagram, Snapchat, Facebook Live, and a pawful of cat-loving sites. In the few minutes we'd been outside, it had gotten liked and reliked, tweeted, posted, quoted, and hashtagged over and over again.

Someone named Rebro775 had commented that it was *Revolutionary.*

Manplan89 called it *Validating in this depraved, misogynistic society*.

A bunch of people had just written in variations on the word *Hot*.

And the one that made me squirm most was a DrNumNum who wrote, *I want some*.

"So freaken stupid," Zoe kept repeating. But she was obviously thrilled. I could feel her trembling next to me as we watched her phone flicker with adoration. Little red hearts winking at us. Gathering all the fanatical fandom from the ether and putting it in the palm of her hand.

Her screen almost blocking out that patch of open skin.

CRAZY SAD LIBS
THE FRIEND WHO WASN'T REALLY A FRIEND

Once upon a time, there was a girl named

_____ .
  [NAME THAT RHYMES WITH "SPANK"]

She lived in a blue house on _____ Street.
                              [FRUIT OR NUT]

She liked to play the piano and wear two different-colored

_____ .
  [PLURAL NOUN]

Hank had a lot of great qualities. She was a great

writer and she could remember all the names of the

_____ .
  [PLURAL NOUN]

But she was a really _____ friend.
                      [SYNONYM FOR "TERRIBLE"]

Lots of people thought that she was _____ ,
                                     [ADJECTIVE]

maybe a little _____ .
               [ADJECTIVE]

But on the inside, she was _____.

[UGLY ADJECTIVE]

And she lied a lot.

One day, _____ did a

[NAME THAT RHYMES WITH "SPANK"]

really mean thing. She broke into her best friend's house!

Yes, girls and boys, that is a serious crime

and _____ could have gone

[NAME THAT RHYMES WITH "SPANK"]

to jail for _____ years!

[NUMBER FROM 99–100]

But no one called the police because

_____ said she only did it

[NAME THAT RHYMES WITH "SPANK"]

to save her friend Zoe's life. And Zoe's parents listened to

that story because Zoe's parents were _____-holes.

[LETTER OF THE ALPHABET]

And then, instead of Hank getting in trouble, Zoe was the

one who got sent away for _____ years.

[NUMBER FROM 99–100]

And none of them lived happily ever after.

CHAPTER 3
spinal freedom

NOT THAT I WANTED TO SIFT THROUGH MORE OF ZOE'S *PUSSYYYYY...*
cat comments or was prepared to go to Bernardo's seven fifteen
FitBidness class with Alli and Zoe at their new gym, but as soon as
I turned the corner back onto my street, I felt a knot of loneliness
lodge in my chest. I could smell the ecofriendly briquettes and
the rack of tempeh or whatever it was that Elan had promised to
come over and grill for us. It was Labor Day after all. And Elan
loved anything involving tempeh or my mom.

Ugh, Elan.

He wasn't a bad guy. He wasn't mean or abusive or addicted
to juggling puppies and knives. His biggest "vice" was sticking
wheatgrass in his coffee. He also loved to tell us about the time
he got caught by a park ranger going off trail in Oregon so he

could photograph a rare mountain lion. Elan loved hiking. He also loved running, swimming, Rollerblading (gross), making his own cashew milk, and recycling old mason jars to turn them into mossy terrariums.

He just wasn't—nor ever could be—my dad.

My dad died almost nine years ago. A heart attack just after he got on the 7:29 A.M. train from Meadowlake, New Jersey, to Penn Station. It was all over in one startling, horrific minute. Mom told me later that someone from his advertising firm was on that same train and tried to give him CPR. You had to wonder what that felt like, to lock lips and puff all your morning breath and hope into someone's dying lungs. Then there were sirens and paramedics, heroic efforts, gasping commuters, and a lost briefcase that would get marched up to our front door eight months later, as if it mattered.

Still, nobody could undead him.

I know there's supposedly a rhyme and a reason for everything (except maybe canned sardines). But I'd like to register a complaint to the Ministries of Mysteriously Poor Timing because my dad's death was really not well-planned.

First off, David Ernest Levinstein was only forty-seven years old when he stopped existing, and he left behind an adoring wife (my mom) and two incredible children under the age of ten (me and Gus), both of whom were going about their day as his pulmonary artery seized, his life flashed before his eyes or at least hopefully he got a whiff of the angels at the end of the tunnel, and then he collapsed.

Second, there was that unreturned call to his mom (Grandma Dot) about her not-so-adjustable curtain rod; that suit he'd never picked up from the dry cleaner's; the leaky gutter; mortgage refinancing; and that we were only halfway through reading the Harry Potter series together.

Third, I had really practiced hard for this day. As in, memorizing and rehearsing my speech about Native American warriorhood eleven times into my Hello Kitty pocket mirror before it was my turn to present to my second-grade class.

There was only a smattering of applause, even though I'd gotten through the whole thing without a single stop. Looking back, I'd easily call my Oneida Tribe Warriors oration the peak of my performing career. But my teacher, Ms. Dennison, wasn't even paying attention. She was standing by the door with Principal Connell doing that thing where her eyes were on me, but her head was tilted toward him as he said something in her ear. Probably the fact that my dad was dead and my mom was in his office shaking and nobody had enough lollipops to make this better.

"Thank you so much for that thorough presentation, Hannah," Ms. Dennison said. "And now I believe Mr. Connell would like to talk to you for a . . ."

Poor Ms. Dennison. She ran out of breath and bit her lower lip nervously. Connell thanked her profusely and told the class he was so impressed with our investigative skills.

Then he turned to me and said ominously, "Bring all your things. I doubt you'll be coming back to class today."

"Oh dawg," said Nicholas Pratt as I stuffed my notebook into my backpack.

I'm hoping he still regrets that stupid statement. I made sure to growl at him on the way out.

As Mr. Connell and I walked down the corridor he started firing questions at me:

"How did you learn all of those things about Native Americans? Were they hard to memorize?"

I hated when adults made up stupid stuff to talk about. Though looking back, I could tell he was really scrambling to keep me engaged. When we got outside his office, he just stood there. I wondered if he needed help opening the door. Talk about embarrassing. After an eon of silence, he said, "Sorry. Your mom will explain."

Mom actually couldn't explain anything. She was a mess. She was wearing her long winter coat and purple sunglasses and I didn't know if she was trying to be a spy or was running from the law. She pulled me into her sweaty chest and rocked me back and forth, back and forth. Humming into my hair.

When she did talk, she said a bunch of vague things about poor diet and cholesterol and how she had begged Daddy to slow down and stop eating so much cheese. (He had been pretty overweight. But I loved banging on his belly like a drum.) I still didn't know that my dad was dead and my life was changed forever. Mom never said the words *dead* or *gone*. She just kept babbling about how she should've known something was wrong and how he was rushing that morning and that he hadn't even taken off the tags on his new dress shirt. Then my little brother, Gus, came into the office with his kindergarten teacher and told us a story about a dinosaur trying on hats. Gus loved to tell long stories. And that day nobody stopped him.

I didn't really get what was going on until we got home, and Gus asked for apple juice, but we didn't have any more apple juice, so he said, "Go get some at the store!" and Mom started weeping, "I can't. I can't."

That's when it became undeniably clear. Because going to the store for juice was nothing to cry about and Mom wouldn't stop. She kept getting shriller and wailier too. I'd never heard a sound this ugly. It made me sad and mad and, above all, scared. Mom's sobs grew and swelled. Soaking through the carpets and pressing against the walls and I felt like I needed to shut all the windows even though it was so hot out, especially for October. Meanwhile, Gus was still whining about being so thirsty he was going to "de-hydronate."

"Dehy*drate*," I told him sharply. I pushed him into the kitchen and grabbed an orange ice pop from the freezer; unwrapped it, and stuck it in a bowl. One minute on HIGH in the microwave and it melted into juice. We passed it back and forth, taking small sips. I felt guilty that I wasn't crying too, but I couldn't make anything come out. When I squeezed my eyes to make tears, there was nothing but static.

Mom did stop crying. Eventually. Or maybe she just got blotted out by all the new voices and footsteps, the doors and cupboards opening and closing, the house phone ringing, and the hushed messages being passed around.

Out of the blue.

Total shock.

Maybe cholesterol, but who really knows?

Service at B'nai Israel on Wednesday at nine thirty.

What a tragedy.

"Do we get to see him at all?" I remember asking Mom. "Like his . . . body?"

"We can see him in our minds," Mom whispered.

"So he's . . ."

Mom shook her head, so I knew not to say anything more.

All I could see in my mind was the fold in my dad's neck where a line of white aftershave always got caught. If I plugged my ears, I could maybe remember the gravelly voice he used to read me books at night. But besides that, it felt like I was always trying to grab scraps of Dad memories from pictures or dreams and tape them together. I was only eight, after all.

The funeral was awful—not that I was expecting a laugh riot. Gus kept pulling at his tie because it was too tight and he felt like he had to burp. Grandma Dot told me over and over again that it was too much, and she was going to die too, which didn't seem fair since it was Dad's day to be dead. I barely saw Mom the whole day—she was just passed from one shoulder to another, dropping tissues along the way. Afterward, lots of people came back to our house to eat bagels and blow their noses. They all said something like, *You're in my prayers* and *Let me know what I can do*—as if that were my job. The worst was the rabbi telling us to hold a special place in our hearts for him. A noble goal, but couldn't he have changed the wording so it wasn't a cardiac pun?

My dad's younger brother, Uncle Ricky, came to stay with us for a month. He was in between jobs and in between girlfriends and seemed to have no idea what to do with his life, but he loved playing with me and Gus. Zoe came over a lot too. Uncle Ricky made us all bacon sandwiches and let us have as many potato chips as we wanted, so that was fun. But it also meant that Mom went upstairs and took a lot of naps. Whenever she wasn't in her room, Uncle Ricky told us to give her space, even though our house seemed to be nothing but space now. It was as if Mom had this outer shell of misery swirling around her, keeping her out of reach. She also kept wearing her long winter coat inside, even as we passed through the holidays and it thawed into spring. Zoe called it her Coat of Grief.

I still didn't know how to thank Zoe for getting me through that year. And really every year since. She helped me remember that I was still alive—coming over to my house every day with a floppy sombrero or a giant bar of chocolate. She wiped Gus's nose when he had a cold and planted whoopee cushions in my bed, determined to make me laugh. When her parents wanted to go to Florida for spring break, she insisted I go with them. And then she picked out a necklace of small pearly shells to bring back for my mom.

I missed my dad. Especially his laugh that was so big it shook the floor. But to be honest, I missed my mom more. She was just so distant and fragile-looking for so long. She took a leave of absence from her job teaching ESL to migrant workers. I wondered if her students felt abandoned too. She was physically there for me and Gus—she got up in the morning when we left for school and she was there at the bus stop when we got off. But there was all this unaccounted-for time in between when I feared she'd just disappear. Hop a train and take it to the last stop. Maybe that's what she did during the day while Gus and I were learning our times tables and taking spelling quizzes. Just drifting.

At home, everything was officially on hold for a long time. The laundry piled up in drifts along the hallway; one of the fire alarms kept chirping to tell us it needed a new battery; the refrigerator stank of forgotten leftovers. One night, the kitchen sink clogged with popcorn kernels, and instead of getting it fixed, Mom suggested rinsing our plates and cups in the bathroom. When I looked up a plumber and called, he said I was very resourceful for a little girl. I told him that he was the first one listed in the phone book with a semidecent customer review. That showed him who was boss.

Mom's best friend Diane is the one who finally got her to put on some lipstick and go out. Diane was really into these adult education classes in our town that were apparently teeming with single men. (Diane was married to a painfully boring man named Al, who rarely spoke. Gus and I constantly caught him farting and then acting like it wasn't him.) It took Mom more than two years to agree to it, but she and Diane took an eight-week class called Pinot and Pottery and brought home lopsided vases. Then they signed up for DIY Cybersecurity, giving me and Gus lectures about online identities. Finding Your Personal Spinal Freedom was supposed to be just a one-day seminar to help with Mom's lower-back pain.

None of us knew it would lead Mom into the arms of one Elan Sayel, doctor of holistic chiropractic sciences.

Elan specialized in lower-back pain and lumbar breathing techniques—which I guess were sexy words to Mom, because she came home from that seminar a new color of giddy. And I will admit, when she walked through our door that night, her neck looked longer and her hunchback of heartache was already softening.

Mom and Elan took things slowly. He called to check up on her sciatic nerve or to mention a new article about the soothing effects of coconut oil. One night, Mom got a babysitter and said she and Diane were going out with "some friends." I camped out in Gus's room because his window was over the driveway. That way I could see if anyone else was in Diane's car when she came to pick up Mom. I stayed up until midnight looking at Elan's website about spiritual redemption by way of arnica salves.

"If he's bald, how come he has a full beard?!" I complained to Gus. "And what medical school did he go to?"

"Uh-huh," slurred Gus. I knew he just wanted to get some sleep.

"He's *so* not Dad," I said definitively. Usually I tried not to talk about Dad with Gus because he got sad that he remembered even less than I did. "I guess that's the whole point, right?"

Gus didn't answer. He was already snoring.

That *was* the whole point. Mom needed to start over. Gus and I had to either get on board or step aside. I wasted months gritting my teeth and scowling at Mom every time she told us she had plans or that her back pain was completely gone. She either never noticed or willfully ignored me. Soon Elan was coming over to cook us dinner and helping Mom plant a vegetable garden in our backyard. For her fiftieth birthday, he got her a fancy mountain bike and they drove up to the Finger Lakes to pedal their way into fitness euphoria.

"Don't you ever get scared that he'll put your mom in a spinal-freedom trance?" Zoe once asked me. It felt good to have an ally in this fight. She agreed that Elan was a little too calm to be human. Also, that he cooked with too much turmeric.

Elan not only loved my mom; he also loved our kitchen. He graced us with his presence at least three nights out of the week now to concoct some vegetarian delicacy that often involved seaweed. He still paid rent on a studio apartment twenty minutes away, but most of his belongings (and camping gear) were in my home. He even had his own key. Which is why I shouldn't have been surprised when I got home from Zoe's house and he was the one to throw open the front door and say, "Well, hello, Miss Almost-Eleventh Grader. How was your day?"

"Hi, Elan. Fine. Is Mom home?" I tried not to use any inflection, lest he think I was excited to talk to him. I no longer tried to stop Elan from coming over, but I also didn't encourage interaction.

"Yes!" He high-fived himself. "Mom's in the kitchen. Gus is upstairs. Grill will be ready in ten minutes. Booya!"

It was sad, really. Elan used so much energy trying to win me over. He was kind. And patient. He even had great posture and these hazel eyes that gazed at Mom without blinking for what felt like hours. The weird part about that was one of his irises drifted sideways. I got confused about where to focus when he was talking to me—which was way too often.

"Hey," I said to Mom as I walked through the kitchen.

"My girl!" Mom cheered.

I tried to kiss her on the cheek, but she was checking the temperature of the oven, so it was more like gumming her jaw.

"Damnit!" she said. "I burned the fennel spears *again*. How did I do that?"

"Just talented, I guess," I said, heading upstairs. Mom was definitely the worst cook I knew. When Gus and I were younger, we sang a song called, "That's Not a House Fire, That's Mom Using the Toaster." I was on piano. Gus came up with the melody and lyrics. I missed our scrappy talent shows with homemade refreshments (aka stale Halloween candy) and multiple costume changes. I would gladly eat Mom's charred pizza bagels for dinner every day for the rest of my life if it meant Elan would disappear.

But Elan was very much a part of our lives.

"Did you know that next weekend it will be exactly *three* years since your mother agreed to date me and consequently turned my world upside down," Elan asked a half hour later as he lifted a glass of rosé on our deck.

"You should make sure nothing spilled out," I muttered.

Gus gave me a swift kick under the table, but Mom and Elan were oblivious.

"And to celebrate," Elan continued, "I was thinking we could all go camping this weekend at Tall Pines. I know it's the first week of school, so you might have other plans, but . . ."

I had to make a concentrated effort not to spit my food across the room. "All together?" I croaked. Gus looked at me and bit his lip. I was pretty sure that he thought that was a horrible idea too, but he would never say it aloud.

"It's a four-person tent, right, hon?" asked Mom.

"Yes, indeed."

This was sounding more catastrophic by the moment.

"There's no way I'm—"

This time Gus kicked me hard. I took a breath and started over. "I mean, first of all, thank you for the invite. But I think I should stay home. As you said, first week of school and . . . plans. Y'know."

"Fair enough," said Mom.

"Gus, you're still welcome to come," said Elan.

"Thanks," said Gus. "Can I think about it?"

"Of course, buddy."

The rest of the dinner was a fascinating discussion of which spices Mom and Elan had used on the barbecued tempeh and how sea salt differed from regular salt. I noticed that Gus was mostly pushing around his food like me but gave myself extra-credit points for not verbalizing my disgust. In fact, I uttered nary a word until Mom realized she'd promised to get a different kind of notebook for Gus and the only store open was going to close soon. Which I was pretty sure was one of her ploys to get me and Elan to connect more.

"You guys good to clean up?" she asked. "Be back in a jiff, I swear."

"No problemo," said Elan before I could answer.

Gus and Mom were already on their way out the door by the time I finished chewing and realized I was stuck alone with this uninvited-yet-so-close-to-permanent guest and a pile of un-eaten fennel. Not to mention the five pans Mom had used in the kitchen.

We cleared the table in silence and I got to work out some of my aggression by scrubbing. Elan was, of course, very helpful, wiping down the counters and table.

"Thanks," I said without thinking.

It was my own fault for opening the door to discussion with him. He put down his dish towel, leaned toward me, and said, "Hey. You're welcome. Thank *you*."

I turned the faucet on harder to drown out our silence. I only had two more glasses to rinse though. And Elan excelled at waiting. After the glasses, I loaded the soap, turned on the dish-washer, and even scoured the sink. Elan just stood there. His feet planted squarely. His breath menacingly calm.

The moment I shut the water off, he said, "Hannah, I know these past few years haven't been the easiest on you, and I just want to express my gratitude to you for allowing me into your life."

I'd never allowed him in. And I'd certainly voted against him making a copy of our key and once *accidentally* tipped over his moped. But this was perhaps the most annoying part of Life with Elan™. I hated how he twisted everything around, so it sounded like he was complimenting me or that he was honored to feel the sting of my disdain. It was probably some espionage tactic—killing or at least coercing the enemy with kindness. He had to realize I was no sucker. I couldn't be played by this onion-breathed mole.

"It's all good," I said forcefully, my jaw tight.

"And I trust that if there's anything you want to discuss, you know I'm here."

I knew he was here, all right. He could not stop being here.

"Because, you know, I think you're really bright and percep-tive, and I wonder when you'll feel brave enough to express some of your feelings aloud."

"Um, *brave* enough?" I asked. I was pretty sure there was steam coming out of my ears and nose at this point.

Elan shook his head and chuckled. As if he'd just done some-thing silly like squeeze out too much toothpaste or put *i* after *e* instead of before. "I mean, *comfortable* enough," he explained.

"Mmhmm." I nodded. Readying myself. "I guess I do have something to say. Though it's more like a question."

"Of course!" Elan chirped eagerly. "Fire away. *Please*."

So I spun toward his open, eager face and asked, "Has your one eye always done that weird thing or do you think you should see a doctor?"

October yada yada.

Not that you care, but

I guess I had more to say after all.

My darling Hank,

It's so odd to me that you haven't written back yet after I shared such intimate, vulnerable feelings with you!

I should probably just write to someone else, but you were right once again—my online relationships have proven pretty fruitless, especially since there's

NO FREAKEN WI-FI HERE!

WTF??!!!

If you have a chance to check up on our video stats, I'd be ever so grateful, my pet.

Ha! That was a joke. Travis already made me dismantle everything. Alli was crying even harder than I was as I did it.

[insert pathetic emoji here]

Anywhos, wanna hear what I learned this morning in Reading Time?

There are these fish in the coral reef called gobies who all have eating disorders!

True story.

I think instead of <u>gobies</u>, they should be called <u>bitchfish</u>.

Get this: Each colony has like seventeen female gobies and one male. The queen goby is the biggest and fattest, and since she's the biggest and fattest, she's the only one allowed to procreate.

Sick, right?

But wait—there's more.

The other gobies are so scared of shaking up the whole animal hierarchy that they'll starve themselves just to stay skinnier than Queen Fatso.

If they put on too much weight, Queenie will push them out of the colony, and then they're done-zo.

Probably attacked by a passing Hankfish.

Actually, that's not even fair.

You never had a great appetite—yet another reason why I vowed to stop eating in front of you last year.

Did you even realize that?

I know exactly what day it was too—June 12.

A beautiful afternoon, actually. The sun was out, the birds were chirping, and a bunch of us went to Yoshi's after school, of course.

You said you weren't hungry, so I didn't get anything either.

And then, at the last minute, you decided to get an order of fries because Hey! Why not, right?

There was not a single cell in your body writhing in confusion or self-loathing. Not a single calculation of how many saturated or unsaturated or polyunsaturated fats could be in that little cardboard boat of yumminess. Or whether adding ketchup (which you did) would equal 25 burpees per lick.

None of that.

I remember standing there, watching you chew that pile of greasy hope. I hated you for being so careless and unpredictable and skinny.

So greasy, grimy, happy, and free.

Queen Goby. Except no matter what you eat or don't eat or how much you exercise or don't exercise you're still smaller than me!

How in the what???

And you know what the worst part about that afternoon was?

You handed me a fry and I spouted some lie about not being hungry or just having had a huge lunch and you just nodded and smiled.

As if you almost _wanted_ or _expected_ me to lie.

CHAPTER 4
missing diana gaia

UNCLE RICKY'S CHEVY MALIBU ALREADY HAD 100,000 MILES ON IT and smelled like hot musk. I didn't care though. It was mine. The most momentous thing I'd done this past summer was pass my driver's test and inherit this vehicle. (I also had to shell out $125 of hard-earned babysitting and organizing-for-old-people money to get a tune-up for this dented but well-loved sedan.) Of course, it was a weird maroonish color and still had the embarrassing vanity plates he'd bought reading HOT RIC. Also, a police scanner still sat on the dashboard because Uncle Ricky loved to test the speed limit.

"Sweet ride," Zoe said as she slid into the passenger seat the next morning. "Oh, hey, Gus," she added, noticing my brother in the backseat. "What's on your face?"

"Nothing," Gus answered. "What's on *your* face?"

"Ha." Zoe shrugged and turned back around. I swatted her knee, so she'd leave Gus alone. If only she'd commented on *my* mustache instead.

I came from a hairy family. There was really no way around that. My dad was from Minneapolis, Minnesota, where I guess they grew an extra layer of hair to stay warm. My mom was vaguely Turkish and had some distant cousin in India, but mostly she was an Ashkenazi Jewish girl from Philly. By the time I was eight years old, my leg fur was so dark and thick that someone at our town pool called me Sasquatch. Mom said I should march back over and tell that idiot about women's lib and a little thing called natural beauty. I didn't. Instead, I started a file of ads for follicle treatments and electrolysis that promised to remove all traces of my pelt but cost more than my parents' mortgage.

I knew Zoe's comment wasn't referring to me though. There was a faint yet undeniable sweep of dust-colored hair on Gus's upper lip, which I purposely hadn't mentioned even though it had been getting more pronounced all summer. Gus was easily embarrassed but stayed quiet about his feelings. When I tried to catch his eye in the rearview mirror to apologize for Zoe's comment, he was staring out his window. Studying the soggy suburban terrain.

It was Gus's first day of high school, and he was acting like it was no big deal, but I worried about how it would affect him. There was the whole getting-from-one-side-of-the-school-to-the-other-in-under-four-minutes challenge. (Our high school was literally half a mile long.) He also happened to have been assigned the strictest Social Studies teacher, and there were new statewide exams for freshman reading comprehension—his worst subject.

Even more than that, I was scared about Gus socially. Not that I was doing so great in that category, but he was a sensitive kid.

Gus was truly one of the coolest people I knew, though I tried not to tell him that since he was and always would be two years younger than me. He was hilarious and freckly and taught himself this magic trick that I still couldn't decrypt where he pulled a quarter out of a raw egg. His room was like a mad scientist's laboratory—strewn with homemade contraptions and mysterious potions. On the windowsill was a pinball machine crafted out of cardboard, yarn, and pom-poms. Above his bed hung a weather station (aka an empty seltzer bottle and some twisted paper clips). Gus was always adding little flourishes or accoutrements to his inventions too. Re-angling a pipe cleaner or painting a lever. Floating about and dabbling here and there in a sort of mad-scientist dance. Gus was an amazing dancer. So lithe and fluid. Our favorite activity together was dressing up in things from Mom's closet and putting on talent shows. For a while, Gus let me paint his nails all different colors and smear big clouds of pink blush onto his cheeks. He had an alter ego named Gusaletta who hosted our shows, speaking in a prim British accent.

But in fifth grade, something happened at school. I never quite got the whole story. Only I knew it involved a lunch aide pointing out Gus's polished nails and calling him "one of *those.*"

Even though Gus acted like it didn't affect him and he strictly forbade Mom from talking to our grade-school principal, things changed after that.

Gus took off all his nail polish and started biting his fingernails so short that they bled a lot. He got very quiet. Then he began having chest pains and saying he couldn't breathe. Sometimes I woke up in the middle of the night to hear him panting and sobbing next to the nightlight in the hall. He became almost completely silent, though there was so much smoldering underneath. His teacher even sent a note home, asking if he should get his hearing tested. Mom took him to our pediatrician, who said there was nothing wrong physically and that these were probably anxiety attacks. Gus came home with a grape lollipop and a CD called *Meditations with Diana Gaia*. It was made by some woman who taught my mom yoga at the Y. All it had on it were different gong noises and someone whispering about breath as a moving entity. Somehow the energy of Diana Gaia was supposed to emerge from those sounds.

And crazy as it sounds—I think it did.

That summer before Gus went into middle school and I started Meadowlake High was actually the most calming, breathfull time in my life. Every night, before bed, Gus came into my room with that CD and we lay on my matted green carpet, listening to Diana Gaia and her gongs. We counted our inhales and exhales, envisioning warm violet light dancing around us. We let Diana Gaia take away all of our worries and send them floating down the river. As I held Gus's hands in mine, like a palm sandwich.

I missed those nights. I'd never told anyone about them—not even Zoe. Not that it was bad. It just didn't feel like it could or should be translated for anybody else besides me and Gus. I wasn't sure I understood it fully myself even.

"Here's good," Gus said, breaking my reverie. His voice was tight and high, which I knew meant he was feeling extra-nervous.

"You sure?" I asked.

We were still a block and a half away from the high school. Gus barely waited for me to come to a full stop though.

"Yeah. I need to walk a little or something. Smell ya later," was all he answered as he pushed open the rusty door and slid out.

"Text me if you need anything," I called. "Hope your day is amazeballs!"

"Balls," he answered softly. Which felt like at least partial victory. Gus and I thought it was ingenious and necessary to use the word *balls* as much as possible. Whenever one of us said it, the other had to repeat it, sort of as an affirmation. I watched Gus heave his backpack up a little higher and then sort of gallop away. I really hoped nobody saw him do that.

Certainly Zoe didn't.

"This is so off the hook," she said, shaking her head at her phone. "Guess how many hits we have now?"

I didn't know who *we* were and *what* we were hitting, so I guessed, "A million gazillion."

"More like *eighty-three thousand*," she answered.

"Wait, what are we talking about?"

"The Meowsers video. Didn't you read my post last night

about how crazy grateful I am and how you and my mom were so supportive and influential in the process?"

"I wasn't really online much last night. You mean the process of sneezing on your camera?"

"Shut your face!" Zoe said, punching me playfully. "I wrote all these nice things about you, Hank." She pulled my hand off the steering wheel and kissed it, leaving a glossy pucker mark. I appreciated her gratitude, but I was still a pretty nervous driver, so I yanked my hand back quickly and searched for a space where I could avoid the whole parallel parking idea.

Zoe was now reading aloud some of the adoring comments from her phone:

> You are too cute.
> This is everything.
> Can you be my new BFF?

"Don't worry; I already told that girl no," Zoe said.

"Wait—are you actually responding to these people?" I asked.

"I was up till two in the morning messaging with this girl in Holland. Her name is Saaskia. Saas-ki-ya? Not sure. Either way, her parents are going through a horrible divorce and she has three cats, but one is really old, so she just *gets* it, y'know?"

"Oh," I said, trying to tamp down the quivering jealousy in my tone.

"It wound up being really soothing and fun. Way better than my usual night terrors."

"Wait—is that still happening? You know you can call me."

"Yeah, it's brutal," Zoe said matter-of-factly. "And I guess I just assumed you didn't want to be up all night right before the first day of school. But it's fine. Honestly. The interwebs is saving me."

"Huh" was all I answered.

Yes, I was concerned that Zoe was still having trouble sleeping. She had gone so many sleepless nights last year that her doctor had prescribed "sleeping enhancement therapy." But most of me was confused and resentful that she was sharing these wee hours of the morning with total strangers. Whenever she pulled out her phone in front of me, I tried to turn it into a joke to hide my frustration. As in, "Can you maybe twit about that later?"

To which she liked to reply, "Sure, as long as you hash my tag."

I lurched into a parking space and turned on the windshield wipers by mistake. Zoe giggled. She also slammed the door shut so hard that the glove compartment swung open in response. HOT RIC had seen better days for sure.

"Can we do Yoshi's?" I asked.

"Sure, I guess."

Across the street from Meadowlake High School was Yoshi's Bagel Shack, home of the saltiest deli meats and the angriest waitstaff in the northern hemisphere. Not that I could blame them. Every school day, Yoshi's was packed with greedy, grabby, I'm-so-independent-yet-my-parents-still-pay-for-my-everything snoots. Today the throngs were ravenous. Groomed and eager.

I wanted to do a psychological study about the effects of massive amounts of carbohydrates on all these overly hormonal teenagers. There was an entire table howling with laughter about a dollop of blueberry cream cheese on some girl's nose and, right next to them, a couple feeding each other the seeds off an everything bagel and making out between bites. The air was so warm and yeasty that I was sure we'd all melt into buns.

Usually, Zoe and I could get in and out of there without talking to anyone but each other. But as I opened one of the beverage coolers to grab an orange juice, I heard behind me, "Zoe, that video was beyond amazing."

"Totally. *Beyond*."

Zoe was being swallowed up by a satellite of girls, led by the fiercely popular Colette McNamara and her BFF Freyja. (Colette was half French, on the track team, and had already lost her virginity. Freyja was Icelandic and spoke only in pouty whispers.)

"Should I just order for both of us?" I called over to Zoe. No response. I guess she was too busy fielding more questions about her new fame.

> *How did you think of that?*
> *Were the whiskers drawn on? I mean, obviously, right?*
> > *But were they?*
> *I'm so impressed you did this. It's huge.*
> *I bet if you make a whole series, you'll get into whatever*
> > *college you want.*
> *Right?*

I was waiting for Zoe to find my gaze and mouth, *Whatever.* We always talked about how artificial these girls were; how even their ponytails were fake. Zoe liked to say that in the rocky seas of teenhood, I was her safe harbor. A little raft of sanity or at least perspective while everyone around us buzzed with status updates and college preparations. Only, at this moment, she seemed happy enough to get carried around Yoshi's on their wave of admiration. She never once looked back to find me. Or maybe she did and my eyes were just too blurry from the glare of her sudden celebrity status. Maybe this was how a star was born— shot out of a cream cheese–filled cannon. One day Zoe was a hyper–theater nerd with her dweeby Sasquatch sidekick. The next she was catapulted into a life of raucous parties, private jets, and monogrammed tracksuits. With Sasquatch left just standing there in her own hairy shadow.

"Next up! Next up! Keep it moving!" Yoshi barked in my face.

"Right, sorry."

By the time I got and paid for our usual breakfast orders— wheat bagel with melted Swiss for me, cinnamon raisin with a side of fat-free cream cheese for Zoe—I could hear the first bell ringing across the street. The shop emptied out like an ant colony all pressing themselves through a pinhole opening.

"Hank!" I heard Zoe call from the crosswalk outside. "Hank, hurry up!"

I caught up to her and her new groupies just as they were saying their goodbyes.

"Wait, Colette, you have to tell Hank what you told me about the record deal."

"Oh yeah! Well, I was just saying that I know this girl who lives in the same town as my cousin outside Seattle and she made this really sad video about how depressed she was and how life was maybe not even worth living and then it went viral and all these people reached out to her even some local musicians because you know like everyone in Seattle is a musician or depressed or probably both but anyway they said please don't be so sad and also these are really haunting words and it should be a song and they recorded it and her single was number one on like a bunch of charts. Plus, she has a record deal and is obviously not sad at all anymore. Okay, see you guys later! Loveyabye!"

"Loveyabye," Zoe echoed softly. Then she turned to me and crossed her eyes. "So crazy, right?" she said. I was so relieved to hear her say that, I started cackling.

"Crazy nuts!" I said. "I mean with a side of nut sauce!"

Zoe didn't find it quite so funny though. "Okay, you don't have to make fun of me, you know."

"Um, excuse me? I'm not making fun of you."

"I mean, it's a little nuts. But I do have almost fifty *thousand* followers. Colette just reposted the video and it's . . ." She held up her phone for me, so I could see the tally of hearts pulsating on her screen. I felt like I was staring into a strobe light.

"Wow," I said. My voice sounded weak and uncertain. Probably because *I* was weak and uncertain. Zoe, on the other hand, stood up tall. She shook out her hair and smeared on another coat of lip gloss. Then she took a deep inhale and turned on her phone camera.

"Hello, my peeps. Thank you for getting me through another dark night. And here I go, off to my first day of junior year!" She blew a kiss to her fans and then rotated the camera to show her viewing audience the front of our high school. She looked like she was going to keep going and get me in the frame too, but I ducked down quickly.

Zoe thought that was hilarious.

"Hank—talk about nuts! I'm not gonna film you, ya big nerd. Look—it's off."

The second bell rang, making us officially late. I knew it wouldn't matter to Zoe, but I had Pre-Calc first period and I really didn't want to start the year on math's bad side. Plus, I was starving.

"Ooh. Don't forget." I handed Zoe the bag with her bagel in it. Or at least I tried to.

"What's this?" She scowled.

"Cinnamon raisin with a side of fat-free."

"Oh." She held it at arm's length as if the bag might also have a live grenade inside. "Did I ask you to get that?"

"No. But . . ." Zoe's eyes were cool and distant. Her lips, sealed shut. I didn't know how to get her to eat this, but looking at her puny shoulders, it felt urgent that she do so. "C'mon," I whined. "Just a bite?"

Zoe pinched her top lip between two fingers, as if trying to find the right words to say to me. Then she slapped on a wide, phony grin and said, "Sure! You know what? I'll have it for lunch."

She took the bag and stuffed it into her backpack, hooking her elbow through mine. "Yum!" she said. "Smells delish!"

If I were anyone else, I might've been fooled by this act of hers. But there was one thing I knew for sure.

Zoe Grace Hammer was a terrible liar.

Whatever.

At a certain point, I started getting a sick thrill from lying.

Gross, right?

Some people were easy to fool, like Alli. She put on her "concerned" face once in a while, but mostly she was just jealous I was giving her hand-me-down leggings. I think Travis was about to call me out on a bunch of bullshit at one point, but then he got caught in his own web of lies, so I guess he didn't feel like he could bring that up in casual conversation.

Poor bastards, huh?

And then once I let that first one escape, it rolled into another, and another. Grabbing everything in its path—scraps of truth and crumbs of someone else's story. It gets so big and sticky. Tumbling down a dirty hill of exaggerations and cover-ups and random details that couldn't possibly make a difference but why the heck not.

Powered by the wind of fairy farts and _what if_ . . .

How's that for some self-pitying poetry, huh?

I know, I know.

Lies don't happen _to_ *people. It's not like a tsunami swept through my brain and reset my truth-o-meter. At some point, I chose to jump in whole hog. And then it got even more exciting, because I had to keep track of all my details—the dizzying count of cuts and calories and concocted alibis.*

"I just ate.

I'm not hungry.

Wow, that cat scratches a lot."

There's a crazy momentum to it all. A rush of adrenaline that you can't get from most sports drinks or slushies, ya know?

I even convinced myself that I was lying to spare everyone else my pain.

If I lied, no one needed to worry.

If I lied, we could all just keep on keepin' on.

So I told another simple, heartfelt lie.

Easier on everyone that way. Right?

CHAPTER 5
laughing on the banks of a fjord

IF YOU'RE LUCKY ENOUGH TO BE BORN IN FINLAND, SCHOOL IS actually a humane process. You learn how to sew your own bathing suit or cook a hot breakfast, and you take one test in your senior year of high school that may or may not affect where you go for university.

Not that I wanted to sew my own bathing suit, but it made more sense than the madness of junior year at Meadowlake High.

Everybody in my grade was either:

a. certifiably insane;

b. hyperventilating about some newly mandated statewide comprehensive-yet-inconclusive assessment tests plus doing enough charity work to make their college applications "stand out";

c. quoting the new *Will you be my pussyyyyy . . . cat?* memes; or

d. all of the above.

Obviously, the answer was *d*. If only real life gave you multiple choices.

Meadowlake was supposedly one of the more easygoing suburbs on the East Coast in terms of academic stress loads. We were even written up in the *New York Times* Real Estate section for having the most adolescent smiles per square mile or something like that. Only, once we got spit out onto the high school lawn, we started getting quizzed on every fact since the Big Bang and had to visit at least three colleges per semester. Some people in my town literally had tutors for their tutors.

By lunchtime, I had already done two practice exams and heard three lectures on how this was the most important and influential year of my academic career. Also, that the future of New Jersey public school funding depended on my scores. (As if my knowledge of Common Core was going to keep our walls from crumbling.) The teachers seemed pissed off and tired. I literally heard two girls behind me in Math whisper:

This could make or break us.

Right???

The only class that felt potentially inspiring or even educational, was Advanced Contemporary American History with Gerry Harvey. Yes, he had two first names. Plus, a lot of pictures of him with older famous people—like Rosa Parks, Ronald Reagan, and some lady with incredible hair and a bedazzled drum kit. Mr. Harvey was known for being the hardest grader in the school and for sneezing so loudly the windows shook. As I walked into the classroom, there were maps of the world taped up on every inch of wall space and in the background was a staticky recording of someone singing "We Shall Overcome."

"So a little about me," Mr. Harvey said, striding around the room. He was a large man, today wearing a checkered shirt that could easily double as a tablecloth. He hummed under his breath as he walked.

"I grew up in a little town outside Raleigh, North Carolina. My mom was a nurse's aide and she made sure we had clothes on our backs and food in our bellies. Me and my brothers marched for Dr. King. We marched for Kent State. We marched to end the Vietnam War. I went to Rutgers and did my master's at Montclair State and I know you're all fascinated but it's important. Because there were times when all I had were the clothes on my back and some sugar packets for my next meal. But I made it. And I learned—the hard way—that there is no such thing as genius or even talent. There's just hard work and dedication. What else? Oh—and I've been teaching in this school system for twenty-five years. I am passionate about history and I have no time for bullshit excuses. Any questions?"

Mr. Harvey got an appreciative rumble from the class for cursing. Then he started passing out name tags for us.

"It'll take me a few days to get all your names," he continued. "I'm trusting you have pens. Remember those?"

There were a few groans and a lot of zippered compartments being opened.

Madison Macomb—who was one of the most annoying overachievers and already owned three Harvard hoodies and a matching car magnet—raised her hand next to me. Mr. Harvey walked right by her, so I guess Madison was forced to take matters into her own hands.

"Um, excuse me? We were told last year that we could take notes on our computers since there's no Wi-Fi and it cuts down on the amount of time we spend transferring our notes at night."

"Is that so?" Mr. Harvey grinned.

Madison nodded eagerly, opening her computer. Mr. Harvey came by and closed it in the same breath.

"Well, I thank you for that information. Right now, however, we are starting off with a little exercise that has nothing to do with your notes or the transference of said notes from one medium to another."

Madison was blinking so fast I thought her eyelashes might catapult off her face. So another Madison—McDougal? Finnemore? (they all melded together for me)—took over where Madison Macomb had left off. "It's just that we have two statewides to prepare for this year and some of us have after-school activities, so we like to—"

"Yes! Statewides!" Mr. Harvey declared, cutting her off. "As I was saying, this class is called Advanced Contemporary American History. Yes, we have a lot of material to cover and I will do my best to give it to you in a cohesive manner. However, we are living in quite a phenomenal and terrifying moment in history. So I'd like to just start by asking, can anyone tell me how many states currently allow guns to be sold without a permit and yet will not allow a woman the right to choose?"

I heard a couple of guesses, but no one was bold enough to speak louder than a mumble. Mr. Harvey stood at the front of the room again, arms folded. It was clear he'd wait as long as it took for us to get it together.

"Okay, let's try this. Anybody know why we currently have troops on the ground in three different regions of the Middle East?"

More murmurs passed around, but nothing intelligible.

"Fascinating," Mr. Harvey said. He pressed a piece of chalk up to his lips. Probably to stop himself from laughing or screaming at our idiocy. "Last question. Who is *this* lady?"

He pointed to the picture of the woman with the sparkly drum kit. Mr. Harvey looked about thirty years younger in that photo, but he still had the same mischievous smile and shiny bald head.

Mr. Harvey paused for just a breath before giving up on us that time.

"Forget it. I know you all love to google everything so go home and look up 'the Queen of Percussion.'" Then he looked straight at Madison Macomb and said, "And no, you don't get extra credit for it, but it's still valuable information. Now! Where were we? Oh yes, getting all excited about those testy tests. Okay, take out your pens or computers or however you feel you can best ingest this information and copy this down. *Now*."

He tugged on the world map at the front of the room so it rolled in on itself with a *snap*. Then he started writing in large angular letters on the chalkboard beneath:

and when we speak we are afraid
our words will not be heard
nor welcomed
but when we are silent
we are still afraid

So it is better to speak
remembering
we were never meant to survive.

—*AUDRE LORDE*

He read the quote aloud to us in a firm, low tone. Doubling back to repeat that last doozy of a line for emphasis.

"So," he continued, "just to be clear. We as a species are not meant to survive. We will expire. You as students in my class will expire a lot sooner if you choose to just sit there. I don't find silence cute or obedient. I find it *lazy*." His eyes roamed the room, glimmering. "Now, given that we are living in a time when immigrants' rights, women's rights, really everyone's rights are being compromised, I'd like to hear some ways in which you are *speaking out and taking action* as part of this democracy. Please, take a few minutes to write a page about this quote and what it means to you."

Madison Macomb needed to know how many words constituted a page and whether it should be double-spaced. Ariel Thompson wanted to know how much this assignment counted toward the whole grade for the semester. There were a barrage of concerns and clarifications, and again I thought about how in Finland there was probably someone my age knotting the hem on her bikini while laughing on the banks of a fjord. If I was ever able to make a family of my own, I would have to move there for the sake of my children.

I opened my new unicorn journal from Zoe and jotted down:

watch the news?

turkey drive for the homeless?

Because those were the only things I'd done that were remotely close to activism.

"Right. So who would like to share with us first?" Mr. Harvey commanded.

This time, he waited for approximately ten seconds. Then he took a copy of some hefty textbook off his desk, raised it over his head, and dropped it to the floor. The *smack* was so deafening, it got a few gasps. Mr. Harvey was pleased. He smiled with all his teeth showing before saying, "Participation is *mandatory*. In this class and in life. So now, who would like to read aloud?"

All the Madisons shot their hands up. I did too, though I had no idea what to say yet. I really didn't want to be first. Or last. Or anywhere in between.

Mr. Harvey nodded approvingly. He let Madison Thompson talk about how she recently went to a life-changing town hall meeting. Madison Ramos said she was part of a social action committee at her church. There were a few accounts of going to DC for the Women's March, and Mike Bendetti asked if online petitions counted, because he signed a ton of those.

Mr. Harvey didn't exactly answer. He stood at the front of the classroom with hands on hips, chewing on the inside of his cheek and taking it all in. Everyone was tumbling and rushing over one another in a storm of words and excuses. I just kept my hand raised, desperately scrolling through my lackluster past in my head. Hoping I could figure out something to report before he got to me.

And there he was. Standing over me with his big jowls and eager eyes. He was demanding but also encouraging.

"Yes? Hannah?"

I opened my notebook to the first page, where I'd written some random thoughts. Or at least that's what I thought I was doing. Only the first page must have been actually the second. And when I flipped back the unicorn cover now, it said in big block Zoe letters:

PUSSY POWER!

"Oh," I heard Mr. Harvey say to me. To my pussified notebook. I shut the book closed and squeaked, "Um, sorry . . . I mean, yeah. Sorry."

"Aha!" boomed Mr. Harvey. "Sorry." Then he said it slower.

73

"Sooorrrry. The most detestable word in the English language. Besides *quinoa*, I guess."

The class chuckled. But Mr. Harvey was not smiling now.

"I joke about it, but I'm deadly serious." Now his eyes were laser-focused on me. "Sorry is never the answer. It's one of those words that I just don't trust."

Forty-three minutes later, I was sitting on top of Weiner Hill, listening to a chorus of *sorry*s. It was incredible how many people came to this place to cry. When Zoe and I first staked out our spot by the chain-link fence as our lunch meet-up two years before, we had no idea it was such a mecca for breakups and meltdowns. It made sense though. Reggie's Weiner Hut was conveniently located directly across from Meadowlake High's gymnasium. It was a hot spot for people to neck over two-dollar milk shakes and French fries. Then they strolled back up the hill for fifth period, arm in arm, sometimes pausing to have a serious—that is, teary—talk about where this relationship was going anyway. And then to end it in a flurry of apologies.

Each lunch—or really, the twenty-nine minutes called lunch when Zoe and I caught up on people-watching and bitching about how horrible our lives were—I was reminded of how small my universe was and how many reasons there were to sob. There was a whole hierarchy to this small tuft of land too—the cliques of the cool or even semi–socially acceptable dotting the brown grass in prescribed order. Preps by the maple tree. Piercings on the crumbling brick wall. Artsy misfits lugging random set pieces through the back entrance to the auditorium and kids from the low-income apartments staking out the one picnic table.

I was feeling really low after that exchange with Mr. Harvey and just wanted to talk to Zoe one-on-one. It wasn't exactly her fault that I'd opened to her PUSSY POWER note, but it did feel like we needed to check in about it. Only Zoe was holding court with Colette, Freyja, and a posse of lacrosse guys that I didn't even recognize. It was hard to catch Zoe for some eye contact. I pulled out my yogurt and the rest of my bagel from breakfast and sat down. I really wanted to see how Gus was doing, but his lunch period was before mine and I knew he wouldn't dare keep his phone on in class.

"Whatcha doin', lady love?" Zoe said. She did a dramatic fall into my lap and I extracted my yogurt cup just before it exploded all over us both. "Oops, sorry about that!" She grinned and gave me a peck on the cheek.

"S'all good. Did you have your bagel already?" I asked.

She narrowed her eyes and tried to push out a smile, but it looked pained.

"Mmmm," she said. Then she tucked her head up under my chin and sang, "Sooorrrry."

Let's not forget the other half of the lie, though.

The believer.

Um, that's you, Hank.

And you know that I know that you know that the world knows you're too smart to have bought any of those make-believes I fed you. Sometimes I watched you pause or raise an eyebrow. And I thought,

Today's the day when she's going to crack me open and make me come clean.

Only you never did.

Whether consciously or not, that was a CHOICE you made.

To accept, ignore, spruce up, and bedazzle all my lies so they fit into your life easily too.

I know, I know. You hate confrontation.

Who knows if you'll even read these words one day.

But it's true.

In some ways you wanted me to lie.

It gave you an excuse to pull away.

And then at some point, I know you started hurling your own lies back at me. Was that fun for you?

There's a hell of a lot more you can do once you decide to live in a pretend world, right?

And yes, the same rules apply, and I could've should've needed to call you out on it. But I was busy.

I guess the point is,

I don't want you to ever whitewash this into your tragedy, Hank.

It's not.

You were dishonest and deceptive, and you betrayed me. More than once.

But I digress.

Where were we?

Oh yes, the joys of lying. Which I guess we're both experts in now. Can you at least admit that yet?

Yours till the coco puffs,

Z

CHAPTER 6

fpoe

I TEXTED GUS DURING LAST PERIOD: *WANT ME TO DRIVE YOUR* balls home?

No thanks, trying out for freshman choirballs, he wrote back.

After walking halfway home by myself, I realized I'd driven to school for the first time today and turned around to get the car. Then I forgot where I'd parked the car and lost another twenty minutes to my sad sense of nondirection. Finally I located HOT RIC in the staff parking lot, with a handwritten warning from the vice principal that I did not have a staff permit and was in danger of being towed. At last I came home.

I had a ludicrous amount of homework—proving some hypothesis in Chemistry, disproving another in Pre-Calculus. One hundred pages of a biography about Cesar Chavez and an openended and unanswerable question about what it means to be an active member of society. I had no idea how to tackle that one. I did do my googling though, and I found out that the Queen of Percussion was a kickass lady named Sheila E. I got lost in a video of her hammering away on the drums for at least an hour. Amazed by her boldness and the number of sequins on her jacket. She was one of those rare musicians who really lived inside the music.

"Helloooooo!" shouted Mom some time later. As I looked up from my computer, I saw the sky was already lowering its shade into night.

"Hey!" I yelled down. "Gus was trying out for choir! I haven't heard from him since three!"

"Got him!" Mom replied. "Come on down and join us! I got you both a delicious treat!"

I was a little terrified that the treat would be Elan and a tub of his special lentil-seaweed chili. Surely Mom wouldn't be that clueless and cruel. Besides, I really wanted to hear how Gus's first day went and obviously I was getting nowhere on my actual assignments.

"Pace yourself," Mom was telling Gus when I came down the stairs. He was inhaling a slice of Sicilian from Village Pizza in the middle of the kitchen. He hadn't even taken off his backpack yet.

"My girl!" Mom cheered, drawing me in for a hug. Her breath was leaping with garlic.

"Whoa."

"I know. Gus and I couldn't help ourselves on the way home. There's two more with pepperoni and three slices with mush-rooms."

Most important, there was no Elan. He was realigning some-one's coccyx or busy with a men's mah-jongg tournament tonight. It didn't matter. I was just thrilled to have this much mozzarella cheese and unaccompanied time with my mom and Gus in the same room. I swiped a plate and a slice from the counter and chomped down gratefully.

"How was Social Studies?" I asked Gus.

"Eh," he answered.

"You find that shortcut behind the gym we practiced?"

He nodded, mouth still too full to elaborate.

"Choir?"

I got a thumbs-up and a grunt for that. I tried reading between the lines, but Gus wouldn't look at me. With his face tilted down I could see that Zoe was right—his upper-lip fuzz was getting darker. As in, moments away from being an undeniable mustache.

"What about *your* day?" Mom asked me. I wanted to tell her that everybody was phony and self-obsessed, and that Zoe was getting dangerously thin. And that instead of running the rat race that was college applications, I wanted to travel to Greece and work on an olive oil farm or build schools and freshwater wells in developing nations while listening to Sheila E.

Only Mom looked so serene. And I didn't want to ruin this family pizza party with my sad life. So I settled on, "All good. The usual."

"How about . . . Did either of you ask any good questions?" This was Mom's favorite conversation starter with us. Only I truly couldn't recall asking a single thing.

Gus swallowed a lump of crust and wiped the pizza grease from his chin with the back of his sweatshirt sleeve before raising his hand.

"Yes," Mom said with a smile. "Gus, you may speak."

"Well, I asked Ms. Nelson whether a thesis statement always had to be summarized at the end of a persuasive essay," said Gus. Mom nodded slowly, obviously pleased. "And then I also asked Mr. Teller how many lockdown drills we would be doing over the course of the school year." I watched Mom take in that information and sort of wince. Last year there had been a school shooting in a high school two counties west of us. One fatality. Gus had been pretty fixated on the story and we even talked as a family about where our meeting point would be if there were ever a violent incident and we couldn't get straight home. I thought after that he'd let it go. But obviously not.

"That's a great question," Mom said. "And what was the answer?"

"Between ten and twelve," Gus reported. "Standard for this part of the country." He did not emote at all. Just put another piece of pizza in his mouth and kept chewing.

Mom looked at me and smiled—a little less brightly now, but still keen to connect.

"And how about you, Miss Hannah Louise?"

"Sorry, but no. I mean, I'm not sorry, but no I didn't ask any questions really. I mean, there's not much time, and we have so much curriculum to cover."

Mom did this awkward thing where she tried to rub my shoulder and Gus's at the same time, but she also had this floppy piece of mushroom pizza in her hand so it sort of shook sauce all over the table.

"Well, I am so proud of you both for having successful first days. And in case you were wondering, my budget meeting went swimmingly and I had a remarkable conference call. So l'chaim!" She lifted her slice in celebration.

Mom still taught ESL part-time. She also did public relations for a human rights nonprofit in Newark, which she said was only mildly stimulating but perfect for her needs. It meant her commute was just twenty minutes and she could be home for dinner with us, which was vital to her.

"Oh! And I looked into getting a few two-person tents for this weekend, just in case you change your mind," she began. "Would that be more fun than a giant tent for all four of us? Maybe you want to invite some friends to come with?"

I had to shut down that line of inquiry before it went anywhere farther down this twiggy trail. I didn't want to hurt her feelings, but I knew she would research every tent on the market if I didn't stop her now.

"Sorry, Mom. There's just a lot of stuff going on this weekend. I'm fine staying here. Gus, you probably have a ton of stuff too, right? First weekend of . . . choir?"

I wanted to give him a better out, but I hadn't really thought through the possibilities. As Mom turned to Gus, I pushed more pizza into my mouth so I couldn't physically say anything stupider on his behalf.

Gus didn't sound like he needed my help anyway though. "Yeah," he said. "I think I'd rather stay home."

"Fair enough. I'll ask Ricky to come stay with you guys." Mom wiped her mouth and gave us a satisfied smile. I wondered if she was contemplating more alone time with Elan in a slippery sleeping bag. Then I started thinking about what they could do together in a sleeping bag and I forgot how to breathe and swallow at the same time. Mom had to thwack me on the back a few times to keep me from choking.

"All right," Mom announced. "Dinner adjourned! I'm sure you two have a bunch of homework and I'll go call Ricky."

Gus gave her the thumbs-up and headed for the stairs.

"Oh and don't forget—school schedule is in effect. Lights out by ten thirty."

Yes, I was almost seventeen years old and had to be in my pajamas by ten on school nights—lights out by ten thirty at the latest. Not something I liked to admit in mixed company. Or to myself for that matter. This was perhaps the lamest trait of my mother's. She was a fanatic about everyone in our family getting eight hours of uninterrupted sleep per night. She always had been, though it didn't really humiliate me until I hit middle school and hosted the most pathetic slumber party in the world. Seriously, I loved and admired my mom. I could even look past the fact that she wore orthotic insteps and still said things like "coolio" and "dis." But her sleep requirements were beyond annoying.

Zoe knew about my sad curfew too. So when my phone buzzed at ten fifteen that night, I was trying to wrap up this Chemistry problem set and felt like it had to be an emergency or else she wouldn't have dared.

Deck door, was all she wrote.

Mom was spooning out her decaf coffee for her morning routine as I tried to slip past her.

"Um, excuse me, young lady. Where are you going?"

"Mom, it's Zoe."

"I've told you that the average teenager needs at least eight to nine hours of sleep per night in order to develop a healthy metabolism, bone strength, and mental—"

"I'm so sorry, Jean," Zoe gushed as I opened the sliding door. Mom had never invited Zoe to call her by her first name, and it still made me cringe.

"It's okay," Mom said in a measured tone. "Just make it quick, please. It's late."

"I know. I totally forgot about the time. I'll be really quick, I promise." Zoe rushed at me and fell into my arms. I could feel her body vibrating as she burrowed her nose into my shoulder. She was so cold and damp that I looked outside to see if there was a monsoon, but everything was dark and dry.

"Is your mom still here?" Zoe scream-whispered.

"Yes," I hissed back. "She lives here."

Mom looked torn between watching us and the clock on the stove. She rinsed out a mug that was already clean and returned it to the dish rack.

"Listen girls, I'll give you a *few minutes* to talk alone, and then . . . you know the drill. It is a school night."

As soon as Mom's foot landed on the first creaky step upstairs, Zoe wormed her hands into my armpits and started tickling me ferociously. She knew all my most ticklish spots too—I was helpless when she did this.

"What . . . is . . . happening?" I eked out in between giggles.

Zoe pulled away from me and flashed her widest, soggiest puppy-dog eyes.

"Please don't be mad at me," she said with a coy smile. "I did this because I think you're incredibly talented and smart and I know you don't like to be in the spotlight but maybe if we're in it together it could be superfun . . . ?" She started doing one of her goofy dances that looked like a rubber chicken on crack. Twirling me around and trying to dip me, but she lost her footing and crashed into the refrigerator door.

"Girls?" called Mom from upstairs.

"All good!" I hollered back. I focused back on Zoe. "You know we have only like eight minutes so please tell me (a) are you drunk, and (b) what is going on?"

"Ha!" Zoe laughed, then tried to steady herself. "Okay, not drunk. As you know, I think that's a waste of calories. But I could use maybe a glass of water. Wait, let me tell you what's happening first."

I got her the glass of water, but she couldn't stop talking long enough to drink it.

"So you know how Alli's been saying that if I get my grades up she would take me to meet her commercial agent?"

I nodded, though I had no memory of this deal and it sounded shady. Zoe was ecstatic, however. Swinging my arms and tap dancing while she narrated her tale.

"So I took this new dose of Ritalin the last two weeks and when I got to school today, Madame Sharp tested me and said I placed out of Beginning French! Which I guess was all Alli needed, because . . ."

Somehow, Zoe wove together her new attention span with a trip to see Alli's commercial agent who apparently didn't have much in the way of work for Alli but loved Zoe's new Meowsers video—calling it "lit." Also, he was the same agent who represented Taylor Swift's pet llama and he had offices in LA and New York, but he enjoyed the grit of New York better because he felt like even the sidewalks were more authentic.

"Zoe!" I begged. "What does this have to do with anything?"

"Right," Zoe continued giddily. "Doesn't matter. Anyway, this is when we get to the part with you, which I hope . . ."

Here she paused to take a deep inhale, forcing out a smile as bright as a billboard. When she breathed out, I felt a cloud of her sugar-free-Bubblemint breath shimmering around me. "Hank, he wants to represent the Pussycat Warriors!"

"The whocat whats?" I asked.

"That's us!" she yipped.

"Huh?"

I was so bewildered and tense. I was not looking forward to Zoe's explanation.

"I mean, I had to come up with a name right there on the spot so I'm sorry if you don't like it, but I feel like this is what we always talked about doing, right?"

"I don't know what it is we're doing," I admitted. "Please, just start from the beginning again."

"*A very good place to staaaaaart*," sang Zoe. She waited for me to recognize the tune or applaud, but I couldn't muster either of those. So she jumped back into her account.

"First of all, he loved the video. *Loved* it. And then he said, 'Do you have any other music?' And I was like, 'Well, I have this band . . .' And then of course, Alli was like, 'You do?' And I said, 'Yes, Mom. I do.'"

"What band?" I had to ask.

"*Our* band!" she said. "The Pussycat Warriors! See, this is what I'm trying to tell you! I think you're so talented on the piano, Hank. I mean, you played at Carnegie Hall! Which I also told him—"

"No."

"Yes! But here's the thing. He was like, 'Music is where it's at *right now*. And this industry is moving fast. Especially teen bop.'"

"Teen bop?"

"Teen pop? I'm not sure exactly how he said it, but I told him we could make really teen-boppy stuff and we would show him one of our music videos this week." She must've seen my face

87

turn all kinds of angry because she stopped herself and said, "Or next week is fine."

"How the hell are we gonna . . . ?"

"Please???" Zoe took both my hands and pressed them to her chest. I could feel her heart thumping so frantically underneath. Like it was pleading.

"But . . ."

"I know," said Zoe. "It's the stupidest idea ever, but it can be really simple. Just piano and vocals, like a hip-hop ballot—"

"You mean ball*ad*?"

"Exactly!" she said, raising herself up and down on her toes. She could literally never stand still. "Oh, thank you, Hank! Thank you thank you you're the bestest *ever*."

I had never said yes. But I also hadn't said no. This was always how it went with Zoe. She was so brash and reckless. So close to euphoria or disaster at every turn. I could never catch up to where she was headed next or what wild vision she was following.

And yet I adored her. I couldn't live without her. She really was my best and *only* friend at this point. Sad but true, I had let most of my other friendships fizzle out around third grade. I even told my sweet neighbor Maribeth that I "didn't have time for other relationships" because Zoe and I were "serious BFFs" and I had to concentrate exclusively on her. Maribeth still lived just across the wooden fence around my backyard, but we hadn't spoken in more than five years. I wondered what kind of smoke-inhalation damage I could get from burned bridges.

Zoe framed my face in her hands and shook me a little. "Hey, if you don't want to do it, I get it," she said in a hushed voice. "I know I'm kinda forcing you. But it's only because I believe in us. You are an incredible musician, Hank. You know that, right?"

Now my heartbeat was the one battering away. The only things vaguely tethering me to earth were Zoe's cool palms. If I'd thought it through, I would have realized she hadn't heard me play piano in years. No one close to me had. But I wanted to trust her so badly.

"And who knows?" Zoe went on, petting my hair tenderly. "Maybe this agent can actually get us some money! Did I tell you the Meowsers video is already number three on CatLife.com and number eighteen on FelineFanatics?"

I really wanted to know who the other seventeen were ahead of her, but I resisted asking.

"Girls, it's after ten thirty, and this is not the way to start your school year," my mom called. I could hear her coming down the stairs and I knew she'd be pissed.

Zoe pulled me back in though. Her face so close, our noses were touching. "I mean, we *have* to, right?" she urged. "This is it! This is what we've been waiting for!"

Then she kissed me so tenderly just next to my ear and whispered, "Pleeeeaaaase," before pulling open our back door and skipping out into the night.

"Make sure to look in your pocket!" she added as she ran down the deck stairs.

Somehow, someway—probably while she was wooing me

with her musical compliments and cuddling—Zoe had slipped one of her little drawings into my hoodie pocket.

"Hannah—*NOW*," growled Mom as I unfolded the scrap of lined paper.

It was two stick figures with bulbous eyeballs. One had a nest of corkscrew hair (me) and the other had a ponytail made of slashes (her). I locked the door and turned out the deck light. I could still see the blue glow of Zoe's phone fading into our backyard. I tried to refold the note and was tucking it away again when I noticed the scrawled heart on the other side.

In ballpoint pen beneath, Zoe had written, *H, you are my FPOE. xoxo, Z.*

There was no moon to help me find her out there now. The backyard was a pool of empty dark.

FPOE? I texted.

Favorite. Pussy. On. Earth, she wrote back.

Best Friends Forever and Ever to Infinity
Addendum

When in the course of not-so-friendly-yet-human events, it
becomes necessary for one friend to dissolve
the suffocating bands that have connected her
with the other, she shall do so.
Preferably in private and not with a captive audience.
Plus, some warning would be nice.

Heretofore and forthwith,
We hold these truths to be self-evident; that all people
are created equal—
fat, thin, short, tall, round, skinny, obnoxiously pretty.
At least that's what they tell me.
What's clear is that we all have feelings.
And we all know how to hurt—each other and ourselves.

So we the people declare this friendship null and void.

CHAPTER 7
commuter's paradise

"**IS THAT A CRACK IN YOUR WINDSHIELD OR ARE YOU JUST HAPPY TO** see me?" Gus said as we waited outside Zoe's house the next morning.

"Ferreals?! HOT RIC, what happened?"

It was pretty minuscule, up in the far-right corner and tripping downward in five small tentacles. Still, between the parking lot misdemeanor yesterday and this glinting fissure, it felt like my stint at car ownership was not going well so far.

"What do you do for a crack?" I asked.

Gus laughed. "You really want me to answer that?"

I'd forgotten how sweet my little brother's smile was, especially since he'd gotten his braces off last summer.

"What?" he said now, scowling at me a little. I guess I was

staring—or really, squinting—at his face. There was a small tide of pink bumps along his upper lip this morning. I'd seen a disposable razor on the shelf in our shower but hadn't thought about why it was there.

"Hey, did you do that because of what happened yesterday?" I asked. I really hoped Zoe hadn't made him feel compelled to shave.

"Do what?"

"Ya know . . ." I pointed below my own nose to explain. Gus just stared at me blankly.

So I tried to make a conversation detour, turning it back on myself. "I mean, I should do something about this 'stache sitch, huh?" I twirled some imaginary handlebars for comedic effect. "I did bleach at the beginning of the summer, but it feels like I need to invest in some longer-lasting procedures. Like, maybe they have a special turtle wax that I can use on both the car and my body . . ."

"Huh," was all Gus said.

"Gettin' a little Schmekel-y, I'd say," I tried.

At least that got a semi-chuckle out of him.

Gus used to find me hilarious. Or at least that's how I like to remember us. Even before Dad died and Mom retreated into her coat, Gus and I took care of each other. We made each other laugh. We constructed huge couch forts and put on elaborate shows that involved way too many costume changes. My favorite one being *Rebbe Schmekel and His Burning Bush*.

I was Rebbe Schmekel, with a long gray beard that dangled

in straggly tufts. It fit around my head with a rubber band and a chip clip for sizing and somehow smelled like wet dog, but I loved it. I stooped forward just like our real rabbi and proclaimed, "I am the rabbi. I come from Mount Sinai. Let us praaaay."

Then Gus jumped out from behind our brown corduroy couch and yelled, "A burning bush!" which launched us into Gus's song:

> *A burning bush ooh ooh*
> *It is so hot hot hot*
> *It is so burning burning burning*
> *Where did it come from? Nobody knows!*
> *But it's still burning whoa whoa!*

Gus's dancing was truly the highlight—he was born knowing how to do impossible things like the worm and a slithering spin. Mom and Dad always went berserk, clapping and hooting when we were done.

Rebbe Schmekel stuck around for a good year or so. Whenever I had playdates from grade school, I'd ask if we could play dress up. If anyone was willing, I showed them my purple tutu and Wonder Woman shield, my Jedi mask and drippy fake jewels. Then, at the last minute, I reached under my dresser and unfolded the special empty pillowcase where I kept my Schmekel beard. I tried to always say something flippant like, "Huh? Where'd this come from?" before sliding the elastic over my head and assuming my slouched posture. It was a good friend-vetting process—Zoe was the only one who ever asked for more of "the Schmekel guy." She put on one of my dad's humongous cardigans and pretended to be Schmekel's best friend, Syd. Her Jewish accent was horrible though.

We never formally retired the Schmekel routine. It was more that once I saw our real rabbi giving my dad's eulogy and then slumping away from the open grave, I didn't see anything fun or funny about him anymore. I was furious that this stooped, withered geezer was still hobbling around, blessing the birds and the bees, life and death and the mystery of it all, while my dad lay lifeless in a box underground.

Also, the sad truth is, I abandoned Schmekel. And Gus, for that matter. Whenever he asked me to rehearse or even put on my disheveled beard, I told him I had other stuff to do. Like baking pink cupcakes with Zoe or planning my sleepover outfits with Zoe or finishing my homework so I could go over to Zoe's house.

I didn't do it intentionally. But I did it nonetheless. And now I had to admit that my little brother was growing up. With or without me.

At 7:47, he leaned his head out the open window and shouted at Zoe's house, "Helloooooo? Anybody home? First bell's gonna ring in just a few!"

"Is it?" I asked.

Not that I was actually surprised. I'd been watching the clock just as closely as Gus, but I thought maybe if I acted like it was no biggie, he could take it less seriously too. It was obvious from the empty driveway and the darkened windows that Zoe and her mom were not home. We'd been idling there for close to fifteen minutes now. I'd already texted and called Zoe multiple times. No response.

"Could we maybe just wait two more minutes before giving up?" I asked Gus.

He grunted something that resembled agreement, then busied himself with rechecking his backpack for the right textbooks and school supplies.

Yes, my brother was a little fanatical about being prepared and on time to everything. Or really, five minutes early, which I found somewhat endearing. Only, with Zoe ten minutes late to everything, I often felt pulled into two different time zones.

Zoe wasn't late, exactly. It was more that she crammed five thousand activities into each hour. Case in point—this morning. My phone started chiming now. First it was a post from Alli—a picture of her and Zoe at the gym with some man who looked like he was made entirely of tendons. Below it read:

> Thank you @RealBodyBernardo for humbling me with his Booty Camp Challenge. My badass teen came too! #betterthanever #mommydaughterbadassery #totestwinsies

Then I got a picture from @Mr.Meowsersz that was his face surrounded by a flock of flushed women and Soul Trainer bikes.

Meowowow! was his caption.

And under it, @RealBodyBernardo weighed in with, **Help! I'm surrounded by the hottest ladies on earth!**

Luckily, Gus didn't see any of these updates. If he did, I knew he'd have some choice words about the fact that Zoe was making us late so she could get in a predawn workout. Really, they were the same words that I was wrestling with in my brain. Only I was too wimpy to admit it.

"You know, she just has a lot going on right now. With her parents and—wait, did I tell you that she and I got representation?"

"Who and what are you talking about?" Gus said.

"Zoe. And me! Starting a band."

"Okay . . . and what does that mean?"

"Good question! Yeah, I'm not totally sure, but it's exciting, right? We're supposed to make a music video and you're welcome to sing or dance in it. And apparently this agent really wants to see our stuff like, in the next week."

"That's great," Gus said in a dull monotone.

"Yeah, it's . . ."

Gus's watch announced that we were now officially late for the first bell. I could feel his frustration smoldering. I just didn't know how to bail on Zoe without her being mad too.

"Okay!" I said with forced brightness. "Let's get going, shall we?" I gritted my teeth and texted Zoe an overcomplicated explanation of how my brother was struggling with this transition to high school and I needed to get him there immediately but if she still needed a ride I could loop back around and skip first period and how maybe in the future we should check in with each other's schedules the night before so there could be clearer communication about morning transportation routines.

Zoe texted back instantly:

No worries hott mama! Luv u madly!

No apology or justification. Only poor spelling and an emoji of a cat blowing kisses.

"Yes! Yes! Seven minutes till the second bell. We can do this, yo!" I gunned the motor and heard HOT RIC's gears scrape and whine.

"Hank, I think you're in neutral," Gus said.

"Of course I am. I knew that. Just testing you. Gotta be ready for your permit. When do you sign up for Driver's Ed anyway? I should take you for a test drive!" My babbling couldn't distract either of us from the fact that we made it precisely a block and a half before getting sucked into the daily parade of minivans that dropped off at the train station.

"Seriously?" Gus fumed.

Our town was "a commuter's paradise" according to all the real estate agents and news anchors in the tristate area. Which sounded like an oxymoron to me, but I guess it kept our property values high and meant that on most weekday mornings we had a line of cars wrapping around the park.

Again, I attempted to redirect Gus's attention though I picked the absolute worst topic for conversation.

"So that lockdown thing. Is that still bothering you?"

"Nah," answered Gus.

"I mean, cuz you said you asked Mr. Teller about procedures . . ."

"Yeah, I just wanted some clarity."

"Okay, well, if you ever want to talk about it. Or . . . yeah."

We sank back into silence as the knot of traffic around us kept expanding.

"How about any fun people in your classes?" I asked.

"I guess."

"Some mildly inspiring teachers?"

"Sure." Gus wasn't making this any easier. I could tell by the way his feet were jittering that he was losing his cool.

"Hey. Gus."

"Yeah?"

"No, you're supposed to say, *Hay is for horses*," I instructed.

"I am?"

"Yeah. Remember, Dad taught us that."

"Oh . . . yeah." I couldn't tell whether he actually remembered or was just humoring me so I'd shut up. Either way, it made me feel even crankier. I didn't understand how Gus could forget vital information like this and I had no idea how to shove these memories back into his brain.

"Forget it. How about this weekend, while Mom's on her wilderness adventure, we watch the entire *Star Wars* series again?"

The last I checked, Gus still had five *Star Wars* posters in his room, and last year he'd written an English paper on the symbolism of Yoda's grammar. I always admired how passionate he felt about this alternate universe and defending Darth Vader's inner turmoil.

"Um, well, I kinda thought you were hanging out with Zoe, so I made some plans."

"Oh right. Uncle Ricky. I'm sure he'd be fine if you canceled."

"No, I'm also doing something with some friends."

"That's awesome! What friends?" I didn't intend it to sound that loud and condescending, but Gus obviously heard it that way.

"Just . . . from choir," he muttered.

I was determined to get him back and show him how truly happy I was for him. Since I obviously wasn't finding the right words to express it, I turned on the *Star Wars* theme music and sang along in a strong vibrato. (Of course, there are no lyrics to the *Star Wars* theme music, so I used the word *balls*.)

Gus flashed me an I'm-more-irked-than-amused grin, but at least it was something. I started my *Star Wars* playlist again and tried drawing Gus in to our game of favorite quotes:

"Fear is the path to the dark side."

"Fear leads to anger," Gus chimed in.

"Anger leads to hate," I added.

Then, in almost-perfect unison, we said: "I sense much balls in you."

I even got a high five from Gus after that, which made me feel mighty triumphant. We hadn't connected in dweebitude like this in what felt like forever.

Only, just as instantaneously, the cord was severed.

I told Gus, "I swear, we'll move as soon as this train pulls out. It's the 8:03. Always packed."

And he said, "You know, Elan used to ride on the 8:03 with Dad."

He said it matter-of-factly. Like it was a mundane bit of trivia.

"Wait—what?" I asked.

"The 8:03," Gus said, pointing outside. As if the actual locomotive was what I didn't understand. "I guess they even sat together once or twice," Gus added.

"Who told you that?" I challenged.

"Elan."

I stomped my foot on the brake, even though we were barely crawling forward.

"Well, that's a lie," I snapped. "Our father did not take the 8:03 train. He took the 7:29."

I could feel Gus's quizzical look, but I kept my focus on the road. "Maybe sometimes he took a later one?" Gus suggested.

"No. Never!" I shot back.

"Oh . . . kay." Gus made this weird sound through his nose. I couldn't tell whether he was sneezing or scoffing at me.

"What? You don't believe me?" I pounced. "Ask Mom. Dad took the 7:29. I know this for a fact because that's why he could only walk us partway to school. Remember? He'd peel off at the corner with the mailbox because he had to catch the 7:29."

"Okay, okay," Gus said, putting up his hands as if in surrender.

"No. You don't remember this?"

"I guess not."

"Well, I'll make you a bet if you don't believe me."

"That's okay," Gus said. "I don't need to make a bet. I believe you. It's fine."

"No, it's *not* fine. I'm sick and tired of Elan telling these stories and trying to rewrite our history. He never rode in with Dad. If he did, I would know that."

"How? Why? What the hell is going on?" Gus asked. All noble questions, but I was not willing to answer any of them. I had a score to settle.

"Here's the deal. If I'm wrong, I'll empty the dishwasher for a week straight and do the recycling cans and . . . whatever. Fold your undies."

"No thanks," Gus replied.

"And if you're wrong—or really, if *Elan* is wrong—then he has to take his tempeh burgers and get the hell out of our house!" The 8:03 pulled away just as I finished my unplanned tirade.

"Whoa," Gus said. As we started moving again, I heard him breathe in and out very slowly. Letting me steep in my nasty tantrum for a full Gaia cycle before he spoke again. "I'm sorry if I upset you. I probably just misheard."

"Misheard what?"

"Doesn't matter," Gus said firmly. "Why don't we say I'm wrong and let's concentrate on getting to school." He was definitely done with this conversation. Only I couldn't let it go.

"But do you think you're wrong? Don't punish yourself if you think you're right." From the train station it was a straight shot down Carlton Avenue to the high school parking lot. As we zipped toward the last light before the entrance, I could hear the late bell clanging. A mess of kids poured out of Yoshi's Bagels, clogging the crosswalk ahead of us.

"I don't think anything," Gus muttered. "I don't think as much as you do. Now please pull over and let me *out*."

I pulled over by the curb, even though I knew there would be a chorus of angry horns blaring at me. I wanted Gus to know that I heard him, and that I respected him immensely and was only getting this fired up because I needed to protect our endangered past. Mom had obviously given up on preserving our family unity, but we could be the generation that turned that around. It was up to us.

"Gus, wait. Can we just—"

He already had the car door open though. When I went to grab his hand I actually yanked off his backpack and scattered his pens all over the front seat.

"Really?!" He scooped up what he could and shut the door.

"Have a good day," I mumbled. Even though I knew he couldn't hear me. Nor could I fix what I'd just done. "Hope it's *balls-tastic*!" I yelled as he ducked into the crowd.

In a galaxy far far away.
So I've been here 3 weeks
2 days
5 hours
and 37 excruciating minutes.
But who's counting?
Answer: Not you, I guess.

Just in case you're jealous, here are some of the rollicking great times
I'm having here!
Today I got to:

1. watch a documentary about the role of the esophagus,
   with all the lights off. Followed by "restorative
   stretching" on a carpet that probably hasn't been
   replaced since the turn of the century;
2. make another collage of airbrushed images from
   celebrity magazines along with words or phrases we
   find misleading like "perfect," "no-carb," and "lose it all
   in 30 days!";
3. eat five meals, each containing some form of either
   peanut butter, whole milk, bread, fruit, pasta, or
   cheese;
4. sit in a circle and talk about how each of these foods
   made me _feel_;
5. have a tête-à-tête with Dr. Marsh, who smells like
   yogurt and likes to ask such unanswerable questions as,

"How do you think you're doing?" and "Do you trust this process?";

6. attend knitting circle (I've been trying to make a scarf, but it looks more like a jockstrap);

7. do blindfolded walking, which is just as terrifying as it sounds and involves us being led in circles, which I guess is a metaphor for life. We capped that torture off with yet another plate of food;

8. go to Drama Therapy with Ducky (and my inner child). Honestly, I can't decide if Ducky is my favorite person in the world or my worst enemy. She's 70-something years old and British. Shaved her hair into a silvery fuzz and is recovering from addictions to sugar, heroin, meth, and several other kinds of self-abuse. She has a puppet with purple skin and orange hair named Missy Me who asks our inner child to come out and play. Missy Me has been asking me for weeks now. It's annoying, and terrifying, and inescapable. I swear, everyone who sits in that seat opposite Missy Me winds up hysterically crying. There's no way past her questions, and yes, she's totally a puppet with plastic eyes and nylon hair and how the hell is she intimidating us into submission??! But it works. And today I was the emotional wreckage in the middle.

P.S. Remind me to tell you the part where I tore at her hair and called her Hank "by mistake."

PPS. Did I mention we can't go to the bathroom unattended

(risk of purging) and I got in trouble for trying to do jumping jacks in the hall? Which I guess is better than the chick who tried to sneak in an enema, but still.

There's more, but I'm too drained to keep writing at the moment.

Missyouloveyouhateyoubye!

CHAPTER 8
bananas and war

MRS. TOOBEY WAS NOT PLEASED.

"What does that mean, 'hip-hop ballad'?" She huffed.

"I don't know. Just, maybe, something more modern?" I said.

"Still doesn't make sense. Get back to your scales. I have to check my meat loaf." She stalked off to her kitchen, her helmet of tight curls jiggling. Before I'd even made it one octave, I heard her screeching, "B-flaaaat!" while slamming the oven door.

I had been coming to the Toobeys' house for piano lessons every Wednesday afternoon for almost a decade and we started the same way every time—monotonous scales from my *Classical Exercises for Musical Precision* book and Mrs. Toobey catching my stumbles even as she bustled around about two rooms away, preparing supper so it'd be ready by five.

Mrs. Toobey was a firm believer in routine. She also had a theory about how our bodies and minds needed to empty and unwind in order to let in the music. To be honest, I appreciated this isolated hour each week, when all I had to do was seek out the next sound. It wasn't like I had somewhere else I'd rather be. Whatever it looked like from the outside or inside, the Toobeys' was the one place I felt I sort of belonged. The world could be spinning out of orbit and I could have twenty more tests to study for, but whenever I walked a block and a half down Harding Road from my house, then made a left onto Owen Drive, I found a little opening through all that nonsense by knocking on the Toobeys' dented storm door.

Mom and Gus both said I had a gift on the piano. Once in a while, Mrs. Toobey herself told me I had great promise. I didn't need to be spectacular though. I just loved sitting on that piano bench and releasing into a different dimension. These weekly lessons were my sanctuary—havens of time and space where no one and nothing else could reach me. The notes told me where to put my fingers and my thoughts. It was all there, just waiting for me to press into and become.

I also loved this crazy, overcrowded house that wound around like a wood-paneled maze. Every inch of wall space was covered in some exotic totem or mask from Mr. and Mrs. Toobey's travels. There were two Steinways pushed together in the middle of the living room and a small jungle of spider plants drooping from different heights. Leaning against the few chairs and blocking the overstuffed bookshelves were huge canvases—usually an homage to either fruit or war.

Mrs. Toobey's husband (whom she always called "Toobey") was the visual artist responsible for these pieces. According to Mom, he once was a prominent urologist (is that really a thing?) but developed early-onset Alzheimer's and now found great relief in painting with tempera. For as long as I'd been going there, Mr. Toobey was part of the strange decor. A specter, often shuffling in and out of rooms in a haze. He spent most of his time painting bright, misshapen bananas and battle-scene montages in the cellar of their dilapidated ranch-style house. Every few weeks there was a new picture on display.

From far away, these images always scared me. But when I got up close, the fruit skin was so delicately textured, the soldiers' spilled blood so thick, I had to marvel.

"Toobey?!" Mrs. Toobey bellowed as I started on the F-sharp scale. She was now chopping something that smelled garlicky. "Toobey! We're going to eat supper in fifty-five minutes!"

He said something back and she repeated even louder, "Supper!" I heard the rush of a faucet followed by a drawer of silverware jingling closed. "What's the holdup?" she continued. "Are you with me?!"

I thought Mrs. Toobey was still barking orders at her husband until she charged through the kitchen doorway, waving a limp carrot in my direction.

"What's going on? You seem moody. Is it that time of month

again or something? What a mess. I'm glad to be done with that."
The thought of Mrs. Toobey as a teenager or even a vaguely sexual being stunned me. I had never seen her in anything besides one of her Mexican-patterned multicolored caftans.

"And what's this with all the glittery schmutz on your eyes? I hate glitter," she told me.

"Thanks?" I answered.

I had to laugh. Or else I'd cry. Mrs. Toobey was always brutally observant. It was rarely a compliment either. But coming from a five-foot-two fireball in cat-eye glasses who'd performed sonatas for two different presidents and toured globally, I somehow felt honored that she paid this much attention to my face or moods. She shook her stub of carrot at me as she spoke. "What do you think I'm going to say?"

"The price of fresh produce is ridiculous?"

"Ha!" At least I could still amuse her. "Nice try. Shoulders down, wrists relaxed, and breathe from your *kishkas*. Like this."

She inflated her belly out like a balloon, her nostrils flaring in sync. As she exhaled, I could smell a hundred different spices and saw a speck of carrot fly across the room.

"Got it?" she asked.

"Got it," I answered. She leaned over me and started up the F-sharp scale until I followed suit.

"Yes," she said, letting me take over. "Yes, yes! Thank you very much. *Exactly*."

Then in one seamless motion she took my *Classical Exercises* book off its little wooden perch and replaced it with a book I

110

knew all too well. The cover said *Claude Debussy* in curly script and below that was an impressionistic rendering of an orange sun melting into a gray shore. There were two fuzzy people in a rowboat close to the binding. I felt a little seasick just looking at the illustration.

"Don't worry," Mrs. Toobey buzzed in my ear. "We'll do it together."

Once upon a time—as in six months ago, when I still believed in rainbows and second chances—I got to play the piano at Carnegie Hall. Or at least I was supposed to. It wasn't in the ginormous concert auditorium where virtuosos and opera stars belted out musical miracles. It was in a toaster-size studio on the fourth floor of the building, with a baby grand piano, twelve students, and big rugs hanging from the walls. I'd had this very same *Claude Debussy* book tucked under my arm. Dog-eared at page fifty-nine.

"Hello, my name is Hannah Levinstein, and this afternoon I will be playing *Arabesque No. 1*," I mumbled. My voice had lost all the bravado and swagger I had years before as a second-grade Oneida tribe reporter.

"What did she say?"

"Lervinstein."

"Leavening?"

"Needs to speak up."

And then to me:

"Whenever you're ready."

I knew this piece by heart. That wasn't the problem. I never had trouble memorizing. My hands pressed those chords and syncopations into my leg while I was walking, reading, watching TV, and even going to the bathroom. I dreamed about the rise and fall of *Arabesque No. 1* over and over.

But the day I went to Carnegie Hall for the Young Maestros of Essex & Bergen Counties auditions, I lost those notes completely. They scuttled under the rugs and seeped through the warped floorboards. My knuckles locked like stiff claws and I shook so hard I could feel my teeth chatter.

"Why don't we try again another day?" asked the judge from North Bergen.

"Sure," agreed the other two, shuffling papers.

"Does that sound okay to you, Miss Lervinsting?"

I slumped out, hunched with disappointment. I looked at my hands, still quaking, and wanted to fling them off the rest of my body. When Mom met me in the hall and asked how it went, I just whispered, "Let's go, please."

A week later, I got a form letter that said the Young Maestros really appreciated my efforts and that there were many worthy candidates. They regretted to inform me that I couldn't be presented a seat in the ensemble at this time but to try, try again. I showed the letter to my mom and told her maybe it was time for me to take a break from piano lessons. I had too much going on with schoolwork and I probably should look into a part-time job before the summer.

"I don't know," Mom said.

Mrs. Toobey would have none of that though. After I missed two weeks in a row with lame excuses, she demanded I come back and then told me those Young Maestros judges were certifiable idiots. She made me hand her my rejection letter and then together we lit it on fire in her bathroom sink.

"Ready. Set. Go!" Mrs. Toobey commanded now. She whipped her hand down the crease of my book so it would stay open and put my fingertips on the keys to begin. "Dooo da da dee da da dooo da da . . . Just ever so lightly," she guided.

Arabesque No. 1 was everything I wanted to be—light and fluid and living on tiptoes. That first progression was always so familiar and comforting, taking me on a magic carpet of arpeggios. Dipping and gliding. Proof that I was continuous. Mrs. Toobey stayed behind me, humming along. Anything felt possible when we were soaring through it together. It was like when I was five and my dad brought me to Harding Road with my purple two-wheeler. He gripped the back of my seat as I rode up and down that stretch so many times. Without him I was sure I'd fly off and get sucked into a gutter. *Stay stay*, I begged him. *Please*.

Only, at some point he had to let go. And, of course, I fell hard.

I started the second section of *Arabesque No. 1* at full tilt. Tripping over my left ring finger, then my right thumb. My hands felt like they were chasing each other. Bouncing and jittering like I'd drunk ten cups of coffee.

"Take your time. Don't think so much. Just *listen*," Mrs. Toobey instructed from across the room. I hadn't realized she'd left my side. Or that her ghostly husband had wandered into the room.

As soon as I saw him, all the notes fell out of me, raucous and wrong. I was weaving and winding all over the place, missing flats and sharps and grinding my teeth. Until I just had to stop.

I heard him let out a pitiful whimper. "Where did it go?" he asked.

Mrs. Toobey nodded her head and said, "It's all right, Toobey. We're good." Then she turned her attention back to me. "Are we good?"

I just shrugged. This was the part of playing the piano that crushed me. Once I stuttered, I could rarely find my way back again. Especially with someone watching.

"My Roslyn can play that piece," Mr. Toobey told me with a big smile. "Da da da da da doo doo doo doo doo doo!" he sang. It was true. As she'd told me before, Mrs. Toobey played this piece to get into Juilliard decades ago. "She's going to Juilliard," Mr. Toobey continued. "Meet at six o'clock, Seventy-Second and Broadway. Maybe we'll get some noodles before catching a bus home." He was so eager to tell me the news. News from over thirty years ago, that is. As he came up to the piano, I could see that the zipper of his baggy tan pants was open partway. I shut my eyes fast, because that was the last thing I wanted to see.

"Okay, let's go, mister," Mrs. Toobey said, taking him by the hand and leading him back toward the kitchen. "I think you're hungry. Should we get ready for supper?"

"Yes, Mommy," he said in a tiny voice. Then he repeated the opening progression of *Arabesque No. 1* again—recalling each flat, sharp, and syncopation perfectly. "Why did she stop?" he added sadly as they shuffled out.

"Keep going!" Mrs. Toobey shouted over her shoulder. "Nice and loud—from the beginning!"

I did try. But it only got worse. My fingers floundering and stabbing at the keys. Skidding to a sour halt.

"Sorry," I said when she came back into the room. It was true. *Sorry* was a total cop-out.

"Don't apologize," she answered brusquely. "I just wonder how we can get you back on track."

"That's why I wanted to try something new," I told her. "Like a hip-hop ballad." It was hard to convince even myself that this made sense. Mrs. Toobey snorted, making no effort to hide her disdain.

"Really?" she said. "You think a *hip-hop ballad* is the answer?"

I didn't. But it was the loudest possibility in my head. Demanding me to try.

It sucks knowing you're not superhuman.

I mean, I never wore a cape and tried to leap over buildings in a single bound. Maybe I should've, right?

But I truly believed that I was the only member of some superior species. That I could survive on the achy slosh of Diet Coke and fumes. The more gnawing and gurgly the stomachache, the taller I stood.

You remember that noodle shop on Center Street—Soba Soba?

Alli took us there after my first gymnastics competition and you and I went halvesies on a pot of wontons big enough to swim through.

Anyway, they opened one in the mall just a hop, skip, and squat thrust away from Primally Fit. I walked by there so many times, totally depleted and starvacious. I'd watch these people all slurping noodles and stuffing their pieholes and I would act all high and mighty, like, no matter how hungry I get I'll never give in.

Never.

I felt so proud of my willpower and dedication. My purely driven stamina.

Alli asked me to go there with her—it was after our first Bernardo class and she was famished, I could tell. So I said sure.

She ordered a ton of food—wontons and noodles and those steamed dumplings with the sweet dipping sauce. It was disgusting how much food there was. And how much I wanted it all.

But I did not touch a single bite. Did not even lift my wooden chopsticks out of their little paper sleeping bag.

116

Alli was too busy scarfing it all down to notice at first, but when she did, she got really mad. Then, of course, she turned on the waterworks and said I had to eat. She was going to get fat as a house and I was going to kill myself and I just had to eat right now!

I told her to stop being so dramatic. I just wasn't hungry.

But she couldn't take it. She had the waiter come and take everything away.

All that wasted food.

And I watched her bawling into her paper napkin as I was thinking, <u>Yes!</u>

<u>I won.</u>

CHAPTER 9

presets

IT WAS HARD TO HEAR ANYTHING OVER THE WHIRR AND GRIND OF Alli's blender. She was making her bionic evening smoothie of probiotics, prebiotics, nucleotides, and, apparently, gravel.

"*Issues*," Zoe told me as I walked into her house. Then she led me past Alli's back and downstairs to the basement, where the blender was only slightly less deafening.

"I swear, my mother is trying to kill me. Psychologically at least."

Apparently, this afternoon had been a doozy of a time in the Hammer/Sinclair household. Alli had insisted that she do backup dancing for the Pussycat Warriors video and had choreographed her own part. Zoe had said no thanks. And maybe a few other things that she regretted, but they had to be said. Alli had responded by locking herself in her bedroom with Mr. Meowsers for an hour and threatening to take a double dose of Prozac. Which, according to Zoe, would probably be a good thing.

"I mean, I know she's in a rough place right now, but she's the one who kicked Travis out."

"She did?" I asked. I had yet to hear any coherent details about Alli and Travis's split. Nor had I dared to ask.

"I dunno," Zoe said through clenched teeth. "I mean who really knows? First it was that Travis was sleeping with Roxanne. Then it was that Travis doesn't know how to provide. Nothing's clear anymore except for Alli's devastating *loneliness* and *despair*. I told her that you and I were staying over at Travis's place Saturday night and she literally clutched her heart."

Zoe slapped her chest and staggered backward for effect. Whenever she impersonated her mom like this it was so spot-on that I shivered a little. Zoe had her dad's eyes for sure, and the flirtatious gleam that had maybe gotten him into this current upheaval. But for the most part, Zoe looked like a miniature version of her mom. Sans the dye job and pixie cut.

"Wait, back up a second." I needed to process this slower. "We're sleeping over at Trav—your dad's?"

"If that's okay with you," Zoe said in a quieter tone. "I know I should've asked you before saying yes. It's just, he's been begging me to come over and I really don't think I can handle it on my own."

"No. I mean, yeah. Let's do it." As lame as it sounds, I felt honored that she was inviting me into this family melee.

"I swear, Hank. You're the one and only person I can count on," Zoe told me. "Do you know Alli literally told me that she and I needed to be *BFFs* now? To which I answered *No way, Alli-ay.* Because (1) that's totally unhealthy for a mother and daughter; and (2) that BFF position is already filled by the one and only Hannah Louise Levinstein, DDS Esquire."

"I'm a dentist and a lawyer?" I asked.

"Ha!" Zoe said, thrilled that I knew what these abbreviations meant. "Yeah, why the heck not? Hank, I swear you're so brilliant, you're gonna get a thousand cum laudes and anything else you want after your name. As opposed to Miss E-Z-O here, which is dyslexic for 'Zoe' by the way."

Zoe came at me and clamped her arms around my waist, trying valiantly to lift me off the ground (like I usually did with her). It was always slightly humiliating when she did this because she struggled to get me up even off my tiptoes, but it sure did feel warm and hopeful to hear her reaffirm my best friend status.

"You are my soul-sister-from-another-mother," Zoe declared. "My life. My anchor. My floaty-vest thingy. Whoa, what's with all the sea references, huh? But seriously, I love you."

"I love you too," I told her. And I meant it. I could never keep up with all the crises that constantly swirled around her, but Zoe was definitely my lifeline too. She could say and do and dare so many terrifyingly vulnerable things. Like wrapping me in these raw moments of affection. Nobody in my life spoke like this besides her.

She pulled me in to her, fast and tight. The top of her head jammed against my chin so hard that I bit the edge of my tongue and whimpered. Or maybe it was Zoe making that noise. I realized she was shaking and letting out little chirpy sobs.

"Did I hurt you?" I asked.

"No! You're the last person who could ever hurt me." She sniffed. "I'm just thinking about how when you go off to college and everyone goes off to college and I'm just left here all alone because I still can't remember the freaken FOIL method for binomials or even tell you what a binomial is . . ."

"But you don't have to," I told her.

"I know, I know. But it's not just that. I just don't want to be all alone. And I know that's what's gonna happen."

"No, no," I insisted. "I'll stay home if you need me to. Or we could travel. Join the Peace Corps and find those sheep."

We had once mapped out a life together in a yurt on a mountain where all we had to do was shear sheep. I'd actually looked into the price of yurts. It would take a ton of babysitting money, but it was entirely possible.

"*Hanky-Panky puddin' pie / You're the sweetest thing in the sky,*" Zoe said between snuffles. "It's okay, it's okay. Maybe this agent thing will lead to *something*. Oh wait! Did I tell you that he said maybe I could model too?"

And immediately Zoe turned the sun back on. She pulled away, wiped her face, and strutted in a narrow circle with her lips all puckery.

"Probably just my face cuz I'm short, but whatever."

"Really?" I gulped. "Is that what you *want*?"

"I don't know what I want," she said. "But I'll tell you this—it sure is nice to have someone compliment you and treat you like a person with artistic vision instead of being told you can't read and you should go on more ADHD meds if you want to ever become someone besides a loser."

I couldn't argue with that. Especially when she pointed her finger at me and added, "I know that's hard for you to imagine, Hank. But try."

I guess even she heard how accusatory that sounded. She did a fast hop-skip-jumping-jack to recalibrate the mood, then smacked a smile back on and said, "Hey! Enough of this dilly-dally yada yada, huh? Let's get to work!"

"Right," I said.

"I can't wait to hear what you came up with at Mrs. Toobey's! Does she totally hate me for quitting? Is her husband still in a walking coma? Ooh, and did you find your matching pussycat costume?"

"Um . . . no, no, and . . . still looking," I reported.

Zoe had taken piano lessons for exactly three weeks about five years ago, but she just couldn't sit still long enough to learn anything. I doubted Mrs. Toobey remembered Zoe's name, let alone had strong emotions about her.

In terms of my pussycat costume, that was a big ol' lie. There was no way I would wear or even look for that. Most likely it was in one of the two dozen contractor bags stuffed into my attic.

The attic was a fire hazard/warehouse full of outgrown clothes, book reports, knickknacks and paddywhacks. It would certainly not fit me, and I couldn't even contemplate going through those dusty bags of memorabilia without sneezing.

"Do I really need to be in the costume too if I'm gonna be sitting behind the piano?" I asked.

"Mmmm, I guess not," Zoe conceded. "But maybe you'll let me pick out something sparkly for you? Ooh! I have a bunch of tops that totally don't fit me anymore."

"Why not?"

"Never mind! I'll get them later. C'mon!"

She pulled me over to her keyboard and plugged it into an outlet. A thousand different lights flickered on—lime green, yellow, and red. It looked like a casino slot machine with a few piano keys stuck on the bottom. I tried to read through all the different tempos and fake-instrument sounds available—violin, clavichord, pipe organ, clarinet, and bagpipe, just for starters. I had no idea what I was going to play, especially on the bagpipe. The keys looked too big and slippery to make any kind of musical sense. I never had figured out what a hip-hop ballad entailed, nor did I do anything about it after my lesson yesterday at the Toobeys'.

"Did I show you?" Zoe jumped in. "It also has presets!" She scooted me over with a sharp hip bump so she could stand behind the keyboard too. "Check it out: samba, reggae, mellow jazz. Ooh, try hip-hop!"

She pressed a button and it felt like we were being dumped

into a drum kit, the beats crashing unevenly around us. There was also a mess of chords, a piercing whistle, and what sounded like a roomful of girls giggling.

"Ummmm, can we turn that down?" I yelled over the din.

Zoe agreed it was a little overwhelming and lowered the volume.

"But maybe you can incorporate that kind of energy or movement?" she asked. "You know, just something to groove to . . ."

"Sure," I said. "Yeah." I could feel her eyes on me as I sat down and turned some more knobs. Samba. Boogie. Something called Ragtime Romp. As if I needed a precise balance of treble, bass, and rhythm to make this kind of music.

Zoe must have known I was faking it. I had never improvised before and all I had in my head was the opening progression of Debussy, though I knew that was the opposite of groovy. I set my hands on the first notes and tried playing it as fast as possible. I sounded a little like I was on fire. Zoe stayed right next to me. Probably too confused to say *Mercy*. After a torturous minute I had to stop myself.

"I'm sorry. This is definitely not what you were looking for, I'm sure—"

"No!" Zoe cut me off. "Don't be sorry! Listen, you are just way too talented for this crap. And I'm making you do something totally stupid and boring and I really appreciate it because I would not be able to do this on my own. So let's do this . . . What if I just show you what I was thinking about and then maybe it'll give you some inspiration?"

"That sounds great."

Zoe took out a piece of loose-leaf paper that had been folded and refolded until it was the size of a stamp. Lots of scribbles and cross-outs had bled through to the back too.

"No. See, I'm already so mortified because you're playing real music and I'm just . . . ugh, I have no idea how to write song lyrics." She crumpled the paper and started shredding it into tiny wisps.

"Wait! Don't do that. I'm sure it's great!" I tried to scoop up the bits of floating lyrics, but Zoe continued to tear the rest of the page while she spoke.

"It's not, Hank. I mean, I want it to be edgy, but it also needs to have a catchy hook and convey a sense of righteous anger, you know?"

"Uh . . . okay. That's a lot to fit in."

"Plus, it has to use the word *pussy*."

"It *has* to?" I handed her a palm-size pile of torn paper. She took it and dumped it on the windowsill without acknowledging it at all.

"Well, Dash is really keen on it being about the word *pussy* and us reclaiming the female body and how we've been disenfranchised but we're stronger than ever . . . ?"

"Dash?" I asked.

"That's my agent. Or—*our* agent?"

She didn't seem sure of anything she was saying, but I nodded as if it were a monumental revelation. "I had a tune to go with it too, but now I can't remember anything. Ugh. Maybe I'm dyslexic in music too."

"No, just keep going," I reassured her. "Show me what you have so far."

"Fine. I'll show you whatever I remember. But I have to face the other way."

Zoe turned away from me and started mumbling in a voice just surfacing above a whisper:

> *I was lost*
> *But now I'm found*
> *Because you're here and there's no fear*
> *When you're around*
> *Cuz you're my pussy!*

I stood there, mummified. Not breathing or moving or acting in any way remotely human. I was really hoping that was a joke. Only, the longer Zoe waited for me to react, the more I knew she was serious. She spun back around and said, "So stupid, right?"

To which the only answer could be, "No. I think it's really . . . powerful."

"For real?"

"I mean, yeah."

She bit her lip and searched my face. Like she wanted to believe me but she knew I had to be lying and she was not going to be the one to call me on it. I wanted to breathe this stilted moment onto some raft of spaciousness and have Diana Gaia take it all away.

"Yeah," I repeated. "Let's find a melody for this."

I went back to the piano to study all those prerecorded rhythms in the key of crazy. Pressing random buttons and humming. Blessedly, Alli chose that instant to interrupt.

"Knock knock!" she called, opening the basement door. "I'm not staying, I swear. Just wanted to let you both know it's almost seven o'clock and I'm heading out for a spin class. I left some of my smoothie for you because it's delicious but I'm just waaaay too full."

For as long as I'd known Alli, she'd been on some unsustainable diet of no sugar, no carbs, no taste. Which she always transgressed and then regretted bitterly—telling me, Zoe, and whoever else was close at hand that she was a *despicable fatty*. All the while being at least two sizes smaller than me. I hated this routine. No wonder Zoe was struggling with her own reflection. But when I looked to Zoe for the expected eye roll, she was at the bottom of the stairs, calling back, "Alli. Wait."

Alli spun around. I hadn't noticed until that moment how red her tiny nose was. There were little pink shadows under her eyes too.

"Listen, I'm sorry about before. I didn't mean to be so harsh," Zoe muttered.

"It's fine," Alli said with a quick shake of her head.

"No, it's not fine," Zoe replied. "I was being a real bitch and I'm sorry."

The floodgates opened then. Alli rushed down the stairs, unleashing huge gasping sobs. Falling into her daughter's fragile arms.

"You shouldn't be the one apologizing, Zoozoo," she lamented. "*I* am. I never meant for this whole situation to be so hard on you. I know you love your dad and he loves you and I can only hope that one day you can forgive me for all of this, but I know that's a lot to ask."

"Alli, *please*. We're in this together." Zoe's voice sounded crackly now too. I tried to busy myself on equalizing the equalizer some more, but Zoe turned around and said, "Right?"

"Poor Hank," Alli answered before I could say anything. "We invite you over to rehearse and then it turns into another sobfest. Ugh, I'm such a mess!"

They both looked at me again, I guess for some answer.

"No, you're . . . fine. You're going through a really hard time," I said.

"That's an understatement," wailed Alli. They drew me into their anguished huddle and I bore my eyes into the floor while they both cried. I tried to make some weepy noises of my own, hoping to blend into their chorus. Until Alli decided enough was enough and she needed to get going.

"Hey!" she said with a sharp sniff. "*You* have to rehearse. And *I* have . . . something to do I'm sure."

"Wait a second. Are you really going for another class? Do you want to rehearse with us instead and then we'll go together?" I couldn't tell whether Zoe actually wanted her mom to stay or not. It sounded more like Zoe was frantic at the idea of Alli exercising without her.

"If that's what you want . . . ?" Alli asked with a coy smile.

"Yeah . . . I mean *yes*," Zoe declared.

"Okay. Well, I did think of some lyrics. Just about, you know, the male hegemony and the urgency of female redemption. Which . . . I don't know. Take them or leave them. I can print them out if you want."

"Sure," answered Zoe.

"Okay, but wait." Alli addressed me now too. "Dash told us that we should film everything. Even if it's a rough cut. 'Film cold, edit hot.' Or whatever he said." Alli took off her lavender jacket and threw it on the ground. Underneath, she had on a matching tank top that obviously had a push-up bra built into it. "I know I look totally ratty. But Hank and I are just background noise, really. Zoe, go get the pussycat top for us. I just washed it."

"Alli."

"Do it."

While Zoe went upstairs to try on her costume, Alli took out her phone and propped it on the windowsill next to the discarded lyric sheet before pressing RECORD. Then she turned on another video camera on a tripod in the corner by the washer, which I had somehow missed.

"Maybe you can be in charge of getting footage from behind?" she asked me. "The more angles we capture, the better." I handed Alli my phone and she set it up on one of the basement stairs so we could record the backs of our heads, I guess. Then, without further ado, she started swimming around the empty basement—her arms, head, and neck undulating.

"That's really . . . pretty," I said.

"Bah," Alli answered with a leap. "Don't you dare put this on YouTube or something like that." The thought had actually never occurred to me. "Hashtag *hasbeen*," she added, smiling at me for approval. Or maybe so I could protest. I did neither.

"If you want to play something hip-hoppy?" she asked, nodding at the keyboard.

"Sure. Yup."

I pressed that trusty hip-hop preset button. Letting that scattered beat eat up the room. Alli started tearing it up now. Lunging and gyrating, waggling her hips and shoulders. Rubbing her hands up and down her torso and shimmying. I didn't know if I was going to laugh or cry. I had never witnessed anything this fearless and exposing. After what felt like an hour but was probably five minutes, she stopped abruptly.

"Phew. Guess an old broad can learn new tricks." She panted. As I fidgeted with more knobs on the keyboard, I heard wild clapping from behind me. Alli and I both turned around.

On the stairs was Zoe, holding herself inside that same drooping hoodie she had had on before—her arms wound so tightly around her middle it looked like a straitjacket. Only with her bare legs sticking out from the bottom hem and bright pink satin ears on top of her head.

"Come on, take that thing off," Alli instructed. She started unzipping Zoe's sweatshirt.

"I didn't know how short the top was," Zoe whined. "It's really . . ."

Even before she had her arms out, I felt my neck tighten, a chill slashing through me.

Zoe was so minuscule.

So drawn and hollow.

Her rib bones stuck out from under a pink satiny bustier like a rickety stepladder. Her stomach was sunken, leaving her hips to jut out in two stark angles. Worst of all, I saw three more red marks carved into her upper inner biceps. They looked so fresh; they glittered with new blood.

"Whoa," Alli said.

"Yeah," I echoed. "Whoa."

I didn't know what Alli's *whoa* meant, but mine could be translated roughly as:

What the hell is going on? How is this acceptable in any way?

Also, *Are you just going to let your daughter kill herself? Am I the only one who finds this horrible?*

"It's too small, right?" Zoe asked. She sounded angry. Without waiting for an answer, she yanked the sweatshirt back from her mom and burrowed inside it. "Forget it. Ugh!"

"Oh, Zoozoo," Alli said. "You look beautiful."

"Stop, please," Zoe said in a low monotone.

"Seriously." Alli sounded like she was pleading. Maybe she was. "You look . . ."

"I said *STOP*." Zoe was barking orders now. "Stop standing there staring. We need to *rehearse*."

Alli went to Zoe and took Zoe's face in her hands. "I get it. I do," she whispered. "But listen, Zoo, you are gorgeous. I mean it. Inside and out. Am I right, Hank?" Alli asked me over her shoulder.

I was still too stunned and horrified to speak.

"Am I right?" Alli urged.

There was no right answer.

"Yeah. Yup. You look . . . gorgeous," I repeated. "You do."

And *that* was the biggest lie I ever told Zoe Grace Hammer.

Or maybe just the worst one.

Dear Hank,

Did you hear about the new emo pizza?

It cuts itself!

("Emo" is how the girls in here talk about someone who's super-emotional.)

Can I tell you a really ugly secret?

The first time I cut myself, I was at your house.

Sick, right?

Wait, it gets uglier.

We were at your place after school because you were fixing my poor excuse for a paper on <u>Animal Farm</u>. I was so embarrassed by how many times I'd misspelled words or forgotten apostrophes. Apostrophe's? You acted like it was no big deal, but we must have sat at your kitchen table for hours. I felt like the biggest idiot ever.

Meanwhile, Gus came home, and he was really upset about something, but I told him just wait till life gets actually hard. Then your mom came home, and she started making dinner. It was taco night and she burned the rice. Not that I was ravenous or anything.

Still, you wouldn't get up until we'd finished my essay. And when we did, the clock said 6:52. Your mom told us that she was amazed at our dedication and that she'd reheat us some beans and had plenty of chips and guac left. (My mom of course had yet to notice I wasn't home and my dad was still at work.)

I said no thank you, like I'd done so many times. You started munching away on dinner and I excused myself to go to the bathroom.

I really just planned to pee. But I saw your row of pink razors on the shower ledge.

I'd read about cutting. I'd even seen some girl vlog about it.

But I didn't know how awesome it could be until that day.

The quick pinch.

The line of blood rising.

The _release_.

It was so quick and effective. I had to laugh. I loved it so much and so immediately. I even thought of telling you about it.

But then I thought, no. NO. This is just for me. This pain and this blood are only mine. Not Hank's. Not anyone's.

I lifted up my shirt and squeezed my bloated tire of belly fat. Then I used that same razor to make three more neat slices.

Marking my territory.

CHAPTER 10
the student, the teacher, and me

THE WEEKEND FORECAST CALLED FOR TORRENTIAL RAIN WITH A chance of hail. Another reason to give thanks that I was not going on Mom and Elan's campiversary trip.

"Who knew it was monsoon season in New Jersey?" Elan said, chuckling as I came downstairs at eight o'clock Saturday morning. Elan had probably been up for hours already. He was just rushing in from tying another tarp to his Subaru's roof rack. He looked like somebody had dumped a bucket of rainwater on his head. Which I wish I'd had the foresight to do, but I can honestly say I didn't.

"Oh, hon," Mom said to him. "It's okay if we have to postpone, y'know."

Honestly, I felt a little bad for her. Mom had never been much of a camper as far as I knew. Currently, she had on so many different rainproof layers that she crackled and creaked as she found me in the doorway to the living room and pulled me in for a hug. "Ooh, Hank. Are we totally crazy?" she asked.

"Define *crazy*," I answered with a starched smile. I knew she didn't want my real answer.

"Not at all," Elan cut in. "We can handle it." He flexed his biceps under his soggy windbreaker, then scratched at his dark beard as if he was a mutt, flicking droplets of water out in every direction.

"Help!" Mom giggled. Maybe this was their version of foreplay. That was not a thought I wanted to think, and now that I had, I couldn't *un*think it. I headed toward the kitchen to pour myself a cup of coffee.

"Hold on, Hank!" Elan said, traipsing after me. "*It is better to travel well than to arrive*," he drawled in a low voice. Then, to make it extra-weird, he grinned at me.

"I'm sorry?"

Elan turned to Mom and said, "Hey, love, did you give her the book?"

"Oops! I'm sorry, sweets. No, I think it's still on the dryer downstairs. I was down there folding laundry and then you handed it to me—"

"No sorrys!" Elan yelped. "It's A-okay in the hizzay!"

I did not know what the heck that meant, nor was I willing to ask him for clarification. Mom squeezed my hand and winked at me. Which could have been her way of communicating that she was ensnared in a sham relationship with a hypnotic male cheerleader and needed me to unleash her from his trance. Or, more likely since she was still chuckling softly to herself, it meant she somehow found his whole act charming.

"Uno momento, my beautiful ladies," Elan said to me and Mom, backing out of the room with a deep bow. "Actually, now I can stick this stuff in the dryer too." He planted his feet firmly so he could take off his sodden jacket and sweatshirt. Which in and of itself seemed like a fair move. Only, as he did so, the bottom of his T-shirt rolled up too, revealing a swatch of his belly hair. It was thick and dark. Like a wild boar's.

"Okay, that's enough!" I squeaked instinctively. I slapped a palm over my eyes to shield me from any more nudity. "Have a great trip and see you later bye!" I spun on my heel and tried to flee to the kitchen before any other flesh was exposed.

"Wait wait wait—*please!*" Mom pleaded. "He wants to give this to you so badly, Hank. Can you please just wait?"

It wasn't fair that Mom was positioning herself on his team. Although I knew it also wasn't fair that I was making up teams in my head. I stood there, counting to infinity while Elan hightailed it down to the basement. I kept my hands over my eyes, though. I really didn't want to connect with my mom or have her tell me how excited she was about this trip.

"Ta-da!" Elan bounded back in with a rectangular package wrapped in turquoise tissue paper.

"Here," he said, his eyes bright with hope as he handed it to me. "Your mom said you were taking a yoga class and I just wanted to share my favorite book of Buddhist teachings."

Elan hadn't tried to bribe me in a while. I used to enjoy the occasional coffee card or chocolate bar from him. But now that we were marking three years with this trespasser, I needed to make it painfully clear that his tricks were not magical to me.

"It's power yoga," I clarified. "It's just part of the new PE requirements at school."

"Awesome!" Elan said, undeterred. "I wish I had found yoga earlier in my life, but I guess the student is only ready when the teachings appear. Or maybe it's the teachings appear when the student is ready? Either way . . ."

He pressed the book into my hands, then kept staring at me like I could finish his sentence. I couldn't though. I couldn't condone what he was doing, preying on my mother, the young widow. I couldn't welcome him into my family or my heart, no matter how earnest and kind he was to me. I hated him.

On cue, Mom tilted her head at me, as if she could hear my thoughts. She thought *hate* was a vulgar, overused term. So okay, I *disliked* Elan tremendously. He smelled like tea tree oil and his eyelashes were too long. He believed in mandals and matcha tea and could name every sprout.

Just to put that in perspective (and give a reality check), my dad smelled like Old Spice and cocktail onions. He drank his coffee black and didn't like vegetables unless they were hidden under ranch dressing. Not that I was comparing, but I would forever be comparing. And my dad once took me on a piggyback ride that lasted three miles, while Dr. Elan here had a whole section on his Spinal Freedom™ website about not carrying anything over ten pounds on your back. (Not that I'd been snooping on him or anything.) So, for that reason and a thousand others, I could not, would not, in a house with a mouse, on a box, with a fox, here or there or anywhere *ever* like this man.

I did accept his book though. And I remembered my manners enough to murmur, "Thanks."

Mom and Elan both looked at me with self-satisfied grins. "Well, then," said Mom. "Wish us luck." She held her arms out for a hug. But I was pretty sure that would lead to a hug with Elan too, or worse still, a three-way smush, so I backed away from it all.

"Good luck! Have fun!" I wrapped both arms around that teachable-moments book and then bounded up the stairs to my room as if I had some very important business there. Yes, it was a bit cold and juvenile of me, especially considering that my mom was heading out into an icy, driving rain with nothing but a rubbery raincoat, a hirsute chiropractor, and some freeze-dried tempeh to keep her warm. But then again, my mother had made her own choices and she would have to suffer her own consequences. No one had forced her into the intrepid arms of Elan the Plucky Pioneer.

I sat on my bed and picked at my toenails until I heard the front door shut. Honestly, my only plan was to try to get another hour or two of sleep. I was more than a little peeved and jealous that Gus was still snoring away in his room, leaving me to be the bon voyage crew. Usually when it rained, I loved just lying on my bed and listening to the drops thrum on the eaves. But as I lay down, it felt like my bed was vibrating. There was some sort of buzzing sound coming from down the hall, as if my house was on top of a giant beehive. I followed the noise, expecting to find a teeming colony of yellow jackets. Instead, it was Gus standing over the bathroom sink. In his hand was a silver wand with chattering blades at the end.

"What's happening?" I asked, squinting at him.

He pressed a switch and the noise stopped. "Sorry, too loud?"

"I don't know. What is that?"

"Electric razor," he replied.

"Why?"

Gus petted his upper lip carefully.

I tried again. "I mean, where'd it come from?"

"Elan," he mumbled.

"I'm sorry, where?" I knew exactly what he'd said. I just wanted him to have to say it again.

"Elan," Gus repeated. A little more audibly this time, but still only looking at the sink drain.

"Fascinating," I said. "You guys are pretty tight now, huh?"

"Um, no," answered Gus. "I mentioned that I was looking for a razor, so he lent me his last night."

I snorted in response. Yes, I knew I was being petty and obnoxious. And yet Elan's name set off a runaway train of indignant anger inside me. He was the one person I could detest without reservation.

"What the hell, Gus? Why didn't you just ask me for help?" I could smell my sour breath as I raged.

Gus looked like he was going to laugh, but then thought better of it and cleared his throat instead. "Because you don't have a . . . beard," he said carefully.

"Whatever. Can I at least get in here to brush my teeth please?"

Before Gus could answer, I pushed past him to the sink and squirted a glob of Crest onto my toothbrush. Then I sawed back and forth viciously, building up a nice froth to complete my rabid-beast look.

"Those things are really dangerous," I told him, pointing at the dormant razor. "It's probably extra-loud because a blade is loose." Minty bubbles flew and dribbled as I spoke.

"Really?" Gus's face was dipping into a worried frown.

"Yup. Didn't you hear about all those product recalls? Super-risky. They can blow a fuse and catch fire, or there was some guy who got electrocuted out in Utah, I think."

"How do you know so much about electric razors?"

"Coulda told you that before. If you asked." I spit a snowball of toothpaste on that last statement and watched it slide through the flecks of Gus's newly shorn facial hair. They looked like those filaments from Wooly Willy—that game Gus and I played as kids where we had to draw on Willy's mustache and sideburns using a magnetic pen. We hadn't played Wooly Willy in eons. Probably never would again. I heard Gus retreat from the bathroom behind me and stomp downstairs.

A few minutes later, I heard the muffled cries of ghouls and zombies leaking out of the den. *RighteousZombieSlayer* was Gus's favorite video game. It involved mazes, machetes, and various forms of the undead. I had no idea how to play, but after two cups of coffee and twenty minutes of reading sad headlines about civil wars and dying coral reefs, I sure felt lonely enough to try. I toasted up two flax-nutmeg-amaranth waffles (courtesy of Dr. Spine) and smothered them with butter before wandering into the Zombie Zone.

I held out the plate of waffle pucks as a peace offering.

"You hungry?" I asked.

"Eh."

"I'll try it if you do."

Gus just shrugged. He clearly did not need me to stay.

"Sorry about before," I mumbled.

"Whatevs," he replied. "S'all good."

"Thanks. But I mean . . ." I wondered who'd taught him to say *whatevs* and if that was somehow cool in the ninth grade or whether it would get him in trouble. Though it seemed like Gus couldn't care less what was cool or not. I watched him blow a tuft of hair out of his eyes and reveal a patch of shiny forehead pimples. If that was me, I'd pick at them and then slather on every vanishing cream invented before being seen in public. Gus just seemed to accept that it was part of his adolescence. Or maybe he hadn't even noticed.

"Can I sit down with you?" I asked.

"Sure," he said. I put the plate down on the coffee table and tried to explain where I was coming from on the whole Elan issue.

"Hey, so I just wanted to say—"

"Wait." Gus cut me off. "Hay is for horses!" He looked at me with a bright, eager smile. "Huh? How'd I do?"

I wanted to hug him so badly. But I didn't want to freak him out.

So instead I said, *"Learned wisely, you have,"* in my best Yoda impersonation.

Dr. Yogurt-Breath: What do you think you are trying to say here?

Me: Nothing. I'm saying nothing. I am nothing.

Dr. Yogurt-Breath: You're something to me. And to a lot of people.

Me: *gag*

CHAPTER 11
backseat zombie slayer

THE ONLY THING WORSE THAN A BACKSEAT DRIVER IS A BACKSEAT zombie slayer. I spent the next two hours next to Gus as he battled the netherworld.

"Die, assface. Die!" he yelled at the television, swerving his body left and right.

"You showed him," I said. "I heard zombies are really self-conscious about their asses."

Gus gave me half a pity laugh for that, but it was better than nothing. He started another attack while I shouted at the TV with him. "He's on your left! Behind the catacombs! No, I mean right. Over there! Get him!"

Gus was disemboweled twice and then beheaded by a

particularly bloody corpse while I shouted out useless directions. At least we were spending some time together though.

"Wait, can zombies even die?" I pressed. "Maybe this is virtual reality where to survive is actually to embrace death!" I thought Gus might be impressed with my profound exploration of zombiehood, but he just kept grunting and shaking his head until he'd used up all his afterlives. At which point he paused the game and turned to me with a tight-lipped smile.

"Right. Now what were you saying, my dearest sister?"

"Ha-ha." I shrugged. "Sorry, am I being superannoying?" He chose not to answer that at all, so I continued. "I just—we haven't hung out in a while and you said you had some friends coming over, which is . . . awesome. And—whoa! When did you do that?" I asked, reaching out to touch his ear. My little brother had a gold stud earring in his right lobe. The skin around it a fiery pink.

Gus swatted me away and shuddered.

"Ow! Don't do that!"

"Sorry. But . . . does Mom know?"

"Yes. Why?"

"No reason. I just . . ." I wondered how Mom had received that news. More than that, I wondered why Gus had told her before telling me. "Wait—when did you . . . ? How did you . . . ? Did you put ointment on it?" Gus waited until I stuttered to a stop before answering.

"I did it yesterday. With a friend from choir. And please do not use the word *ointment* in my presence ever again." Gus scrunched up his nose. At least he hadn't outgrown his sweet freckles.

"Got it."

"Thank you so much. And if you'll excuse me, I'd like to play one more round on my own."

"Right. Yup. Just . . . for reference, when are you expecting your friends and how long are they staying?"

"Just for reference . . . I dunno exactly. We'll be in the basement." Gus tilted his head like he was choosing his words very deliberately. "Is that okay with you?"

"Totes! Just let me know if . . . you need anything."

Which clearly, Gus did not. As I made my way back to the kitchen, I ducked into the basement, which had always been a dumping ground for half-folded laundry, overgrown Halloween costumes, and metal filing cabinets spilling over with tax receipts, book reports, outdated warranties. Only today it had been re-arranged and swept clean. The cabinets were shoved back into their rightful corners; the washer and dryer were empty and silent. There was a string of chili pepper lights strung from one end of the room to the other. In the center of the room was an old area rug that used to be in Gus's bedroom, with a frog flying a helicopter over clouds shaped like the alphabet. There was also a metal card table covered in a navy bedsheet, and five folding chairs.

"Wow," I said to the empty room. "Classy."

I knew I should just let Gus do his own thing, but I couldn't take the mystery of it all. I popped my head back into the TV room and tried to be extra-subtle.

"Just wondering if you need any help cleaning up downstairs or . . ."

147

"Hank. I could hear you on the basement stairs. It's fine. We're doing a campaign."

"Oh! Like student government?"

Now it was Gus's turn to laugh. "Um, like D&D," he explained.

"Right." I knew Gus had been reading up on Dungeons & Dragons last year and had met some gamers online, but I didn't know he was still serious about it. "That's really cool."

There was no part of me that was curious about role-playing games until this very minute. I'd always been a little judgy and snooty of people who got into these alternate lives full of wizardry and otherworldly beasts. Only now could I see how this could be fun and even kinder than the real world. Gus must have seen some pitiful look in my eyes, because before I could say another word, he told me, "I'd invite you to join, but it's my first time as DM and we just set our characters."

"No worries! Of course! DM? That's awesome!"

"Hank, do you know what DM means?"

"Dude . . . Man?" I guessed.

"Close. Dungeon Master," Gus explained.

"Right. Keepin' you on your toes. All hail the Dungeon Master!" I folded myself into a deep curtsy for him. Gus just shook his head and chuckled. As in, *Boy, it's amusing how clueless you are.*

"Okeydoke," I said. "Well, I'll be upstairs doing . . . something. Just shout if you need me."

"Sounds like a plan."

Not that I didn't have an obnoxious amount of homework left to keep me occupied. Or preoccupied. Although I never really understood the difference between those two words so then that sent me down a rabbit hole of nerditude, looking up the Latin roots for *occupied* and *preoccupied* and finding out they both involved seizing and grasping and then thinking about all the things I wanted to seize or grasp.

A piercing *beeeeep* jolted me awake around 12:30. It smelled like someone was cooking tires downstairs.

"Gus?" I yelled. There was a lot of hooting and cackling going on, so I was pretty sure no one was on fire. "Gus!"

"Aw, shit!" was all I heard in response. Followed by "Daaaamn" and "Gross, dude. Get that out of here."

When I got down to the kitchen, I was blasted by a heavy, greasy fog. The window over the sink was open, and Gus was outside on our deck with a metal tray that was smoking like a cauldron. Next to him were three gangly boys and a girl in denim overalls holding my mom's striped umbrella over herself and Gus. She stood so confidently, with wide shoulders and a short shock of turquoise hair. Gus must've said something to her, because the girl looked up and they both waved at me.

"Nothin' to see here!" Gus called. He tried to laugh but it turned into a cough. "Hey, guys! Say hello to my sister."

"Hey, sister," mumbled one of the guys standing out in the rain.

"Sister. I think I have one of those," said another.

"Sorry about the smoke," shouted the third. "We were just trying to melt some cheese on . . . stuff and then . . ." He unraveled into a snorty kind of laugh that made me feel embarrassed. Not that I was some paragon of graceful adulthood, but these guys were all limbs and smells—dangling somewhere between childhood and adolescence in a pimply, awkward phase.

But then the girl took over. Whoever this girl was, she was unafraid. She flung open our back door and walked into the kitchen with a smile that took up most of her face. Her cheeks got involved too—wide and rosy, practically shoving her eyes closed. She looked almost like a snowman, getting progressively rounder as she went down.

"Hey," she said. "I'm really sorry we almost burned down your entire house." She stuck out a doughy-looking hand for me to shake. "By the way, hi. I'm Tata."

"Tata?! As in . . . ?"

"Yeah." She pushed her ample rack out at me. "My little sister couldn't pronounce 'Tara' when she was a baby, so she called me 'Tata' and it stuck." I still hadn't taken her hand, so she dropped it by her side and said, "Comin' in for a hug instead."

She was warm and thick, her arms tucking me in tight. We were just about the same height, and even though the rest of the kitchen reeked of burned cheddar, Tata's neck smelled a little like a Creamsicle. I noticed a colorful skull tattoo just below her left ear as we broke apart.

"That's Hank!" Gus called from outside.

"Awesome! I've heard so much about you!" said Tata.

"Uh-oh," I responded. "Like what?"

Tata looked at Gus and then smiled at me. "I don't know. Maybe that you were really cool and a kickass piano player and the best big sister ever."

"Really?" The backs of my ears were getting hot and I wondered how much of that Gus actually said. He was still outside though, fanning his tray of cheesy burnedness under the umbrella.

"Okay, boys! We've done enough damage here. Let's move it on out!" Tata circled her hand above her head like a lasso. The guys shoving and poking each other as they meandered toward the back door to meet her.

"See ya later, Gus!" shouted Tata. "Nice to meet you, Hank!"

"Yeah, you too!" I called after her. And I meant it.

"So . . . Tata's cool," I told Gus a few minutes later when he'd come back inside.

"Yep."

"Is she?"

"I think we just established that she is." He overenunciated, as if I were hard of hearing rather than just incredibly annoying.

"Okay, I'll butt out," I said. "Just . . . thank you for saying those nice things about me. And I'm really happy that you have some nice new friends."

"Thanks. And sure."

I really missed Gus in that moment. Despite—or maybe because of—the fact that he was standing right in front of me. Already at least two inches taller than me, in fact. And no matter how much facial hair was forcing its way between us, I felt darn lucky to call him my little brother.

"You and Uncle Ricky doing something fun tonight?" I asked. I was seriously wishing I could tag along, even though I knew Zoe was counting on me now.

"Yeah, I think we're gonna catch an early movie and then maybe go ax throwing."

"Whoa. Manly."

Gus smiled. "Looks like you're gonna be busy too."

"What do you mean?"

"Aren't you part of that music video thing? Tata was actually showing me the events page that Zoe made. It already looks like a ton of people are going," Gus said. There was something tentative in his voice now. Like he wished he hadn't started this conversation.

"I'm not sure what you're talking about, but . . ."

Gus swiped through a few pages on his phone and then handed it to me. The screen was covered in cat stripes and in hot-pink letters it read:

Be Part of Our New Pussycat Warriors Music Video!

Apparently, I was cohosting an event with her, chez the Hartwicks. Zoe had already collected ninety-eight people who promised to attend, plus a disco ball, "libations," and someone's cousin's smoke machine. More upsetting was the series of photos that she'd included on the page. Most of them were of Pepe le Meowsers, but there were a few of Zoe peeking seductively over her bare shoulder, along with a short testimonial from her that I was too scared to watch. The comments underneath were alarming enough.

Nerdknocker (3 hours ago)
Love these soooooo much! You look hottt!

Alakazoom (1 hour ago)

I'll be your pussycat. Meow!

Fred2003 (20 minutes ago)

what is your name I think we have a lot in common also I

produce movies and want to meet for coffee?

I didn't know who these faceless people were, but I hated them all.

"What the hell is this?" I demanded. I didn't want to shoot the messenger, but Gus was the only one available to receive all my fearful anger at the moment.

"I don't—don't know," Gus stammered. I could hear him chewing on the strings of his hoodie nervously. "And also . . . have you seen this?" He took the phone from me and clicked on a link before handing it back.

There was a thirty-second video of Zoe and Pepe le Meowsers basically tonguing each other.

"Okay, you know what?" I shoved the phone back at him. "Why are you watching this? Why are *we* watching this?"

"I don't know. I thought you were one of the pussy people or—"

"No!" I cut him off. I loved my little brother fiercely, but hearing the word *pussy* come out of his mouth was just too much.

"I appreciate your . . . attention, but please put that away. I will take care of this situation."

"Oh-kay," Gus said, brow furrowed.

"Actually, can you just send me the link so I can figure out what creeps are posting comments?"

"Sure. But why is that your job?" he asked.

"Because she's my best friend!" I yelled.

Gus nodded thoughtfully before saying, "Is she though?"

His thorny question hung in the air between us as the front door opened and Uncle Ricky came in dripping.

"Two of each animal! Gather them quick!" he boomed. Uncle Ricky was born without volume control, so we really never had a conversation that didn't echo throughout the house.

"Hey, FU!" Gus answered. *FU* stood for *Favorite Uncle*, among other things.

"Hey hey!" Uncle Ricky answered. "What? Nothing from the Hankster?"

I was too busy scrolling through my own phone now, trying to get to the comments under Zoe's video. Uncle Ricky shed some of his soggy clothes and shuffled up behind the couch.

"Whoa, are we watching porn as a family now?" he asked. Then he busted out laughing at his own joke, which I found thoroughly unamusing.

I slammed my phone down and snarled, "Okay, that's not only gross; it's illegal, because she's not even eighteen."

Uncle Ricky put his hands up in mock defense and shook his head.

"Also, don't you guys have some movie to watch or axes to throw?" I added.

"Well, I haven't even looked up the movie times yet," Uncle

154

Ricky started. "I thought maybe I could dry off, grab a snack, and then maybe we'll head out around four?"

Gus must have heard me steaming. He stood up and announced that he really wanted to go see something as soon as possible. Like, it was urgent that he see this movie that was probably playing only at two. They could get eggs at the diner on the way back. Or Chinese takeout. He started ushering Uncle Ricky back toward the front door as he spoke. I knew it was Gus's way of giving me some space and I was truly grateful, but I was also too frayed to thank him.

As they headed outside, I texted Zoe in all caps: DANCE PARTY?

She wrote back right away: So stupid. Lol.

BUT WHAT DOES IT MEAN? I persisted.

Will explain in person. Promised Alli I'd do Booty Camp class with her first tho so meet me at gym @ 3? We can change for party in locker room and use their fancy hair products.

I wrote back: I DON'T UNDERSTAND.

Pretty please with everything on top?

I heard it was November out in the real world.

But enough about me!

Or you!

Or the "us" that was destined to one day topple over and break into me and you again.

Check out some of my newest and dearest celebrity crushes who either self-destructed or rose from the ashes to tell the tale!

(See—we get homework in here too.)

Karen Anne Carpenter (March 2, 1950–February 4, 1983)

Brilliant American songstress and drummer. She had a voice that tripped and trilled. She also defined bell-bottoms and free love. Until she <u>died from anorexia</u>. In those days, people could still go to the pharmacy and get drugs that would make you vomit, so Karen did that in between singing gigs. It made her heart so weak that it eventually gave out. The saddest part is that Karen sang this awesome song called "We've Only Just Begun" and it really does sound like hope with whipped cream on top.

Gilda Radner (June 28, 1946–May 20, 1989)

My mom's all-time hero, and I have to admit she was freaken funny and brilliant. She was on the first season of <u>Saturday Night Live</u>. There's this one skit where she dances with Steve

Martin and I just want to float away on her skirt. She also had a ton of eating disorders though, and she wrote this beautiful book about how she wanted to do right by her body. She got cancer really young and she kept on making people laugh even while she was dying.

Kesha Rose Sebert (aka Kesha)

Is a motherf-cken woman! Her <u>Rainbow</u> album is the only thing keeping me (somewhat) sane in here. Do you remember all that crap and abuse she went through with her old producer? And it led right into an eating-disorder nosedive for her. I've been reading these amazing interviews with her that make me weep. How she felt so forsaken and alone. How she sat in rehab and asked the universe for a sign. And now she's kicking ass.

Zayn Malik (aka the silent sexy guy from One Direction)

Okay, first because he has righteous eyebrows. Also, because he broke out to perform on his own and there is something so sad about his voice. Which is maybe why he had to sing. To get out his inner sadness. He spoke openly about battling his eating disorders and I think that's extra-hard to do if you're a guy.

Zosia Mamet

When I first saw her acting, I thought she came from another planet. She spoke so fast that I felt dizzy but in a good way. And then I heard her talk about her relationship with her body and how she doesn't want to hide from or with eating disorders anymore. One of my favorite Zosia quotes:

"Wouldn't you rather be your real self instead of an unrealistic idea of perfection?"

I'm just not sure I can answer that yet.

CHAPTER 12
booty camp 101

THERE WAS A POCKET OF TIME IN MY LIFE WHEN THE EAGLE BROOK
Mall represented freedom and hope. Zoe and I had to be eleven
before we were allowed to roam there unchaperoned, and even
then, it was just for two hours while one of our moms hid on
another floor trying on sunglasses or eating salads by the in-
door waterfall. The mall was obscenely big and constantly being
expanded. Zoe and I used to save up all our allowance to go
there and get cotton candy–flavored lip gloss, beaded headbands,
bedazzled mirrors, and invisible-ink pens. I even lost a tooth at
the Popcorn Hut and Zoe got her period for the first time at the
movie theater in the basement.

I knew some people from our high school still came here a lot.
There were rumors that Brendan Montague was caught sniffing

glue in the parking lot elevator and Nikki DeFelice had gotten felt up in the photo booth. But the last time I'd come here was at least three years ago. Stepping into the mall this afternoon was a little like falling into a vat of scented candle wax. There were a lot of nail salons promising cuticle renewal. Also, a kids' designer clothing boutique and a lingerie shop called Adult Secrets. The top two floors were now the recently opened gym/spa/way of life called Primally Fit. This was where Zoe and I had agreed to meet before our sleepover.

Once through the revolving doors, I was greeted by a seven-foot-tall pillar of muscle whose name tag read KARLA.

"Welcome to Primally Fit! Do you want to take control of your body and your life because if you do there's a new member special going on for two more weeks it's so awesome I swear it changed my life and I mean that!"

Karla had no time for punctuation or inflection. She didn't even wait for me to answer her before accosting the next person through the revolving door behind me. Lucky for me, there were five more Amazonian specimens behind the front desk waiting to pounce. I heard about how Primally Fit was founded by a destitute diabetic who started with sugarless gum and jumping jacks and now lived in Bel Air and managed fifteen franchises worldwide. Also how Primally Fit instructors were each groomed and indoctrinated by other certified Primally Fit instructors. And I was told again about that special for new members, which was going on for two more weeks and would totally change my life.

160

"Sorry, I'm here to meet a friend. She's in a class called Boot Camp?"

"Boot Camp?" one of the women said.

"Boot Camp . . ." Another got busy looking it up on a computer.

"Do you mean Bernardo's Total Body and Booty Camp?" chimed in Karla.

Everyone behind the desk started wiggling their hips and cheering. "Booty camp! Booty camp! Booty booty booty camp!"

"I think that class already started."

"Yeah, didn't it start like a half hour ago?"

"He will *not* let people come in late."

"I'm not actually taking the class," I started to explain. Then I realized the women were talking to one another, not to me. So I murmured, "Thanks," and started wandering toward the other end of the room.

Or I thought it was the other end of the room. In fact, it took me almost fifteen minutes to locate Zoe in this aerobics metropolis—the gym was so sprawling that I wandered through a day-care corner, a juice bar, a salon, and a small gift shop before locating the Booty Camp Training Center.

"Really?!" a man I had to assume was Bernardo screamed into his headset. "That's all you can give me? I do not believe you, ladies. This is not okay!" There were only a half dozen women still upright in the Booty Camp 101 class—including Alli and Zoe, of course. The rest of the group was bent over, tucking heads between knees or chugging water.

"You want that perfect booty, don't you?" Bernardo taunted. "How bad you want it? How bad? So bad it's good, right? So good it's baaaaad. Am I right?" Turning up the incessant techno beats. "Who's gonna be my booty queen, huh?" He caught me staring and gave me a smarmy wink. Then whipped his head back to face the class and bellowed, "Twenty burpees, on my count. Go!" He catapulted himself back onto the little stage at the front of the studio and started squatting and thrusting and push-upping with groans. Nobody could keep up with him now. I felt dizzy just watching.

"I swear just five minutes left," Zoe gasped at me, her eyes still focused only on Bernardo. I was seriously tempted to go hide in the pit of brightly colored plastic balls and suck my thumb with all the toddlers who'd been abandoned for a good sweat. Even with their wailing, it seemed much more soothing than listening to Bernardo berate these exhausted women. As the music got more and more frenetic, so did the class. Ab-crunching and mountain-climbing so ferociously, it sounded like a roomful of feral squirrels fighting. Bernardo stepped over their bodies slowly, snarling as he looked at himself in the wall of mirrors.

"C'mon! You want results? You want to see *change* in this world? Stop wasting my time and show me your—"

I had never been so grateful for the sound of an egg timer going off.

"And tiiiiiiiime," Bernardo announced. There were a few weak hoots and some pitiful applause from the sidelines. Whoever was left on the floor collapsed gratefully onto a gym mat.

Bernardo was miraculously transformed into a gentleman, smiling delicately.

"Nice work today, everyone. Really impressive," he said, striding around the room like a peacock—reaching out an arm here and there to help people up. When he lifted up Alli, they came nose to nose.

"*Really* nice," he said into her sweaty hair. She was still breathing too quickly to make real words, but when he offered to buy everyone a watermelon-flaxseed shot at the juice bar, she nodded vigorously and tripped after him. Zoe grabbed my hand and pulled me out of the gaggle of spent women.

"Ridonkulous, right?" she said. I could see her pulse throbbing in her neck. "You have to try it one day though. C'mon! Let me give you a tour of this place."

She showed me around the gym as if it were her second home, pointing out the different trainers and state-of-the-art elliptical machines that could simulate unpaved roads and overgrown marsh. I had no idea how that could be desirable, but Zoe said it was what all the professional marathoners used. There were classes in Zumba, kickboxing, Zumba-boxing, and archery. Also, three racquetball courts, a steam room, a sauna, and a sideways shower that Zoe called "orgasmic."

"Kinda nuts, but kinda cool, right?" Zoe asked.

"Sure," I answered, following her back out into another nautilus machine torture chamber. This place gave me the heebies. No matter what they painted on these walls, everything in the entire gym felt overexposed and frantic. There were so many sinewy bodies sauntering by. So many hungry eyes and sunken cheeks. Tracking each other's form. Stepping on scales. Huffing and puffing, practically in unison.

Alli waved us over to the juice bar to officially meet Bernardo. She slammed me into her in a forceful, smelly embrace.

"So glad you could make it," she rasped at me. "Did Zoe tell you about Bernardo coming here from Portugal on a dancing scholarship and working with Beyoncé?"

I nodded even though Alli's gaze was fixed on Bernardo the whole time. And possibly shooting eye lasers at the clutch of ladies still surrounding him.

"What? You do not introduce me?" Bernardo said, pulling on Zoe's ponytail so sharply that her neck jerked backward. "Let me guess—this is your twin sister?" He and Alli both laughed at how preposterous that sounded.

"This is Hannah, my best friend in the whole world," Zoe said. She tucked a clump of hair behind my ear and rested her head on my shoulder. "She really is the best. And the sweetest. And the realest and kindest. Hannah banana, I don't deserve you."

Bernardo nodded in agreement as we just stood there, being ogled. "This is very lovely," he told us. "Yes, you know. The women. They are who make us. Am I right?"

Yes!

Woo-hoo!

Oh Bernardo!

The flushed female chorus around him cheered like he'd just validated or maybe invented our gender. Bernardo was pleased.

164

"Hannaba Nana," he told me. "Please come for a free trial class anytime. I can get you passes to the sauna too."

"Bernardo!" Alli said, swatting at his hairy forearm. As if talking to me about this promotion made him a naughty boy. "It's a *far infrared sauna*," she explained to me, still catching her breath.

"Wow," I said. Because somewhere, somehow, someone must've been impressed by that detail. I also didn't want to invite any explanations about why I should be amazed. Bernardo gave me another penetrating look and then Zoe told her mom that we would be sauna-ing and showering if anyone needed us.

I didn't last very long in the acclaimed far infrared sauna. Probably too far or infrared for my composition. Plus, the whole time we were in there, I couldn't see past my fingertips and I felt like I was breathing in pine-scented car exhaust.

"Sorry. A little. Too. Dry," I panted.

"No prob. Meet you by the lockers. Don't forget to try the sideways shower!" Zoe said as I hurled myself out of the hot box.

My left armpit and hip were thoroughly pleased by the sideways shower. The rest of me was just confused. It took me twice as long to rinse myself off and I was pretty sure my left eardrum was power washed by the time I escaped. Still, I got dressed, swished some complimentary mouthwash, and studied a large bulletin board with colorful flyers boasting courses like Self-Acceptance and Teeth Whitening, Know Your Boundaries, and my favorite: Who Are You if Not You?

"Didn't you love it?" Zoe gushed as she emerged from a cloud of eucalyptus. Then she squinted a little. "Ooh, is that what you're wearing?"

"That was the plan," I answered. I had decided on my favorite batik pants with elephants marching on them and my *Unicorns Fart Rainbows* T-shirt. Which to me equaled fancy.

"Awesome," Zoe said quickly. She pulled her towel around her even tighter. "You know, this is why I love you so much, Hank. Because you don't give a shit or get all hung up on what's cool. You're so awesome. And so much wiser and smarter and realer than anyone else I know. I just wish I had a smidge of your balls."

I felt her words slap the wet tiles but didn't know how to react.

"Balls," I repeated out of habit.

Zoe smiled, trying to remember what the rule about *balls* was. "Jinx!" she squeaked.

"No, just *balls*," I told her.

"I say 'balls'?"

"You said it, then I say it."

"Then I say it again?"

"Never mind," I told her.

"No, I want to get it right. Please?" Zoe whined.

"Just—balls."

"Okay, *balls*," she repeated. I gave her the thumbs-up, primarily so we could move on.

"Did you see the ridonkulous number of hair products by the sink? You *have* to try some," she urged.

I knew she was genuinely excited by cosmetics, but I also

sensed that she was trying to get me out of the locker room while she undressed.

If I was brave, I would have stayed planted there so Zoe would have been forced to show me her body again—this time the full thing. So she couldn't hide anymore, and I couldn't hide anymore, and the truth could set us free.

But instead I wandered over to the bank of sinks and squirted about eight different gels and foams into my hand. I smeared so many different textures into my hair, it looked like shellac. Then I tried rinsing it out in one of the sinks and flipping it upside down to embrace its chaotic waves.

"Where'd you get those curls?" asked an older woman behind me. Before I could answer, she told me wistfully, "I used to have curls like that." She was combing back her short salt-and-pepper tufts and she had a white towel fastened around her ribs. Her dark breasts were bare, dangling like heavy brown coins. Daring me to gape.

"You can have them," I suggested sheepishly. I hated my hair, but I felt like she'd lost her curls to some cruel robber or disease.

"Bless your heart," the woman said with a quiet chuckle. Then her voice dropped an octave as she noticed Zoe come in. "Oh dear," the woman muttered, shaking her head and sucking her lips into a tight line.

I wasn't sure exactly what the woman was reacting to, but Zoe was definitely a sight. She was in the polka-dotted shorts with black tights underneath; a sheer pink tank top over a black bra underneath, and black lace-up boots with hot-pink laces. There were patches of glittery body gel on her cheeks and shoulders and she wore neon-pink lipstick. Basically, she looked like a misguided meteor. Plunking down a bag filled with shimmery eyeshadows, she said, "Still have to do the rest of the face. I'm not a natural beauty like you."

I just glared at her because there was no way anyone would ever honestly call me a natural beauty, and I didn't know whether it was the lights in there or the eucalyptus stimulation, but even Zoe's face looked watery and frail. Her arms hung out of her top like limp toothpicks. And was that foundation smoothed onto the "cat scratches" on her biceps?

Zoe fished through her eyeliners and pulled over a stool so she'd be tall enough to work on me. "I'm gonna give us both purple whiskers and a pink nose. Is that okay?"

I just shrugged. Because I still hadn't found a way to say no.

"What are you doing, honey?" the bare-chested woman asked.

"Oh. It's for a silly video we're making," Zoe told her. "We're supposed to be cats."

"No," the woman said, shuffling closer. She scanned Zoe's body in the mirror. Her face working its way into a steady, grim stare. "What are you *doing*?"

"What? Who, me?" Zoe replied.

"Yes. *You*." She caught Zoe's eyes in the mirror and wouldn't let go. "What are you doing to your poor body?"

Zoe's smile started drooping, and I could see her nostrils quivering.

"You come in here how many times now?" the woman

continued. "All jumpy and bouncy and running from your own shadow. You're wearing yourself ragged."

"I like to . . . exercise," Zoe told her in a quivery voice.

"I know you do," the woman shot back. Then she softened her voice a bit and tried again. "I know you do. But you can't keep going like this. You know that? You need to put some *fuel* in your body."

Zoe nodded her head at the woman and said, "Thank you. I'll do that." All the while rolling her eyes for me.

The woman caught her mid-eye roll and clucked her tongue.

"You can mock me, young lady. But it's true."

"No, I wasn't mocking," Zoe insisted.

"You need a hot meal. You need to stop this nonsense."

"Okay, I *will*." Zoe sounded like she was pleading for the woman to stop now.

But the woman wasn't done. "Because this is not pretty," she told Zoe. Then, in case I hadn't paid attention yet, she turned around and said it to my face. "This is not pretty at all."

"We're going to eat something right after this," I told her. I just wanted her to stop glaring at us.

"A really big meal," Zoe chimed in merrily. She stepped in front of the mirror and started painting my face. So I couldn't see the woman's reaction.

I could only hear her heave a sigh and walk away.

Hey, Hank! I know you like math.

So I wrote you a word problem:

The National Association of Anorexia Nervosa and Associated Disorders says that at least 30 million people in America have anorexia nervosa, bulimia, or other fun eating disorders.

According to the American Journal of Public Health, about 1 in 4 adolescents participate in nonsuicidal self-injury.

If 30 million anorexic people (cuz we don't take up that much room) are traveling south on a train going 85 miles per hour, and 1/3 as many are cutting themselves while traveling north at 73 miles per hour, when will they collide, how many will have suicidal ideation, and will anyone actually care?

CHAPTER 13
this much

"PLEASE, EVERYONE, WON'T YOU GIVE ZOE YOUR ATTENTION?" YELPED
James Hartwick III.

If life was hard for pitiful ol' me, it must have been triply hard
for James. He and his twin sister, Amelia, were British transplants,
and their parents were both brilliant anthropologists who were
constantly flying overseas to give lectures or offer the newest data
to the United Nations. James was in a lot of my classes and was
constantly staying after the bell to check in with our teachers and
make sure he was living up to his potential. James took himself
and his potential a little too seriously. At seventeen, he already
looked a little stooped over from the weight of it all. He wore
thick bifocals and wrung his hands a lot too.

Amelia, on the other hand, lived life on her tiptoes. Bouncing through the halls at school and always finding a reason to shriek gleefully. Zoe told me that Amelia could run a six-minute mile if she wanted, but she was usually too busy gossiping at practice or planning her next party. If her parents were going to stick them in this huge echoey house and have a nanny feed them soup when they had colds, then Amelia was determined to get what she was due as a teenager. And that meant, when her parents were away, she invited everyone she knew and strung up Christmas lights in zigzags around the basement. She also told Zoe that she was determined to lose her virginity in her parents' bed, which made me shudder.

Despite Amelia's best intentions though, the Hartwick parties usually stayed pretty tame. Just a mess of horny careless teenagers trying to get drunk. James greeted everyone at the door, nodding in his bashful way. He always looked shocked when people remembered his name. There was a pool table, a wraparound leather couch where people made out or played video games or both, and a pinball machine that got jammed or tilted. I could never find a place to sit or stand, so I was part of the wandering crew. Awkwardly moving from corner to corner, complaining about how lame our lives were and how our lives got lamer every year and it was all the fault of our lame parents who had punished us with their genes of lame-itude.

Tonight was more crowded than usual. The rain was keeping everyone pressed together inside. Amelia was directing people to the middle of the room while James struggled to move the couch back. (There were a few people who sat there on the couch as he drove his shoulder into it, but James was too humble to ask them to scoot over or get up.)

"You guys. Listen up!" Amelia stood on the pool table and explained that this was a once-in-a-lifetime chance for her dear friend Zoe. We were all going to learn a few moves that Zoe had gotten from her *professional choreographer, Bernardo.* There were also multiple cameras set up around the room to capture it all. But the most important thing was for us to *act natural.*

As if anyone our age in a sweaty basement with confusing emotions and desires knew what acting natural meant.

"This is serious!" Amelia continued. "Zoe's agent said that if this video is good enough, he can get her on season three of *Dance for Me Now!* And next week she's flying out to LA to meet like *everyone.* So let's give it up for . . . Zoe!"

I felt my breath get shallow and uneven. I had never heard about this plan to go to LA next week, nor had I heard anything about *Dance for Me Now!* I needed to pull Zoe into a corner so I could check in and make sure this was just another Amelia Hartwick embellishment. Only that was impossible now. The party had taken on a fierce, new momentum. Everyone around me was scrambling to hug Zoe or grab a can of beer from one of the coolers before our dance instruction began. I wanted to tell them all not to be fooled by her glitter and glam. I knew for a fact that underneath the makeup and cat ears she was all sharp angles and knobby joints.

There was just too much shoving and squealing. A few beefy guys from our big-on-pep-rallies-low-on-actual-scoring school lacrosse team lifted Zoe on top of the couch so she could teach everyone Bernardo's seductive moves.

"Oh yeah!"

"Work it, girl!"

"Look how tiny she is!"

"Wait, where's Hank?" I heard Zoe say. "Has anyone seen Hank?"

I didn't answer. Instead, I pushed farther out through the crowd so I could lean against one of the basement walls and just observe. The room was teeming with Zoe admirers, oohing and aahing at her moves. Catcalling and purring. Yes, I was the only one who knew she continued to sleep with a nightlight on and that she believed in Santa Claus until she was twelve. I knew she still had to do most math problems by counting on her fingers and was terrified of cockroaches. I knew Zoe better than anyone else here. And yet I had no idea how long she had been lying to me and trying to cover it up with powder that was two shades too dark for her sallow skin. I wanted it to be just this past summer that she'd changed so much, but really, hadn't she been "too busy for lunch" most of our high school career and didn't she disappear into the bathroom for long periods of time and always come out reeking of aspartame, chomping on a fresh stick of gum?

I had nobody but myself to blame for being this blind—or really, for strapping on my own blinders. Even a topless stranger in the gym could name the glaring reality better than me.

"Hank! I need you," I heard Zoe call again, but I kept snaking my way toward the side door. I needed to put some distance between myself and this whiskered stick figure and see that we were separate entities. I'd been attached to that teeny hip bone for so many years. I had considered it my honor and privilege to be at Zoe's beck and call like this—to achingly anticipate her every need. To live inside her dreams and become an extension of her.

No longer. I just couldn't anymore.

When I stepped outside, the rain was still emptying itself in sheets from the sky, so I tucked myself into a little corner of the driveway, sheltered by the roof's overhang. I closed my eyes and took in a long drink of night sky as I weighed my options:

1. I could call Gus and Uncle Ricky and force myself into their plans. They were probably grabbing dinner by now and of course I hadn't eaten with Zoe.
2. I could drive myself home and hide under the covers and file a missing person report for myself.
3. I could just pretend I was a puddle and go to sleep.

The woman from the gym with the unapologetically sagging boobs kept glaring at me in my head. Telling me this wasn't pretty. That something needed to be done.

"No," I told the rain. "Fuck no!"

"Excuse me?" said a squeaky voice with a British accent.

"Oh, sorry. James, is that you?"

I could just make out his blurred profile against the rainy background. He was standing a few feet away under the next corner's overhang, taking a drag on a cigarette. He quickly snuffed it out on the ground and said, "Yes. Yup. It's me, James. Are you enjoying yourself, I hope?"

"Sure," I lied. "I mean, it's a great party."

"Is it? Oh, I'm so glad." He moved closer to the gutter light, so I could see him put on a polite smile for me. Only, he looked so weary and waterlogged. I thought about the last time Amelia had conned James into hosting a party and he had retreated to the laundry room because Amelia threatened to play truth or dare.

"James, did you have any idea this was going to be a whole . . . thing tonight?" I asked.

"No," he admitted. "It's fine, it's fine. I'm just a bit nervous that my parents are going to catch wind."

The pain in his voice undid me. I wanted to scoot over and give him a hug just for being so earnest and concerned. But that would probably make both of us shudder with embarrassment. So instead I made him a promise.

"Listen. I'll make sure this doesn't get out on social media, okay? Would that help?"

"Oh yes! Immensely! But is that possible?"

"Sure. Yes," I told him. Though I had no idea how.

Just then the Hartwicks' door slammed open. A flare of colored lights and steamy beer stink cut through the night.

"Ooh, there you are! Hanky-Pank! Yay!" Zoe shot through the doorway and into my arms. I didn't know if she was drunk or just overly excited. I heard the *swish* of her satiny shorts and the *thonk* of her boots crashing through the calm and landing on top of me.

"Didn't you hear me? I need you on the dance floor! Ahh, this

176

fresh air feels great. Oh, hey, James. Mind if I borrow Hank for a bit?"

"Of course not," said James obediently.

"Hmmm," Zoe said even before the door closed behind us. "Anything you want to tell me about you and James Hartwick III?" She snickered.

"No," I told her. "Except that I don't think Amelia told him about the whole dance thing and he's worried that if people post videos of it, his parents will find out and then . . ."

"Ha! Is that what he told you?" Zoe steered me through the clusters of clammy bodies toward Amelia, who was taking in a long hit from a joint. "Amelia!" Zoe shouted in her face. "You need to talk to your brother. He's freaking out!"

Amelia burst into a hyena-style cackle and Zoe squeezed my hand tight, navigating us toward the couch.

"Hanky!" Zoe yelled in my ear. "I got you!" The room was closing in on us again. Ten different people were clamoring for Zoe's attention so they could make sure she approved of the dance moves they'd memorized. Zoe grinned graciously and gave lots of fist bumps. As if we were walking into a political rally and she'd just been announced the queen of everything. The hip-hop beat was being piped into the room so loudly, it sent tremors up through my empty gut.

There were three earsplitting *meow*s from the speakers and then everyone in the room *meow*ed back. People started rolling their hips in unison. Raising two fingers on either side of their heads to look like cat ears. Zoe pushed all the people ahead of us out of the way and got us to the center of the dance floor. It was so packed and steamy now, even the floor felt slick.

"Just follow me!" Zoe called over the music.

"Yup," I whimpered.

That was the one skill set I actually knew I had. I could always imitate Zoe Hammer. I'd done it for most of my life and had made it my undeclared mission statement. I matched each shimmy and hip grind perfectly. I found her rhythm and saw how seamlessly the rest just fell into place. After all, Zoe was my one constant in life. The vortex of the same storm she was creating. There was soon a circle of dancers around us, clapping and meowing. Cheering for us as we wound around each other, bopping in perfect sync.

Zoe hooked her skeletal arms around my neck and gazed at me with wide, glinting eyes. She wasn't drunk at all. She was serious and sober.

"You can catch me, right?" she asked.

"Yes," I replied. This was a test of my devotion and a calculation of how much she weighed, and it was all being caught on video, so if I didn't do it, I'd ruin whatever we had left. I nodded, trying to bend my knees and clench my middle for inner support.

"Totally," I added.

"I swear, Hank. I love you more than anyone in this whole stupid room."

"I love you too," I said.

"I mean it." Her voice was low and rumbly now. "Do you believe me?"

"Yes."

"You're so freaken smart and beautiful and real and kind. And I know I haven't always been the friend you needed, and I just wish you knew how much you mean to me."

"Thanks," I said. If she didn't jump soon, I was going to tip over from nervous anticipation.

"Do you love me?" Zoe whispered in my ear.

"Of course."

"How much?" she insisted.

"So much," I said. Which would always be true.

Zoe's eyes crinkled as she pulled away from me. She shuffled backward for a running start and dove into my arms. I caught her easily, cradling her like a newborn. The crowd whooped.

"This much?" Zoe asked. She grabbed me by the back of my neck and pulled me in for a kiss. A real kiss that took all the air out of the night and turned everything to now. Somewhere beyond us, there were hoots and growls of appreciation. Or maybe that was thunder. I had the feeling that everything and everyone was caught inside this moment and yet we were all alone. I felt the edge of her tongue poking at my lips. Salty and sweet and slippery with pink. As she pulled me into her tide of warm recklessness.

My legs were trembling. My left arm was sparking with pins and needles. But if I put her down, it would all be gone.

So I stayed there, clutching on to my little girl.

One last time.

TIME CAPSULE

We had to do this time capsule exercise the other day and it broke me in half. Because I realized that I had nothing from today that I wanted to keep. And all I wanted were a million parts of yesterday. Or really, from a lot of yesterdays ago. I want to go back to the way we were when we first got those kitty-cat costumes in ballet class. When we stuck our bellies out and colored them with lipstick and our biggest worry was getting caught eating chunks of butter or running out of crayons.

Do you remember the time we made a lemonade stand and used all the profits on glow-in-the-dark tattoos that never glowed in the dark?

Do you remember that game where we hid in your pantry and pretended we were police arresting the vacuum cleaner?

Sometimes these memories are so clear and bright in my head that my eyes sting and my chest caves in. Because we can't go back. Time just doesn't work that way. Even if you hurl your clock against the wall. Even if you scream at all your counselors and slap your inner child silly. Time will never slow down or even pause.

Silver lining: I guess we're not stuck here anymore either.

CHAPTER 14
red dye #5

TRAVIS WAS EXPECTING US BY 11:00 P.M., WHICH MEANT WE needed to leave the Hartwicks' by 10:40 at the latest, and I was hoping for better directions than Zoe's "You get off Route 22 and then take that main road down until you see a Starbucks and I think a yarn store . . . ?"

It was already 11:20 by the time we slinked out of the Hartwicks' basement. I hadn't touched a single sip of warm beer and I don't think Zoe had either. But we were both tipsy from the rush of sudden, passionate fame. After our kiss on the dance floor, the party got a lot steamier. People piling onto one another and doing a lot of grinding and twerking. I had to admit, it was a relief to just get lost in the middle of this madness, sweating out my vicious fears and frustrations. But by eleven o'clock, the

Hartwicks had two neighbors threatening to call the police because of the noise levels and James looked like he was going to have an aneurysm from anxiety.

He turned down the music and announced, "Thank you all so much for coming but I'm afraid we have to close up now."

Amelia jumped onto a coffee table and screamed, "Afterparty in my bedroom!" Then lost her balance and crashed into a speaker.

I could hear her cackling as James shouted over her, "Please! We will have a party again. Just get home safe and thank you, this has been a wonderful time."

Most everyone from the party started spilling out onto the wet driveway then. The rain wasn't quite torrential anymore, but the wind was picking up and it was definitely still coming down. I tried to pull Zoe straight to my car, only she was surrounded by a tight posse of new fans trailing her toward the HOT RIC–mobile.

"Hey, I don't mean to be a jerk, but isn't your dad waiting for us?" I said.

"Boo!" said Zoe.

"Yeah, boo!" echoed Colette McNamara.

"Do we really have to go?" Zoe whined. She looked at me with wide, pleading eyes while Freyja whispered, "Don't go! Don't go!"

I tried to look really interested in the dripping gutters on the side of the house because I had nothing to say besides, *Why are you making me the bad guy?* Zoe must have sensed my discomfort. She took my hand in hers and put it on her heart.

"No, it's not Hank's fault," she told the soggy crowd. "And have no fear! The Pussycat Warriors shall return!"

As we got into my car, a handful of people pounded on the trunk, like we were zooming off to a glorious honeymoon. I was sure I'd lose a muffler or at the very least get a few dents, but Zoe loved it. She climbed into the backseat and blew kisses as I drove away.

"So stupid, right?" she asked. "Seriously though, don't you wish we could just dance all night?"

"Uh-huh."

Out of the corner of my eye, I saw Zoe plop herself back into the passenger seat and start tracing spiky circles into the fog on her window. Or maybe it was a cat—I couldn't tell. Then she swiped the design away and grunted. She was also digging her fingernails into her thighs now while she knocked her forehead against the window and audibly fumed.

"What's . . . why are you doing that?" I asked.

She sniffed and swiped at her eyes with the back of her hand.

"It's just—I hate this!" She kicked the glove compartment door and it flew open, spewing a stack of papers I was supposed to sign but never did. "Sorry," Zoe said in a softer voice now.

"Sorry doesn't . . ." I lost my nerve on that argument. "Can you tell me what's going on?" I tried.

"Ha!" Zoe laughed bitterly. The vivacious ringleader I'd danced with just a few minutes ago was gone. In her place was a wretched ball of gloom. "I mean, was that not the most awesome party?" she moaned. "And now we have to leave it to hang out with fucken

Travis in his beige bachelor pad of patheticness? It's just *not fair*." Her misery kept swelling as she sank lower into her seat.

"I'm sorry," I said. "I thought you wanted to go. Or at least you wanted me to come with you—"

"Yes!" Zoe cut me off. "Yes. I really want you to come with me. I'm very grateful you're coming with me. I'm just having a hard time. I can't explain it more than that, okay?" Her phone buzzed but she refused to answer it. "And, of course, now Travis is calling yet again to ask where we are."

I thought it would actually be helpful to talk to Travis, considering we didn't know which way to go after getting off the highway, but I wasn't about to suggest that to Zoe. Instead, I said, "Hey, how about this? I'm superthirsty and I'd love to look up exactly where Travis's building is, so what if we pulled into ye olde Quicky Yum FoodMart and split a slushie?"

Zoe was silent.

"Or I'll just get something and you . . . can try on sunglasses?"

I heard Zoe gulp, and took that as a yes.

We used to stop at Quicky Yum FoodMart for slushies on the way back from ballet class when we were in grade school. Or really, I think we did it once. Maybe twice. By third grade, Zoe had been moved up to the accelerated dance program and had started gymnastics on the other side of town, so we didn't get to carpool anymore. But I wanted to stretch out that one memory as far as it would go without snapping.

As we walked into the mart, I felt Zoe's pointy elbow dig into my rib.

"Be right back," she said. "Gotta pee."

There was nothing quick or yummy about this place. It looked like it had been updated since I'd last been there, but in a really haphazard way. A strip of wood paneling and a sign that said, YEEHAW! over the hall to the bathrooms. A shiny new incubator for the hot dogs to lazily roll upon under a heat lamp. Security cameras in every corner. (Their latest burglary was all over the *Nightly News* and involved people dressed as angry clowns.)

Tonight, the Quicky Yum FoodMart was completely empty except for the cashier. She was facing away from us as we came in, but even as she whipped her head around, I couldn't tell if she was fifteen or forty. Her jet-black ponytail was pulled back tight and high, then cascaded down her back almost to her butt. Her olive skin and fuchsia lip liner were both glistening and hypnotic. She looked at me and Zoe, then at the clock above the cash register and back at us again. It was clear she had plans tonight after closing and she didn't want us interfering with that.

"Hold on, I have to finish my job, you know!" she barked into her phone. "And you have to get here by midnight to pick me up!" Then she held up her phone to face me and said, "Am I right?"

"Totally," I said. Which cracked her up. It got even funnier to her as she did the instant replay:

"Did you hear that? I said 'Am I right?' And she was all, 'Totally.'" Then she looked up at me and winked. "I like you. You're funny."

I liked her too. She was decked out in a purple T-shirt that read *Keep Calm and Carry My Sh*t*. The bottom was cut into uneven strips of fringe, ending just above her acid-washed jeans and curvy hips. Her name tag said HI MY NAME IS SHARON.

I wanted to ask Sharon if she was really happy or if it was just for show. If she felt like she could trust whoever was on that phone with her heart or if the whole idea of mutual respect and loyalty was untenable. Did she have a best friend or a best enemy or was it better to just be alone?

"What's up? Can I help you?" Sharon asked.

"Oh—no. I mean, I'm gonna get something but I'll be right back."

"'Kay," Sharon answered. "We close in twenty."

"Yup."

I picked up three different bags of tortilla chips before making my way to the slushie machine. Zoe was back from the bathroom, standing in front of the Diet Orange with her cup half full. Smacking her lips and mumbling.

"I don't think this is diet," she said, without looking at me. "Is this diet?"

"It says Diet Orange."

"Yeah, I know, but . . ." Zoe took another sip, then jolted her head back. "No. No no no no," she steamed. She rushed over to the counter to consult with a higher authority. The fact that Sharon was still on the phone only made Zoe get louder.

"'Scuse me?" she called. When Sharon didn't respond immediately, Zoe jutted her arm out and waved her hand in front of

Sharon's face. "'Scuse me! Sorry. Is this diet? I pulled the thing that said Diet Orange, but this doesn't taste like it's diet."

Sharon turned toward Zoe in what looked like slow motion. Probably because Zoe was so wild in comparison.

"Hold on," Sharon rumbled into the phone. Then she tightened her ponytail and said to Zoe, "Can. I. Help. You?"

"Yes!" Zoe yelped. "Thank you. Yes! I just need to know—I mean, can you just taste this? I swear I don't have cooties or anything. I just need to know that it's diet because I have a thing with sugar."

Sharon rubbed the side of her jaw and squinted. As if Zoe's frantic chatter needed to be decoded.

"You want me to—?"

"Please!" Zoe pounced. "I'll pay for it either way. I swear. I just need to know. Because if it's sugar then . . ." She shook her head to erase that possibility.

Sharon picked up her phone again and said, "Yeah, something's going on. Lemme call you back, 'kay?"

I hid behind the rotating rack of personalized mini-license plates, shivering. The underwire of my bra had caught all the sweat from dancing and it was at least twenty degrees colder in here than in the Hartwicks' basement. I wanted so badly to be anywhere but here and anyone but me.

"Now let me get this straight. You think this has sugar in it, so you want me to drink it for you?" asked Sharon.

"Just a taste. *Please*. I need to know what's in it. It's my *right* to know!" Zoe pushed the cup so forcefully at Sharon that it almost tipped over into her acid-washed lap.

"Okay. *Whoa.*" Sharon put both her hands up to shield her face. "You're a little bit—" Sharon pressed her bright lips together instead of finishing that sentence. She took a deep breath and tried again. "Now I'm not supposed to touch a customer's food, but . . ."

"It's okay! I'm telling you to!" Zoe gushed.

Sharon cocked her head and drew her eyebrows into an angry peak.

"I mean, I'm *asking* you to," Zoe said. "Please."

Sharon brought the cup up to her mouth. She lifted a single fuchsia fingernail out as if at a proper tea party, then slurped noisily.

"Hmmm," she said, putting the cup down again.

"Does it taste like diet to you?" Zoe demanded.

"I guess."

"But what does that mean?" Zoe sounded close to tears now. "I need to know. I mean, don't you have the nutritional breakdown in a binder or something? Or even just a label. It's required by the FDA. It's the *law.*"

"Wait, what?" Sharon was losing her patience now. She peered up at one of the security cameras and squinted.

Meanwhile, Zoe spun around to enlist me in her cause. "You know what I'm talking about, don't you, Hank?" Her bottom lashes were dark and wet.

"I . . . m-maybe," I stuttered.

"Come on! *Please*."

Sharon was the one who actually stepped up to the plate and said, "It's sugar and water and orange dye number three."

"But you just said it was diet!"

"Okay, then it's fake sugar and water and red dye number five."

She looked at me and shrugged. I knew I should thank her, or gently escort Zoe off the premises, but I couldn't move. I wondered if those security cameras were going to send out some sort of bat signal soon to alert the authorities.

"No!" Zoe stamped her foot like an outraged toddler. "I'm not buying this until you tell me the real ingredients."

"Oh, wait. Is that a threat?" Sharon's cheeks were not so warm now. Her nostril flare made it clear that she had done more than her share of coddling and Zoe was going to pay for that slushie and a whole lot more in a second.

"No," Zoe said defeatedly. "Of course, I'm gonna buy it. I was just making a statement because I wish . . . I wish—" I could hear her choking back a sob while she unzipped her wallet and put some bills on the counter. But I couldn't watch her scrawny shoulders anymore—I had to shut my eyes. It was all just too bewildering and sad. Zoe sucked in a miserable breath and said in one long exhale: "Thanks you can keep the change Hank take your time I'll meet you outside sorry I'm such a pathetic mess everyone."

I heard the light jangle of bells as she pushed the door open, but I still wouldn't let myself look until it was followed by the suction of the door closing again. I gave the personalized license plates a little spin; maybe it could look like I was really interested in a souvenir instead of witnessing Zoe implode. I could feel Sharon's eyes still on me though. So I grabbed a bottle of water and a powdered doughnut. Bringing that plus all three bags of chips to the counter.

"Sorry about that," I mumbled.

"Why are *you* sorry?" asked Sharon.

"Well . . . yeah."

She rang me up in silence and I thanked her and said sorry again. Once again, proving Mr. Harvey's theory that *sorry* only made things muddier. I was pretty sure Sharon didn't like me or think I was funny anymore.

I went back to the car, but Zoe wasn't in the passenger seat.

"Zoo?" I looked under the seats, sorting through different horrific abduction scenes in my brain. She'd only been gone for a minute, maybe two. "No," I told myself. Her stuff was right here on the seat. There was no sign of breaking and entering. I opened the trunk and moved Uncle Rick's spare tire to the side. Unearthing nothing. Then walked around to the driver's side. My pulse quickening.

"Zoe?" I called into the street. "Zoo!" I cupped my hands and pointed my voice at the sky.

She didn't answer. At least not with words. But I heard something behind me, almost imperceptible. As if everything were growing quieter. Leading me to her. The rain had sedated itself to a soft, steady white noise.

Huuuuuuussssssh.

And maybe it wasn't her crouched just behind the air pump for deflated tires. Because everything was so dark and who could be sure. If I brought this moment up as evidence, she would find a thousand ways to deny it.

Only there were her boots with the hot-pink laces. The sharp edge of a polka-dotted hip.

She was hidden in the shadow of a dumpster. Almost completely silent. Except for a small retching sound. A little whinny and then a splash.

And I knew now for sure. I had my irrefutable proof, even if I turned the other way and plugged my ears. I knew this was my best friend, Zoe Grace Hammer.

Making herself sick.

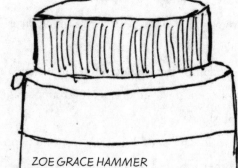

ZOE GRACE HAMMER

52 Silver Birch Dr.
Meadowlake, NJ 00792
Prescription: BRAIN-SCRAMBLER

TAKE ONE TABLET BY MOUTH EVERY
HOUR ON THE HOUR
UNTIL YOU'RE NOT SUCH A PATHETIC
FREAK ANYMORE.

AS MANY REFILLS AS NEEDED.
NO DR. AUTHORIZATION
NECESSARY.

CHAPTER 15
sycamore estates

I'D LOVE TO SAY I COAXED ZOE GENTLY BACK INTO THE CAR AND VOWED to find her the help and support she needed. That I rocked her wounded, weakened body gently in my arms as she sobbed. Or even that I took a deep breath and thoughtfully considered my options.

But I didn't. I sat behind the steering wheel squeezing my hands into fists. Feeling the whole night shake. Longing to drive off into the darkness, or better yet, hitch a ride to wherever Sharon was going.

"I got directions to Travis's," Zoe said when she got in the car. She made no pretense or excuse for being somewhere else while I waited. Just handed me her phone so I could follow the map and then cranked some horrible new teen sensation called

"BabyWantsIt" through HOT RIC's speakers. I drove a hefty fifteen miles per hour above the speed limit, just to see if the police scanner would make a noise or flash some lights. We were too far away though. Out of range.

Whoever named Travis's apartment building the Sycamore Estates was obviously trying to make a joke. There was not a single tree in the sparsely lit parking lot nor in the sad strip of marshy grass leading up to the three front steps. The only thing vaguely estate-ly was the fact that there was a checkered parquet floor and a lopsided chandelier just beyond the security doors. Still, Travis greeted us in the lobby with a proud smile and wide-open arms, as if he were going to give us a tour of the Parthenon.

"Ladies! So glad you made it!" he cheered. "I was worried." He pulled Zoe toward him, which I think was intended as a hug but looked more like a body slam.

"The party was actually still going when we left," Zoe informed him coldly.

"Really?" Travis kept that smile plastered tightly onto his face. "That must've been some party." Then he gave me a gracious but awkward bow. "A pleasure to see you again, Hannah," he said stiffly.

"*Hank*," Zoe corrected.

"Thanks," I said in my tiniest voice.

"No. Thank *you*," Travis answered. He spun around as if there were more to see here. "So there are mailboxes behind that wall and they're upgrading the common room." He waited for us to react. I tried to smile ever so slightly though I knew his eyes were fixed on Zoe's glower. "Whatever, right?!" He pressed on. "You're so embarrassing, Dad!" he said, mocking himself. Even though Zoe rarely called him Dad and it looked like she couldn't be bothered to even mock him.

He led us up two flights in a cold, dim stairwell. (The elevator was broken.) The hallways smelled like lemon disinfectant and new carpet. Zoe had made a good point about it feeling like a beige coffin in there. Not that I was anything close to an interior decorator, but the walls almost sagged from loneliness.

"Voilà!" Travis said, ramming open his apartment door with a forced flourish. "It ain't much, but it's somethin'! Right? Put your bags down anywhere and let me show you around."

It was really just one big room, separated by a (beige) Formica counter between the kitchen and the bedroom/living room. "You ladies can have the new futon," he proposed. "It unfolds really easily."

The mattress was bare, with a pile of pale folded sheets on one end. The only other furniture was a blindingly bright floor lamp, a TV on a small wooden stand, and Travis's guitar leaning against a closet door.

"This is great," I said as cheerfully as I could muster.

"You hook up the Wi-Fi yet?" was all Zoe said.

Travis answered us both with the same hollow-looking grin and nod.

I wandered over to the two large windows overlooking the parking lot. Or, really, the narrow wall between them. There was a four-by-five framed photograph of Zoe when she was probably two years old, in a frilly yellow bathing suit. She was sailing through the air and there were two arms outstretched below, ready to catch her. Her toddler belly was so round and bright. So gleefully airborne. But the photo was too faint to make out whose arms they were.

"So sweet," I said. "Who is this?"

"Zoozoo, of course!" Travis replied.

"Oh, yeah. I meant, who's gonna catch her?"

Travis looked at Zoe with long, somber eyes. Zoe shrugged, then sat down and started unlacing her boots.

"Well, it's a bit of a debate in our house," Travis explained. "I think that was on our trip to Disney World and I was in the pool, playing with her. But Zoe and her mom remember it a bit differently." He breathed carefully before asking Zoe, "Is that a fair assessment?"

"Whatever," she answered.

"No, but I want to represent all sides of the story. If you have a different version of what happened, please." Travis had always struck me as a sturdy man, with thick shoulders and a short, sandy-colored beard. It was hard to watch him stand over Zoe now, so dependent on her approval.

Zoe didn't seem too excited by her newfound power over

her dad anyway. She lined up her boots under the futon and said, "Can we just let it go, Travis? I mean, you said yourself—whatever happened, happened. Either you were there, or you weren't. Can't go back in time and prove it."

"True, true," Travis said, wallowing in the uncertain stillness. I took another quick glance at that picture. I wanted to see if I could prove they were Travis's arms reaching out, ready and waiting. I shuffled forward, then back. To one side and another. Switching focus from one eye to the other and squinting. But I was just making myself off balance and tired. I didn't want to try to unravel this mystery anymore.

Meanwhile, Zoe had picked up Travis's guitar and started plucking out notes.

"You gigging a lot these days?" she asked. She pulled a business card from the top fret and handed it to me. It said:

TRAVIS J. HAMMER

973-434-0808

SINGER • SONGWRITER • COMPOSER • *DREAMER*

I tried to hand the card back to Zoe, but she just sneered.

"Please, take it, Hank," said Travis. "I just got a whole bunch of them. And if you hear of anyone looking for acoustic music for a function . . ."

"So, lots of gigs?" Zoe pressed.

"I mean, I just moved last month," Travis answered.

"I know, but I thought that was one of your priorities now,

right? You need to get back to your music and really take stock of what's important? How's the Uber-ing going, by the way?"

"Fine, I guess. It takes a bit of time to build up reviews or . . ." Travis cleared his throat and clapped his hands, determined to reset. "Well, moving on! You ladies hungry? Thirsty?"

"Sure," I said.

"Not really," Zoe said over me.

"I thought you were coming a little while ago, so I set out some snacks. It's not much but . . ." He disappeared into the matchbox-size kitchen and then returned with a plate of dimpled crackers and some chunks of orange cheese. "I wasn't sure what you would both eat, but . . . it's something called cashew cheese? Nondairy. Non . . . something."

Zoe looked at the plate and sniffed. "Thanks so much. You first," Zoe challenged him. I could hear Travis's jaw clicking as he steeled himself to take a bite. He looked at me with wide eyes.

"Please, Hank. Join me," he begged.

"Oh . . . kay."

I didn't know how I'd gotten caught inside their hungry silence. Their eyes darting between the plate, each other, and me. I was pretty famished, but certainly not for this. The fake cheese felt drier than the crackers.

"Poor Hank," said Zoe. "Maybe something to drink, Trav?"

"Oops! Of course!" He scurried back to retrieve a two-liter bottle of Diet Coke and some Dixie cups. Zoe held one up to the overhead light. The waxy coating looked like shifting clouds.

"You do a lot of entertaining with these?" she asked with a smirk.

"Ha-ha-ha!" Travis forced out a laugh. Ignoring the fact that the joke was on him. "You are my first and favorite guests."

"Really?" Zoe asked. Her eyes were blazing at me. "What about Roxanne?"

"I told you, I'm not seeing Roxanne anymore," Travis said in a pleading voice.

"Then who's the lucky lady?" Zoe continued.

"There's no lucky lady. As I said, I'm using this time to figure out how I can be a better co-parent and a better person, and just be more honest with myself and those I love."

It seemed like a heartfelt response to me, but Zoe was thoroughly unimpressed. "Yeah, you already told me all that. I just don't know how true it is. You know, once someone breaks your trust, it's hard to believe them ever again."

Travis hung his head like a child being reprimanded. As it dipped lower, I saw a circle of thinning hair on the top of his head. I wondered if divorce could cause baldness.

Zoe walked by Travis and his sad-looking refreshments while I stuffed another cracker in my mouth. At least chewing gave me a focus for all my aggression and longing for this night to be over.

Zoe yanked open the refrigerator door as if expecting a hidden lover to tumble out.

"Wow. A stick of butter and some pale ale," she reported. "Not your best moment, huh?"

"Listen, I understand you're upset," Travis said in a shaky

voice. "And I know that I didn't handle this whole situation very well. But I'm trying, Zoo. I'm trying my hardest."

"Really, Travis? You want to do this right now? In front of *Hank*?!"

Both Travis and Zoe whipped around to devour me with their urgent glares. I waved, which made no sense, but I needed something to do.

"I can head home," I squeaked. "I probably should, actually. My uncle's there . . ."

"You promised me you'd stay," Zoe said. Her lower lip jutted out in a fierce pout.

"Yes, please stay," Travis said. "We don't have to talk about this now. We can watch some TV and get some sleep. Or I bought a deck of cards." He started flitting around the kitchen, opening and closing cabinets. "I asked them to get the cable going before you came, but you know how that goes . . ."

Zoe grasped my hand and rolled herself into my side. "I'm sorry he's doing this," she whispered in my ear though it was definitely loud enough for Travis to hear too. "This is exactly why I needed you here. I swear, I'd kill myself if you weren't."

I didn't want to be in the middle of this standoff anymore. I needed them both to know that if they were looking for me to be the lifeboat, I was already deflated and currently sinking. There was so much fiery hurt and resentment coming from both their faces though. All I could do to tamp down the flames was give a dull "Oh-kay."

"Thank you thank you thank you," Zoe gushed. Squeezing my palm so hard I could hear two knuckles crack. "Here, let's at least have a drink, shall we?" She reached for the bottle of Diet Coke, unscrewed the cap, and took a long slug. Then she passed it to me so I could drink some too.

"I do have cups," her dad said. He didn't hand them to us though. Just stood in the dim kitchen, waiting for something—anything—to change.

"No way!" Zoe yelled. "Okay, you both want to see some awesome shots of the dance?" Travis and I both jolted toward her, so eager for the diversion. Zoe was making her way over to the futon, fielding a bunch of texts and video footage on her phone that was cracking her up.

I should have made sure she was watching me as I came up beside her. I should have waited until she was seated or at least facing in my general direction before I attempted to hand her back the two-liter bottle of soda. I should have, but of course, I didn't. I thought she'd grabbed it, so I let go. And then both of us just watched—dumbly mesmerized—as it tumbled onto the futon and started emptying itself onto the floor.

"Wah-wah," Zoe sang, like the sound on a game show when the answer was wrong and you'd lost your chance at the final round.

"I'm so sorry I'm so sorry," I blathered. The bottle was gurgling and spitting out dark bubbles all over the mattress and wall-to-wall carpeting.

"No problem," said Travis in a singsong that sounded too high for him. He swooped down to pick up the bottle while I went back to the kitchen to search for paper towels. There were exactly two squares left on the roll, which sank quickly into the brown puddle. Then he scurried over to the closet by his front door and took out a faded Mets T-shirt. He dropped it on the carpet and started mopping up the mess. I bent down to help him, but Zoe grabbed my arm and pulled me back up.

"It's fine. Right, Travis?" asked Zoe.

"Oh sure," he answered. "Just want you girls to be able to sleep here comfortably."

I winced. He was now on his hands and knees in front of us, squirting dish soap into the stained mattress, then smearing it frantically. Every once in a while running back to the kitchen sink to wring out the saturated towel and starting anew.

I didn't know what the rules of this game were, but it felt cruel. Zoe was scrolling through more pictures on her phone, acting like she couldn't see her dad toiling away, even though his shoulder was grazing our legs. I'd never seen her act this horrible to Travis. Or to anyone, for that matter. But Travis especially— she had always adored him. Wedging herself into the crook of his elbow and begging him to sing us a new tune. I didn't know why I thought of it at this moment, but I had a distinct memory of Travis carrying Zoe from the car after we came home late from the movies one night. I was so jealous of the way he tucked her into his chest. Protecting her even from the sheen of a street-light with his mighty embrace. I pretended I was asleep too, just in case he thought to sweep me into his arms also. (But when Alli opened my door, I popped up quickly.)

Whatever Travis Hammer had done, he was still a great dad, in my book at least. And yet, there he was, crawling on the carpet in front of us. Forsaken in a sea of dish soap bubbles.

"Ugh. How do I still have this double chin?" Zoe grumbled next to me. She deleted an unflattering picture.

"Impossible," I said, reaching for the phone. But she shut it off and hid it behind her butt, flipping her attention back to the room.

"How's it going, Travis? You need us to make a rain check for this sleepover?" she asked, standing up.

This was too much, even for Travis. He stood up quickly and faced Zoe straight on. I was so relieved to see that he was still taller than her. By at least a foot. He held the saturated T-shirt out behind him, each drip making a muted *plop*.

"We're going to make this work," he said determinedly. "I'm going to run out to that 7-Eleven on the corner to pick up some more paper towels and maybe another bottle of soda. I will be right back." His words were clipped and nonnegotiable.

"Great," Zoe answered. Which was the closest she'd come to saying anything kind all night.

Travis didn't move though. He took a deep breath through his nose and said in a voice just skimming above the surface of a whisper, "I know you're not hungry now, but maybe I could get something for the morning? Like English muffins or some fruit?"

I nodded. Mainly just to have something to do. I was already trying to figure out how to sneak out of this apartment before dawn and I certainly didn't need Travis to feed me, but his jaw looked so heavy and pained that I said, "That sounds great, thanks."

"Yeah," added Zoe. "Maybe if they have Rice Krispies. Or some grapes."

Travis and I exhaled in unison. It was such a simple, calm request.

"Of course! Yes!" he blurted. "I love Rice Krispies too!"

His smile so hopeful it hurt.

As soon as the door clicked shut, Zoe checked the peephole and attached the chain lock on top. "All right," she said. "Before you call me a monster and feel all sorry for him, just come here. Look!"

She led me back into the kitchen and opened up the refrigerator again.

"Behind the butter," she said.

I stood on tiptoes but couldn't tell what I was looking for. "More butter?" I guessed. Zoe was unamused.

"*Move.*" She pushed in front of me and took down a small Ziploc with shreds of dry green leaves in it. She shook it in front of my face.

"I'll give you a hint. It's not oregano, and it rhymes with *flarijuana.*" She was so excited, she was doing a little dance like a boxer getting ready for a prizefight.

"Do you think he . . . ?"

"Uses it? Duh. Sells it? Possibly. Either way, it's totally illegal and I have to mention it in court so Alli gets more alimony."

She took out her phone again and snapped a picture.

"I didn't know you were going to court," I said, feeling weak.

Zoe rolled her eyes. "I wasn't going to, but if he has the money for drugs, he should be giving us more too. He's a shithead, Hank. I know it's hard for you to see that when he plays all sweet and innocent but trust me. *He is*."

She started opening random cabinets and drawers, though I had no idea what kind of incriminating evidence she was seeking.

"But maybe it's . . . medical. And he's your *dad*."

"*Was* my dad," she corrected, opening and closing the refrigerator one more time with a ferocious swing. She was done tearing open the kitchen and was moving on to the bathroom. I followed her in. It was beige and cavernous. Surprisingly big, with a metal handrail by the toilet and another in the shower stall.

"Is this a retirement community?" I asked.

"Ha! No, but I'll tell him you said that."

"No, please." I wanted to take back everything about this night—what I'd said, where I'd been, how I'd waited and listened to everything unravel. Zoe was emptying out her dad's toiletries bag now. Holding up pill bottles and listing all the reasons he was unfit as a father.

"Vitamin C, vitamin D, Mega Maca," she said. "Thank you very much!" She twisted the cap open and popped one in her mouth. Turned on the faucet and leaned over, slurping from the stream.

"You want?" She offered me the open bottle, but I waved it away.

"We also have your uppers here—" She lined up a few more

bottles and a small plastic bag that was full of brown capsules. "Why not, right?" She opened the bag and stuck a capsule under her nose, inhaling deeply and wincing.

Another slurp and it slid down her throat.

"Why are you looking at me like that?" she asked. "I swear, it's all herbal."

"But what do they do?" I had visions of her being whisked off in a stretcher to get her stomach pumped.

"A whole lot of nothing, really," she answered. "Some of them keep you up; some of them make you feel totally relaxed. Travis swore all last winter that if I took two glucosamines and called him in the morning, I'd have perfect attention span and joint health. Plus maybe I'd stop crying myself to sleep. You see how great that worked."

She shook some more bottles at me, then threw open a narrow closet next to Travis's shower. Staring at his two spare rolls of toilet paper on the otherwise bare shelves. "It's his fault that I'm like this!"

"Like what?" I asked.

"Ha!" Zoe cackled. "Nice one, Hank. Invincible! Unstoppable! The most obnoxiously self-centered brat on Earth! Ready to destroy everything in her wake!"

She started unwinding the toilet paper and then threw the rolls to the floor. Stomping and raging.

"Aha!" she yelled, picking off a small blue bottle of cologne from a shelf and waving it in front of my face. She was one screech away from rabid, her eyes pulsating.

"What am I looking at now?" I whined.

"He never wore cologne before! I bet it's from Roxanne. Did I tell you they met in church choir? How lame is *that*?"

"Wait—so if he has cologne, that means he's sleeping with someone?" I honestly didn't follow her logic. But Zoe had no time to explain.

"*Hallelujah!*" she sang. "I bet there's Viagra in here too. And condoms. Unless he's trying to get her pregnant, so he can fuck up a whole new family." Now Zoe was ripping open the drawers under the sink, checking the empty garbage can, even turning on the shower for hidden traces of something. It was so scary to see her like this. Anger throbbing in her forehead and coloring her skin a raw red.

"Why are you just standing there?" she growled.

"I'm—"

"Hank, you can get suckered into his sad routine if you want, but just know he's lying to you too. The whole *taking some time to figure things out* is bullshit. There's always another woman. That's just the way men are. They can only think with their dicks!"

"But maybe . . ." I had nothing to fill in that blank. I just wanted Zoe to take a breath and be wrong. From inside the bathroom, I heard a key clicking into the apartment's front-door lock. Zoe and I both shuddered as the knob squeaked and the chain caught his momentum.

"Hello?" Travis called. "Zoe? Hank? Hey, I think you might've locked the top lock by mistake," he said. He knocked lightly on the door. It had to be past 1:00 A.M. by now and I was sure he didn't want to wake any of his new neighbors. "Girls?"

Zoe shook her head at me and put a finger to her lips as she tiptoed out of the bathroom to stand facing the front door. I, of course, followed.

"Girls?!" Travis sounded like he was getting scared. I heard him fumbling with the chain and cursing under his breath. He closed the door and then opened it again, his panting getting more forceful. Then I heard Zoe's cell phone ringing. So did she.

Instead of saying hello, she answered with, "Hammer residence! How may I direct your call?"

"Zoe, please. Don't do this." I could hear his voice in stereo—low and close. "C'mon, honey."

"Just tell me, did Roxanne get a boob job, or are they naturally perky?" Zoe demanded into the phone.

"What are you talking about—"

"You know, someone should tell the minister about what's going on in that choir. Are you both still going to rehearsals or was that all a front?"

"I enjoy singing in the church choir, and I believe Roxanne does too, but that has no bearing on—"

"Ha-ha!" Zoe howled. "Told ya!" She shoved the phone at me, baring her teeth in a grimace.

"No, you're not listening," Travis pleaded. "Just let me in so we can talk."

It was too much. Even if he had slept with this vixen Roxanne.

Even if he had five different families located in five different states. He was a grown man begging to come into his own, sad home. He was her *father*.

"What?" Zoe snarled at me. Then she answered her own question. "I know you think I'm *so* mean and you'd never do anything like this to your dad. Well, guess what, Hank? We can't all be perfect like you."

"I didn't say I was perfect." I tried to stand still and tall even though everything inside me was quivering with hurt.

Zoe's wrath terrified me. I'd seen her depressed before. I'd heard her rant about her parents' dysfunction. But this was a whole new dimension of pain. It seemed to infect her like a consumption. Her tears melting into her cheeks.

"Just get out of here already!" she seethed. "You know you want to! I'm disgusting and horrible and I deserve to be alone. Go!"

"Hank." Travis sounded like he had crouched down in the hallway, beseeching me from that slip of space between the floor and the sill. "Please. I know this is awkward. But can you just reach up and unhook the chain?"

I gazed at the door. Then back at Zoe. Her eyes hard with fury. Her nostrils flaring. She raised a brow as if to say, *I dare you.*

It didn't matter what he'd done or hadn't done. Whether he made her believe in the power of glucosamine or took her to Disney World. Zoe had no idea how lucky she was to have her dad *alive*—trying to repair as much as he could. Trying to feed her and piece her back together. She had no idea how many people she was hurting and taking for granted. She acted like she was entitled to all the anger and despair in the universe, while I was the one who'd been literally abandoned by everyone in my life.

Before I could talk myself out of it, I slid past Zoe, unhooked the chain lock, and yanked open the door. Travis pitched forward with his bags, catching the knob on his forehead as he crumpled to his knees with a pitiful grunt.

"I'm . . . sorry," I said to the room.

"It's okay," Travis said, gasping.

"No it's not!" Zoe wailed. "Nothing's okay. And nothing's gonna be okay!" She threw herself onto the wet futon, rolling around and flailing her arms. Travis gathered himself up and went over to console her, but she swatted him away.

"I hate you!" she shrieked. "You too, Hank! I hate you both so much! I really do!"

Everything stung. My eyes filled with water. So did my mouth. Zoe burrowed herself into the dry corner of the mattress, tucking her legs under her until she looked like a partly polka-dotted turtle. Her spine sticking out in a ridge down her shell.

I looked at Travis as he gazed at her. Only, I had no idea what he saw. There was a little egg-shaped welt blossoming above his right eye and he was blinking a lot. He rustled through his plastic bags as if he could find something in there to douse this fire. Ultimately he decided the only thing left to do was cover her in a semi-damp sheet.

She stayed knotted in that tight, fetal position. The only

movement was the slowing rise and fall of her hunched shoulder blades. Travis and I continued to watch. Until she must have fallen asleep, because her arms loosened and one slipped out of the cover to dangle on the floor.

I saw three more neat scratches peeking out of her left sleeve at the wrist. Startlingly pink and clear. I reached forward to tuck her arm back in and then stopped.

I couldn't be in charge of covering her up anymore.

I couldn't ignore those scars, disguise them, or strike any more deals.

In that moment, I came to understand that there was no saving Zoe Hammer. At least not on my own. Her misery was too big for this room; for this friendship. She was starving and wretched and too jagged to touch. She pulled her arm back in to her side and flipped to face the other wall. I watched her resettle and wondered what life was going to be like without her as my best friend.

Travis silently laid down a blanket and pillow for me on the floor next to the soggy futon. I brushed my teeth without even running the water because I didn't want to risk waking Zoe up.

When I came out of the bathroom, Travis said, "I'm sorry this has been so hard on her." He looked at me as if I could be the one to forgive him.

"I'm just . . . here," I answered.

Then I buried myself under that stiff blanket and tried to will myself to sleep. Most of the night I just gazed up at the speckled tiles of Travis's ceiling though. Listening to the rain thrumming, the spray of passing car wheels, the *clink* and *ping* of his deluged gutters. I knew time was passing, but the morning couldn't come fast enough.

I knew I was leaving. And I just wanted to go.

Wednesday. Half past the freckle.

Listen, I know it's not <u>all</u> your fault, Hank.

I wish it was, really. But the more I sit in these therapy sessions and stuff my face with rice pudding, I see it's not. I want to blame you for every missed day of school and every reactionary journal entry and every mindful meditation on self-reflective, nonjudgmental bullshit in here.

It's not you though.

What is it, you ask?

Huh. It's everything.

I mean Mommy issues, Daddy issues, who-am-I, and why-am-I-here issues.

<u>Nobody look at me!</u>

<u>Everybody look at me!</u>

<u>Why do I feel like a giant hole that can never be filled?!</u>

I keep having this recurring nightmare that I'll start buttering a dinner roll and never stop. I'll just keep adding more and more butter. Spreading it all over my roll, then my face. My hands, lips, eyebrows, hair.

Because I could, you know.

Hank—the scariest thing is that the more I eat, the hungrier I get.

And that's not your fault.

That's just who I am.

CHAPTER 16
purple hearts

THE RAIN WAS GONE, BUT THE SKY LOOKED BEATEN UP AND BRUISED.
There was a blanket of wet leaves on the ground and gusts of
red, orange, and yellow stragglers still swirling. The streets and
tree trunks were drying in splotchy patchworks. Everything
sodden but somehow brighter.

I had set my phone to wake me at sunrise and managed to slip
out before Travis and Zoe were up. My right shoulder felt limp
from being twisted under me and I wasn't sure if I'd actually
slept more than thirty minutes, but at least I could say it was a
new day. Maybe it was my imagination, but even in this half-hour
drive home, I saw the low-slung hammock of clouds lift just a
sliver and some fresh lavender sky peek through.

I passed the VFW hall that had a pot of fake daisies on its step year-round and a flag that was always at half-mast. The Dunkin' Donuts where Mom used to take us to get our birthday breakfasts, until it was shut down because of health-code violations, which made me rethink every Munchkin I'd ever munched. There was still caution tape strung up near the entrance, flapping and billowing wildly from the remnants of the storm. And, of course, there was Seasons Change, a patio furniture and lawn ornamentation shop that somehow stayed in business even though I'd never seen a single person go in or a single chaise longue chair go out.

I wondered if anyone would miss me if I just kept driving. I could swing by the Jewish Community Center and find new reasons to be Jewish in a community. Or sneak into the zoo and try to be fascinated with the new panda exhibit. I had zero navigational skills, but I did know Mom had a cousin up in Vermont and if I found her address somehow and pointed myself north, maybe I'd get there in time for the first snowfall.

I needed more cash to make it on the road though. Plus my bladder was already creaking since I'd skipped my morning pee. I crept in through the side door of my house, ready to tiptoe past the pullout couch where Uncle Ricky usually slept when he stayed over, but nobody was there. Not a single throw pillow was out of place either.

"Hello?" I asked.

No answer.

"Hello?" I said again. There were no other cars in the driveway except for HOT RIC.

WHERE ARE YOU? I texted Gus and Uncle Ricky.

215

In bed, Uncle Ricky answered.

Whose? I asked.

Ha-ha! My own.

Did you tell me you and Gus were staying at your place?

I don't know. Did I? How was your pussycat crusade?

I didn't have the energy to come up with a response, so I tossed my phone onto the couch and stormed upstairs. I started turning on all the light switches. (Somehow, someway, maybe that would scare away all the demons of anger clogging my brain?)

"It's not *my* pussycat crusade!" I screamed at the empty hallway. "I am not a part of that. I cannot be part of that anymore!"

I marched into my parents' room. My *parents'*. Not Elan's. Which was why it was totally inappropriate for him to have his gray-and-green-plaid flannel shirt slung over the back of my mom's ancient rocking chair. It was also highly disrespectful for him to have his little pot of lip balm, his waterproof watch, and a puddle of loose change spread out on my dad's side of the dresser. I was about to knock Elan's change onto the floor in the most ineffective act of protest in history when I saw the lopsided green bowl I made for Mom in third grade. It was still on her night table, holding the shells we'd collected as a family at least a decade ago. When we were whole.

I collapsed onto Mom's side of the bed. Trying to shriek out all my miserable, helpless confusion into her lavender-patterned quilt. I missed my mom more than ever right about now. I certainly wasn't going to interrupt her wilderness adventure to tell her though. She was probably doing sun salutations with Elan or gathering chestnuts for their breakfast. I hoped they hadn't been washed out to sea or buried in a mudslide.

I lay there for a while, but my eyelids refused to lower. It was too sloggy and still in there. I had never really been alone in my house before. Every leaf touching a window and every sip of air under a sill seemed magnified and threatening to me. I wanted to punch the world in its throat and scream until I shattered glass. Only I couldn't find the strength to do either.

So I settled for playing the piano instead. I just needed to make some noise. Mrs. Toobey always said music could express the inexpressible. And that a piano could weep for you, if given the chance. Pulling out my *Debussy* book, I gazed at those dreamy boaters on the cover. Desperate to climb onto their old-fashioned rowboat and drift into their pastel world. I started with scales. Slowly. Methodically. Then I transitioned into *Arabesque No. 1*. Tiptoeing over the keys at first. Then leaning in as I'd seen Mrs. Toobey do so many times. Searching, searching for a way in.

I couldn't find it though. Stumbling onto a D-flat, I fell off in the middle of a crescendo and couldn't figure out how to go back and get it right. I kept trying to rewind a few stanzas and start again. Each time tripping myself up in a new way. It was sounding less and less ethereal now and more and more like Oompa Loompas farting. I got rough. Almost violent. Purposely hitting a sharp instead of a flat. Running the slower phrases together and mashing all the pauses into a cacophonous pileup. Until I was smacking the keys with my palms and stamping on the pedals. Slamming the piano lid up and down so hard, the rusty hinges were crying.

"Well hello to you too!" shouted Uncle Ricky, laughing as he and Gus barged through the front door.

I stood up so quickly that I knocked the piano bench backward. It ricocheted against the wall, then scraped the back of my calves and crumpled me forward. I didn't let out a squeak of protest though. I already felt too vulnerable just knowing he'd heard me. Plus, he seemed to be more concerned with another conversation he was having on the phone.

"That was your daughter, tickling the ivories," he reported. "Here, you want to talk to her?"

Uncle Ricky handed me his phone and mouthed, *She's fine.* Which, of course, only made me fear the worst.

"Mom?"

"Hank!" Mom exclaimed. "Oh, Hanky, did you have fun last night at the party?"

"Doesn't matter. What's going on?"

"Well, the good news is, we're on our way home," she said. Her voice sounded distracted now. "No, this is fine, hon. I'm talking to Hank."

"Hey, Hank!" I heard Elan yell in the background.

"So, yeah, we should be home in a few hours or so. I don't even know what time it is though."

"Nine-ish!" chimed in Elan. I could have told her that. But Mom was already midsentence describing how the campsite they'd reserved was a brown lake of mud and she wasn't wearing the right shoes for this kind of travel. The trail had really taken a beating in the storm—lots of branches and debris and honestly, she'd always been a klutz, but it was only a hairline fracture, which meant the recovery time would be much less. At least that was the hope.

"Wait, Mom, what?"

"I know, so ridiculous, right?" she replied. "But listen, I'm only hearing half your words because we're driving through some pretty steep mountains. Is this Route 25, hon? Route 282?"

She got into another muffled conversation with Elan that only made the story more convoluted. They were on Route 25, but only for a few miles and it was a detour because Route 282 was flooded. Or maybe that was 828. These darn country roads.

"Mom!" I tried shouting my way into the narrative. "Mom?!"

"Well, either way . . . ," she continued. "Soon . . . rest . . . bagels . . ."

I hung up the phone, feeling all kinds of mad.

"Can someone please explain what happened and what's broken?" I demanded.

"Sure! In here!" called Uncle Ricky from the kitchen. He and Gus were setting out a delicious-looking spread of egg-and-cheese sandwiches, onion bagels, and two plastic tubs of cream cheese. "I love my man Yoshi," said Uncle Ricky. "But he really needs to broaden his cream cheese selection. Even just chives."

Gus was grabbing some knives from the silverware drawer while Uncle Ricky unwrapped a loaf of sourdough bread that was still steaming.

"I know. Not needed," Uncle Ricky admitted. "But literally straight out of the oven." He took a big sniff from the end of the bread and then stuck it under my nose so I could get a whiff.

"No!" I said, a little more harshly than I'd intended. Gus spun around from the counter with wide eyes. "Please," I said in a lower tone. "I would like to know what happened to my mom."

"Right," said Uncle Ricky. "Sorry, Gus and I were kinda famished when we came in here. So it sounds like your mom tripped on a root or something. Thought she twisted her ankle, wanted to keep going. But Elan insisted on getting her to an ER for X-rays. The nearest one was another forty miles north. Good thing he did though, because a hairline fracture is nothing to ignore. Plus I guess the campsite was entirely washed out."

"But where did they sleep?"

"I think they were in the ER all night," Gus said, pouring a cup of coffee. "Mom said she fell asleep for a few hours once they gave her some painkillers, but Elan didn't even have a chair."

"I know you don't like him, Hank. But you have to admit, he's a good guy," Uncle Ricky said with his mouth full of cream cheese.

"I don't *not* like him," I sneered. "I just don't want him acting like . . ."

Gus stuck a warm egg-and-cheese sandwich in my hand so I wouldn't have to come up with an end to that sentence. I thought briefly of refusing, but I was drooling from all the salty smells. The air was so warm and doughy, and the coffee pot gurgled and clicked.

And yet part of me couldn't give up this fight. I still felt like I was the only one left to defend my father's honor.

"Actually, Uncle Ricky, I bet you can set the record straight," I said.

"Sure," he said with a big grin.

"What record?" asked Gus as he dropped a blob of scrambled egg on the table.

I certainly didn't need to push it further. The past twelve hours had shown me just how shattered a family could get when one side was pitted against the other. But there were just so many frayed wires inside me, looking to ignite. "So Gus and I were having a debate because Elan says that my dad took the 8:03 train to Penn Station and I think he took the 7:29. Actually, I *know* he took the 7:29. But maybe you can verify?"

Uncle Ricky looked from me to Gus and back to me again. Waiting for us to tell him it was a joke, I suppose. "Ummm . . ."

"Hello! Do you know what I'm talking about?"

"Not . . . really," answered Uncle Ricky. His face was wide and unconcerned. Which only fueled my indignation.

"Didn't you work with Dad one summer?" I pounced. "And you slept over here on Sunday nights a bunch of times and took the train in with him. Why doesn't anybody remember these details except for me?!"

Uncle Ricky kept shaking his head slowly. His lips were pressed together in a thin line now; I'd definitely scared him with my temper. "Hank, I am truly sorry I can't give you the information you want," he said in the most somber tone I'd heard from him.

"It's okay," I mumbled. "It's . . . whatever." I got myself a mug of coffee and rewrapped my breakfast sandwich so I could take it upstairs and hide in my room until I came up with another plan. I thought maybe I'd draw Mom a get-well card with those smelly markers I'd hung on to since first grade. I knew those cards did absolutely nothing in terms of healing, but at least it would give me an activity and maybe the fumes would knock me out.

"Actually, Hank, can I talk to you for a second upstairs?" Gus asked.

"Sure." I shrugged. He was probably going to feed me a quote from Diana Gaia about letting go and accepting the infinite. Which was great in theory but currently impossible to practice. "I know, I'm acting like a bitch," I told him as we got to the top of the stairs. "I just have a lot going on and I'm not in the mood to give Elan a Purple Heart for saving Mom in the woods."

Gus gently pushed me into my room. "Yeah, the Elan stuff we can talk about another time," he told me. "I'm just worried . . . um, so do you know what's going on with your video?"

"*My* video?"

He shut the door behind us. "Yeah," Gus said gravely.

"What are you talking about?"

He held out his phone so I could watch him type in the words:
PUSSYCAT WARRIORS HOT KISS

Just so I knew that life could get worse. Much worse.

A brief list of unrealistic promises these masochistic monsters disguised as health professionals have now made to me:

1. If I eat peanut butter and whole-milk yogurt at every meal, I will feel energetic, exuberant, and optimistic about life!
2. Every pound I gain will make me more fun and determined. I have so much to say and do and _be_ and the world can't wait to see what a go-getter I am!
3. Eating slowly and mindfully will help me understand my body's wants and desires and I will know how it feels to be truly satiated!
4. Instead of cutting myself, I must apologize to my body and thank it for its beauty, resilience, and strength. If I do this three times a day (and stay away from razors), I won't ever feel the urge to cut again.
5. My relationships with my parents and loved ones will be richer and stronger, based on mutual respect and honesty!
6. I will get to go home when I'm ready to go home.
7. They will determine what "ready" means.

CHAPTER 17
every creature

I GUESS 5,828 PEOPLE HAD ALREADY WATCHED THE VIDEO AND decided I was a *righteous lesbian*. Also that I was *awkward, brave,* and *a little like Hagrid and Einstein had a love child, right?*

The comments were mostly misinformed and/or presumptuous. A few of them were heart-wrenching—talking about how they wanted to express same-sex love like this but were too afraid. Then there were a few that really disturbed me. Describing how they wanted to watch us in slow motion and do things to make us both yowl. The comment that made me drop my phone just said: *BONER.*

Gus sat next to me the whole time while I scrolled through. We were on my floor, with our backs up against the door so nobody could come in. I wanted to tell him to shield his eyes or that he didn't have to stay, but I felt like the warmth of his shoulder next to mine was the only secure thing.

"I'm sorry you're seeing this," I kept telling him. "It's not what I thought . . . It's not what I meant . . ."

"Stop apologizing," Gus said.

"I need to delete it. Is there any way I can do that?"

Gus shook his head sadly. "The settings are locked. Looks like ZGH2002 is the only one who can change that."

"Yup," I said, feeling more defeated. ZGH2002 was obviously Zoe Grace Hammer. I tried calling, texting, and pinging her on every app I had. No response.

At some point, Gus said, "I think your best bet is actually going to her house." Though I didn't want him to be, I knew he was right. Gus promised to field all of Uncle Ricky's nosy questions and to let me know if anything else happened online.

There was definitely someone home at Zoe's house. I could hear the thud of feet rushing down the stairs and sporadic yipping noises. It took me a few minutes to summon up the courage to knock on the door though. As pitiful as it sounds, I couldn't remember a single time I'd come here to ask for something. I'd certainly gotten plenty—hand-me-downs and stickers, fresh-baked cookies and pinkie-swear secrets. But I'd never stood outside their dome-shaped wooden door trying to put my words together plaintively. I couldn't hand them Girl Scout cookies or a pamphlet about Jehovah or solar panel estimates. I just had to ring the doorbell and state my case.

"Who is it?! Just a second!" yelled Alli. She flung open the door and barely registered I was there before she peered over my shoulder to see if I'd brought anyone better with me. Specifically, her daughter.

"Wait. You don't have Zoe?"

"No, sorry. I came over because she wasn't answering any of my messages."

"Of course she's not," Alli snapped. She let me in and closed the door before unleashing tears and yelling, "Why is my life such a fucken mess?!"

I was pretty sure she did not want me to take a stab at answering that.

"You know why she's not answering our messages? Because she's too busy listening to Travis's bullshit excuses. Or maybe she's getting her nails done with Roxanne or taking more meetings with *my* agent. And meanwhile—"

Alli dropped to her knees and started hammering on the floor with her fists. "Come on, Meowsers. This isn't funny!" She grabbed a remote control from the coffee table and skidded it under the couch, possibly to scare the cat out of hiding. But still nothing happened.

I crouched down to see what was going on. "Is the cat . . . ?"

"Okay?!" Alli screeched. "No! He's not. And your friend Zoe was supposed to be in charge of him, but instead she left this out, open, next to a half-eaten yogurt and now he's totally batshit crazy!"

I couldn't tell whether she was angry or terrified. She showed me an empty prescription bottle for Ritalin. Holding it up to the light so her face turned a wavy amber color as I looked through it.

"How much was in it?" I asked.

"No idea." Alli moaned. "He was tearing up the place when I came in. I think he ate one of my scarves. But then when I went to hold him, he dove under the couch and now he's just hissing every time I come near. Can cats OD on this stuff? They probably can, right?"

I nodded and shook my head and shrugged all at the same time.

I peered under the couch. I could hear Meowsers grunting. Then the scurry of feet and the creak of couch coils as he darted back and forth. When I caught a glimpse of his face, it was even scarier. His eyes were wide, pale buttons in the dark.

"I think maybe you need to take him in to the vet," I said timidly.

"I know!" Alli wept. She sounded like she was honestly in pain. "I'm just trying to get him out of here, but he won't let me touch him. Which is probably a metaphor for everyone else in my life. And who knows where the hell Zoe is or how to get in touch with her. Not to mention I look like hell and am I supposed to take him to an emergency room, or do they even have those for animals? They do, right? Animals have emergencies too!"

"Yes," I said. Even though I had no idea if it was true. Then I looked up veterinary ERs on my phone while Alli got an umbrella and tried scooting Meowsers out from under the couch again. He was sort of coughing now, pacing under the couch like a feral beast. She pushed him out just enough to grab a front paw, but he wriggled free easily. Then he started hurling himself around the living room, ricocheting off the molding and clawing at the radiator cover. It was terrifying to watch him zig and zag, tuck and roll. Alli stood in the middle of the room, turning around and trying to lure him by clicking her tongue.

"You can take him straight to Valley Veterinarians on Parker," I told her.

"But I can't even catch him," she whined.

We watched Meowsers streaking across the room and skidding into an end table. Tipping over a basket of blankets and pawing frantically at the fringed edges. That basket was actually what saved us. Alli snapped to attention, crept over, and flipped the basket on top of him like a wicker cage. He was shuddering violently, tucked into a ball.

"Shhhhhh," Alli told him. "We're gonna get you some help now." Then she turned to me and said, "Maybe . . . I'll go figure out where Zoe is and you can just drop this guy off at the vet's?"

"No," I said sternly, startling both myself and Alli.

I had never uttered that word to anyone in Zoe's family before. I told Alli that I would go look for Zoe and she was in charge of the cat. Then I helped her load Mr. Meowsers into his little travel bag and watched her drive away without saying thank you or goodbye to me. I stood in her driveway for a few minutes after she left, feeling everything vibrate around me—the echo of

Meowsers's disturbed mews, his paws scratching the bare floor. The rev of Alli's engine curling around the corner and fading.

And further back in my memory-scape, the soft click of Travis's key in the door and the gleeful scurry of Zoe's feet running to greet him. The crinkling of cellophane wrappers as we dumped out our Halloween buckets on Zoe's bedroom floor. The clang of her bathroom radiator and the whine of her kitchen faucet. Everything this house contained. All the pancake breakfasts and bubble-gum-scented pillow fights. I needed to let them all go. To pull them out of my head and heart and throw them to the wind.

It took way too long to locate Zoe.

I knew she wouldn't answer me, so I dug out Travis's business card from my wallet and tried texting him instead:

> Hi, this is Hank. Thank you for the sleepover. Is Zoe still at your place?
>
> HANK! Thank YOU for being such a great friend to my daughter.
>
> Zoe is at the gym.

Of course she was.

Then Travis followed up with a series of texts:

> *Maybe we could chat for a few minutes today or tomorrow?*
>
> *No presh*
>
> *It would just be great to get your perspective*
>
> *Thnx*

I knew he was concerned, and I didn't mean to punish him with my silence. But I was also fielding strange new friend requests and comments about when the next PussyCat Warriors performance would be happening. I thought of poor James Hartwick III and the promise I'd already broken. I needed to get Zoe and shut off that video.

The stench at Primally Fit was particularly ripe when I walked in. I almost preferred the smell of mingling BO to all the coconut-pomegranate-ocean-mist spritzes they had blasting out of their motion-detector air fresheners. Someone new and extra-perky was bobbling behind the front desk.

"Welcome to Primally Fit! Do you want to take control of your body and your life? I'm Ashleigh and I can't wait to help you get started!"

"Thanks, Ashleigh. Actually, I've come here before. I'm not a member though. I'm just looking for a friend," I told her.

"Great! Just swipe your key fob or enter the last four digits of your social security number on the screen to your left."

"No, that's the thing. I don't have a fob because I'm not a member."

"No prob!" Ashleigh winked. "Just try your last four digits then."

"I don't think that's gonna work either. Because of the non-member thing. So can I just look around and see if my friend is here in one of the classes?"

"I'm sorry." Ashleigh made a big pouty face to show me that she was really empathizing with my disappointment. "We only allow members or their guests into classes."

"Right." I sucked in a deep breath to steady myself because

I felt close to tearing at Ashleigh's smooth pink cheeks. "I am not here to take a class. I am not here to become a guest or a member. I am here to talk to someone *else* who is currently in a class."

"Oh!" Ashleigh said brightly. Then she thought about it some more and went back to frowning. "Oh. I'm not sure what to tell you. Most of our classes run fifty minutes, so the next one should be getting out at 11:50 A.M."

"Great. I'm not going to be able to wait that long because this is sort of an emergency, but if you just swipe something so I can come through, I'd really appreciate it."

"Emergency?" Ashleigh narrowed her eyes and scanned me up and down, as if looking for an oozing wound or some other sign that I was imperiled. I had nothing to show her except a nasty nostril flare of growing anger. She picked up a small walkie-talkie from under the shelf separating us and spoke into it. "Derrick, this is Ashleigh at the front desk. We have a *non*member here with an emergency . . . ?"

She looked back at me with her rehearsed smile and said it would be just a minute if I wanted to take a seat.

"Nope, I don't," I told her. Then I ducked under the metal turnstile to her left and heard the off-key warning sound that must've indicated GYM INTRUDER GYM INTRUDER. I put a little spring in my step and started galloping toward the steam rooms.

"Excuse me? Excuse me?"

Maybe I should've had a healthy dose of fear or at least

unease. But when I heard Bernardo shouting in Studio B, *"Are you kidding me? Stop wasting my time, ladies!"* I knew I was close. And I was committed to getting Zoe out of this nuthouse.

I heard Ashleigh get called over to some lady whose Stair-Master wasn't climbing stairs fast enough. Which gave me just enough time and space to skip into a side hallway and navigate my way to the women's locker room. There were two women in front of the mirrors discussing how a juice cleanse had saved their sex lives. Another was stepping on and off the scale repeatedly. I tucked myself behind a striped shower curtain near the row of lockers Zoe had shown me the other day. I even took off my boots and mismatched socks, rolling up my pants legs so my wardrobe couldn't give me away.

Zoe came in last from the Sunday Booty Camp crew. I shivered hearing someone tell her, "You amaze me," and her answering, "Bah. But thanks."

There was a cluster of women going up to have juices with Bernardo. Another two bemoaned all the carpools they were late for.

"Tell your mom we missed her," said someone in between gum smacks.

Then I watched all the other shadows leave the room and heard the click of Zoe's toilet stall lock. She said, "Hello?" to see if anyone answered.

No one did.

I squeezed my boots and socks to my chest and just listened.

This time, when Zoe made herself sick, I knew the sound. I winced, but I was not surprised. I waited until she flushed and came out of her stall, then I pulled open the shower curtain.

"What?" she said. "I mean, hey."

"Hey."

Her breath made an acid cloud between us.

"Zoe," I said haltingly. "How long are you gonna keep doing this?"

"What are you talking about? I'm going to the bathroom."

"With your feet facing the toilet?" I asked.

She blinked quickly. Her skin so taut and colorless. Her lips clenched tightly as she tried to scorch me with her glare.

"You can't keep—"

She cut me off sharply. "Thanks for your concern, Hank. I think we already went over this at Travis's though. You don't have to worry about me anymore. We're done."

She took a piece of gum out of her running-shorts pocket and unwrapped it, popping it into her mouth. Then she headed to the bank of sinks in the next room. Cupping her hands under the water and splashing her face. There were small hollows under her cheekbones. Her teeth looked slick and tinged with yellow.

"If you'll excuse me," she said to my reflection behind her, "I have a twelve o'clock class."

"Um, no," I told her.

Zoe cocked her head as if she hadn't heard me correctly.

"No, you don't," I said—louder this time. I looked at her startled face in the mirror, then waited for her to turn around and face me in person.

"I know you hate me and you hate your family and your life. And you're right—there's nothing I can do about that. But your cat is very ill from possibly eating your pills, so I'm taking you to meet Alli at the vet's office. And while you're there, waiting to see whether your cat survives, you have to take down that video of us kissing."

My words quivered and my armpits were soaking through my shirt, but at least I got it all out without collapsing.

Zoe, on the other hand, looked stony and sure. She narrowed her eyes at me. "I *have* to?" she said.

"Yes," I answered, sounding less sure of myself now. I hadn't even thought of the possibility that she'd refuse. "Please?" I added. I felt like I was pedaling frantically on a bike with no chain attached or doing one of those horrible swim tests at the Y where we were forced to tread water for two minutes straight.

Zoe didn't answer me. Instead she called her mom and I listened as they battled it out about who wanted this cat to begin with and how much the twelve o'clock class meant to them and what sacrifice was all about.

"So stupid," Zoe spat bitterly after she hung up. "I bet you love being right all the time, Hank. Don't you?"

I didn't know how to answer that, so I just stood there, waiting for her to pack up her things.

I drove her to Valley Veterinarians in icy silence. There was a big statue of a German shepherd in front whose paint was peeling around the ears. Also, a parking lot to the side and a long row of kennels stretching back into a line of trees. The howls and yowls clattering around us.

I stopped in front of the big wooden door. There were so many scratches and grooves worn into it from paws of all sizes.

There was a sign above the top molding that read: EVERY CREATURE IS SACRED.

"Um, I don't think this is a parking space," said Zoe.

"Yeah," I said. "It's not. But you can get out now. I'm not staying."

"Seriously?" I couldn't even bring myself to look at her face as she gathered her gym bag and got out of the car. Slamming the door shut with a savage whack. It shook me to the core, but it was the closest thing to triumph that I'd ever felt with Zoe.

Only it was over before it began. I switched HOT RIC into what I thought was drive but must have been reverse. So instead of a victory lap, I rammed the back of my car directly into the statue of the German shepherd. Knocking off the statue's snout and sending my chin into the steering wheel.

"You okay?" said a man emerging from the clinic with a yipping lapdog.

"Yup," I said numbly. Or really, the opposite of numb. Like

everything felt so hot and close and I couldn't find any place soft to land. I reached up to check that my head was still attached to my neck. It was. Also, there was no blood.

"You popped a taillight," the man said.

"That's okay," I yelped, speeding away.

A brief list of side effects from this "rehabilitation" process that these same health professionals just neglected to mention:

1. Approximately 80% of my waking hours here are spent crying.
2. My ankles are so swollen they don't fit into any of my socks.
3. I'm not allowed to look in the mirror, but I can feel myself aging exponentially.
4. I miss my mommy and daddy.
5. I miss who I was when I had a mommy and daddy instead of an Alli and a Travis and all their bullshit excuses for parenting. Sometimes I think we would all be better off if they had just left me on some tour bus for _Beauty and the Beast_ and I was raised by a pack of wild stagehands.
6. And that's not a cue for you to say no no! or to try to save me in some way. I'm just in a moment.
7. I miss you, Hank.
8. A lot.
9. And even though I want to hate you and stab you with one of my plastic sporks or pelt you with butter patties in your sleep, I hurt all over with missing you.
10. Yesterday I asked Dr. Yogurt-Breath when I would be set free and he looked at my weight chart and said possibly by the holidays. Which should make me shout hooray and dance a celebratory jig, right? But

at this point, I don't know what to expect from the
world outside.

I mean, I haven't been able to go to the bathroom unattended or look
in a mirror for almost two months. I go to sleep at ten and I wake up
at seven. My biggest responsibilities are writing in my meditative
journal and finishing my dessert. I wear flannel pretty much day and
night. I have no idea what I look like or what those numbers in my
weight chart say. And I have to admit, I feel safer that way.

So, there's that.

CHAPTER 18
writing the script

TRAVIS WASN'T EXPECTING ME.

I wasn't expecting me either.

I could blame it on the brain jangling I'd just endured from smacking into a canine statue. But really, my heart is what led me back to the turnpike and up to the Sycamore Estates. I really felt like I'd run out of other options. At least that's my version of the story. And I'm sticking with it.

"Hello, hello!" Travis answered his intercom before the first ring was complete. Making it impossible for me to bail.

"Hi, Travis. It's Hank."

"It's who?"

"Hannah. Levinstein."

"Oh! Yes! Did you leave something here?"

"No. Maybe. Could you just let me in?"

"Of course. Of course!"

I took the stairs two at a time. I needed to do this and get it over with as quickly and painlessly as possible. If that was possible.

Travis had the door already open for me. It looked like he was in the middle of trying to feng shui his three pieces of furniture. Maybe so he could cover up the soda stains on his beige carpet.

"Sorry about the mess," he said. "I didn't know I was having company."

"I'm not company," I said—a little more curtly than I'd intended. "I'm just here because I have to tell you something and it won't take very long but . . . yeah."

Travis closed the door behind me and gestured toward the futon, which was now in the middle of the room with a lamp on the floor beside it.

"You wanna sit down?" he posed.

"Sure."

I waited for him to sit down first so I could perch myself on the other end. Not so much because I feared being next to him. It was more that I felt like I needed as much space as possible to unknot all these images in my head.

"Okay," I said. "I have to tell you some things that are not fun and I'm sorry to be the one telling you this but . . ." I took in a big gulp of air and tried to get out everything in that one breath. How sick Zoe was. How she was wearing clothes that fit her in

240

the first grade and posting videos of us that made me nervous. How much she was hurting and lying and overexercising and puking. How I'd witnessed her pillaging his medications and seen those cuts too symmetrical to be from a cat.

"No." I heard Travis moan. "Oh, no no no."

"I'm sorry," I muttered.

"No, *I'm* sorry," he told me. "Okay, so let me just get a few things straight," he added. Then he started firing out questions at me, like did I think Zoe was doing this to get back at him? Did I think she was taking other drugs too? Could it be that she'd lost weight just from stress? What about, did she ever talk about . . . trying to "end it all"?

"Not that I know of," I answered slowly. "But I do think that she needs help. Like, professional help."

"Right. Right. So would that be like a therapist or . . . ?" I didn't even try to answer that one. I just wanted Travis to take charge and fix the situation. Only he obviously was not picking up on my frustration. "Okay," he told me. "We got this. You and me, Hank. We can get her the help she needs and save her. Right?"

We got this. We can get her the help she needs.

I shook my head no. I had been part of this we-some for practically my whole life. ZoenHank. BFFAETI.

"I'm sorry," I said softly. "I don't think I can do this anymore."

"Oh no. You *have* to!" barked Travis. I felt my chest tighten and my gut seize. Travis cleared his throat and started over. His voice dropped to a soft sorrowful tone. "Sorry. What I meant was, *please*, Hank. I know this can't be fun for you either. Zoe has

241

been your pal for so long now. Can you just help me find her or figure out what to do next?"

He got his laptop from the kitchen and started googling information on self-harm and eating disorders. He kept muttering and opening up new tabs. It was clear he was completely overwhelmed.

"Can I just try something?" I asked.

"Please!" He pushed the laptop at me. "I'll get us both some water."

I found a few eating disorder clinics relatively close by. One in Philadelphia that seemed to have rolling hills and great reviews. Another in New York City that looked more like a spa, with chandeliers as big as my house.

"Cheers." Travis handed me a Dixie cup full of water and knocked one back himself. When he saw me looking at him blankly, he added, "I'm just . . . celebrating progress I guess."

I showed him what I'd discovered so far, and he looked over the sites carefully.

"So . . . I should check in and see where Alli is in all this, right?"

"I don't think so," I replied. "I mean, I think she's in some big-time denial." I had already gotten three different alerts from Alli's Instagram feed showing me pictures of Meowsers hooked up to an IV, his feline pupils dilated. Then there was a whole slideshow of Alli and the young male vet with their arms around each other over the drugged-out cat. The last picture was of Alli and Zoe back at Primally Fit gym. The caption said:

242

I guess the only perk of having your cat in the hospital is that you can still get to the afternoon BodybyBernardo class! #BodybyBernardo #fitforlife #singlewhitemom

Travis sort of whimpered after he saw that.

"Okay. So it's just us doing this."

"Uh—"

"I mean, *me*," he corrected. "But how do I get her into one of these places? I can't just blindfold her and stuff her in the backseat."

All I could think of was that lady in the gym again, with her boobs hanging out. So open and vulnerable and stern all at once.

"I mean, there must be tips on how to make an intervention. I bet there are even scripts for what to say," I told him.

"*Scripts?*" That was the magical word for Travis. His face was lit up with purpose and momentum now. After all, he was the tragically misunderstood Beast. For the next half hour, he pored over the computer, compiling different ideas from the Internet about effective interventions. He read his script out loud to me as he wrote it:

"*Step one: Start with love.* So, I'm gonna try to use phrases like, *You're one of the most important people in my life,* and *I believe in you.*"

"Sounds good," I said.

"*Step two: Describe specific troubling behaviors and use 'I' statements.* Okay, I think that's like, *When you don't eat, I feel scared.*"

Again, he looked to me for approval.

"Sure." I gave him the thumbs-up.

Step three was a little harder for Travis to wrap his head

around. It was about detailing what could happen if the addiction went untreated.

"But we don't know that she's addicted to anything, really," Travis said. "I mean, if she went into my herbs, that's kinda like eating an extra salad."

"*No*," I said resolutely. "She's addicted to hurting herself and starving herself and making herself sick. Those are harmful addictions. She could die."

Travis hung his head. "Okay. You're right," he mumbled.

Step four was about picking the right place to take the patient for rehab, and step five was showing love and support throughout the entire process.

"Can't cross your legs during an intervention," Travis informed me.

"Really?"

He tilted his screen toward me, so I could see the series of informational cartoons he'd been studying. We were supposed to sit with our feet planted and our arms open. According to the illustrations, it also helped if we were wearing bright colors and bulky sweaters.

"Okay. So when do you want to do this?" Travis asked. "I mean, I can usually memorize my lines pretty quickly. But I know you have a busy schedule."

"I can only do this if we do it now," I told him.

We drove back to Meadowlake in separate cars. It was close to three o'clock now and Zoe and Alli still weren't back from the gym. I really just wanted to get home and see Mom. Gus texted me that she and Elan had gotten back around two and she looked good but was lying down for a nap.

How's it going over there? Gus asked.

Oh, y'know. Just hangin' with Travis, waiting to do an intervention, and rethinking the past 16 years of my life. Good times.

Balls, Gus responded.

Balls, indeed.

Travis knocked on my car window and said that maybe we should park our cars around the corner and wait inside. (He still had a key.) It felt like the worst surprise party in the history of surprises, but I agreed to his plan. It all felt so illicit. I didn't know which one of us was shaking more as we crept through the side door and positioned ourselves in the living room. Travis debated about whether we should sit in the dark or turn on a few lamps for ambience. I voted for one lamp. He made it two. I tried to look really involved with something on my phone while he paced along the edge of the room. Reading through the notes he'd printed out at home. Rehearsing his lines.

And then . . .

All the waiting and planning and predicting and avoiding. As soon as Alli and Zoe walked into the house, it was like we all got sucked into this vortex of anguish and anger.

Alli was the first to shriek. "Holy crap! What are you doing here?!"

Then Zoe crashed into the room. "What the hell?" she yelled. "Did you break in?"

Travis tried to speak calmly. He kept opening his arms to hug Zoe, then letting them fall again. He was clutching those notes desperately; his voice fluttering and cracking.

I believe in you.

When you don't eat, I feel scared.

Zoe plugged her ears and stamped her feet. Screaming at him to get the hell out of her house. Alli was pleading, "The cat is so sick. Can't we talk about this some other time?"

Then the moment I'd dreaded the most: Travis turned to me and said, "Hannah, did you want to add anything?"

I wished I wasn't close enough to see the tide of emotions flushing through Zoe's face. Her tiny body quaking and turning even whiter with rage.

"Hank?!" she bellowed. "Hank!" She stomped and fumed. "Hannah! Louise! Levinstein! Was this *your idea*?"

She planted herself directly in front of me and I watched the knob of her sternum rising and falling so fast. The silence between us thick and barbed.

"Was it?" she repeated.

"I—I—yes," I stammered. She looked at me like I'd just smacked her across the dreams and she was going to torch my village. But I couldn't turn back now. "Because I love you and I want you to—"

"Stop it!" Zoe hissed at me. Her green eyes so cold and hard. Contracting into bright marbles of hate. "Stop it all, Hank. Stop pretending that you're doing this for me. You know you're not. You are a jealous, vengeful bitch. You want everything of mine. You want my body, you want my career, you want my life."

"I—no. I—" I shook my head wildly. I couldn't find words. There were too many feelings caught in my throat.

"Don't ever speak to me again, Hannah Levinstein," Zoe ordered. Her bottom eyelashes were collecting heavy, angry tears. "You can pretend that you're some sad hero but you're not. Do you hear me? You're *not*. Now *leave me the fuck alone and don't ever come back!*"

As I've said, I always did what Zoe told me to do.

Even that day. The last day I ever saw her or called her my friend.

I was vaguely aware of Travis shaking my hand goodbye. Also, of Alli weeping on the couch. When I got outside, there was a parking ticket for $150 on HOT RIC because not only was I illegally parked but I also had a broken taillight from my earlier fiasco.

But what I remember most was how much easier it was to breathe once I got outside.

Dear Hank,

So you may have noticed that I took a little break from writing you. Maybe you didn't. Honestly, I was hurt you didn't write back. But when I said that to one of the counselors here, she was like,

<u>Didn't you tell her you never wanted to see her again?</u>

And I was all, yeah but...

I'm sorry, Hank. I do want to see you again.

Somehow.

Someway.

I'm not sure if that's something you want too though.

Isn't it crazy how we make all these plans and act like we can map out our futures when in reality, it's all so beyond our control?

I mean, I know time keeps clicking forward.

I know it's too late to go back and fix things.

I know I have to start here, wherever the hell here is.

So maybe we could get to know each other again?

Feel free to answer as many or as few of these get-to-reknow-you questions as you like. I know you're busy.

1. How did Spanish with Señor Farber go this semester? Does he still get those goobers in the corners of his mouth?

2. What's going on with your mom and Elan?

3. Is it true Yoshi's had a fire and closed for three weeks?

4. What do you do when you haven't showered in three

days but you kind of love the smell of your own toe
cheese? (Not that I'd know.)

5. How's Gus doing at Meadowlake?

6. Can you tell him hi for me, please?

7. If I made you a jockstrap/scarf in Knitting here, would
   you maybe wear it?

8. What are you playing on the piano these days?

9. Will you be my friend if I come back twenty pounds
   heavier?

10. Will you be my friend if I come back at all?

And really the most important question, which I should have asked
long ago:

Do you know I admire you?

CHAPTER 19
the cleanup song

I CAME HOME SHAKY AND SORE. HOT RIC'S BACK RIGHT WHEEL WAS rattling and the glove compartment refused to close at all. Everything was spilled out across the front seat—including my exhausted psyche. I tried to inch into our driveway, but Uncle Ricky's new convertible and Elan's Subaru had taken up most of the space. Also, in front of the garage there was a tall aluminum ladder set up. Uncle Ricky was manning the bottom, with one beefy arm draped over the crossbar for safety and what sounded like a steady monologue about his love of Upstate New York as the sound track. Twelve feet above him, scooping out my house's gutters, was Elan.

Of course, he was the first to notice me and waved enthusiastically to welcome me home.

He truly wasn't a bad guy. This I knew.

And yet I needed a minute or an eon to gather my thoughts. Or at least to sift through the fuzz in my brain and find something to say besides *Aaaaaaaagh!*

I parked on the street and just looked at my house for a few breaths. This had been my home for my entire life. We still had the same light-gray siding and the one drooping shutter on the upstairs bathroom window. The front door was bright red, but Gus and I had painted it and it had telltale streaks of childhood artistry. We had told my mom we'd redo it for so long. Just like we'd promised to get on a ladder and clean the gutters. And then I said I'd call the guy to come and do that. (Which devolved into me giving Mom a coupon last Mother's Day that said I WILL CALL THE GUTTER GUY. She smiled, then tucked it into a pocket.)

There were so many handyman projects that I knew really irked her. Like the basement window needing insulation and the hole on the side of the garbage enclosure from a fiercely determined raccoon. Mom had a little list of tasks that were on the refrigerator. At the top it read ONE DAY. I kept planning to look into it—to craft some DIY mesh that stumped the raccoon or to greet her with a brightly repainted front door. But I never did.

Yet another reason why Elan was now the hero of this story. Standing on that ladder, scooping out globs of mangled leaves and twigs from the gutter, he was finally making good on my unmet promise. I couldn't blame him, really. This was one thing my mom desperately wanted—someone to help patch up all the cracks and drafts that had become our home. There was just one bush that looked like it could be alive. A splotch of green in a cluster of dried-leaf goodbyes.

I watched Uncle Ricky hand Elan one of my pink beach pails from the summer trips we used to take up to Maine. I hadn't used it in years, but I knew it was mine because it had big bumpy eyes on its side. It used to have squid legs drawn on too, only they'd faded from so many years of salty sea air. Mom and I went on countless shell walks with that bucket—gathering wampum, sea glass, and snail carcasses. I was never that great a swimmer and the water in Maine was always so cold. But those walks with Mom—I lived for those walks.

Now Elan was depositing all the gutter grime in my bucket. His hand dripping with brown muck.

I really wanted to shout, *Stop, thief! That's my squid bucket you're stealing! And my house and my mom and my soggy leaves and my life!*

But, of course, I hadn't used that pail in at least eight years—if not more. Truthfully, I didn't even know it was missing until this moment. Or that it was in our house the whole time.

"Aha!" Uncle Ricky shouted as soon as I opened the car door. "Liberace has returned!"

"Hey," I answered. I'd honestly forgotten about my dismal piano recital from hours before and didn't want to relive it anytime soon.

"Seriously," Uncle Ricky called up to Elan. "Have you ever heard this girl play the piano? She's amazing."

"So I hear!" Elan responded. He pulled out what looked like a waterlogged birds' nest and placed it in my bucket. "Hey, Hank. Sorry I'm using your bucket. It was the only one we could find. But I swear I'll get you a new one."

Uncle Ricky found that hilarious. His round frame shook with laughter.

"I told him not to worry about it," he told me between guffaws. "But he was so worried it was some precious squid heirloom. So seriously, if you want to be mad at someone, be mad at me."

"I'm not mad. I'm just tired," I told him. Uncle Ricky let go of the ladder to give me a hug that was tight enough to squeeze all the air out of me. Then he twisted my left arm around my back, which was his favorite move to do ever since he started a jiu-jitsu class last year. But I'd also taken a class in self-defense and knew how to wriggle free. I threw in a headbutt to his chest to prove I meant business.

"Uncle!" Uncle Ricky shouted.

"Ricky!" I shouted back.

That made him quake with laughter again. While he was momentarily speechless, Elan informed me that my mom was upstairs lying down and that she would love to see me.

"Thanks," I told him. I knew I should thank him for so many things—like making sure my mom went to the hospital and then getting her safely home and putting up with my bullshit cranky attitude not to mention dealing with whatever sludge he was now digging out of my gutter. But at this moment, that one *thanks* would have to do.

If my mom was excited to see me, she sure hid it well. She was snoring passionately when I came into her room. Her foot was propped up on a pillow and shrouded in a thick cast that went up to her knee.

Though I'd seen my mom disappear emotionally, I had rarely seen her physically incapacitated like this before. Or maybe I had and had just turned away. Through rain, sleet, hail, or chicken pox, to me she had always appeared upright. The only time I remembered her sick was after we had Chinese food one time and she ran to the bathroom, and when I heard her throw up, I cried so hard that she had to come out and console me. That was all I knew—I could not accept her being anything less than steely and indestructible. She was the only thing holding up our rickety family, after all.

I looked at her now, so serene and beautiful. Her eyelids fluttering ever so slightly. Shuttling her between dreams. She smelled like Johnson's baby powder and her Swedish hand cream. Her dark hair was wet from what I hoped was a delicious shower. On her night table was a glass of seltzer still spitting up bubbles and a bottle of Tylenol. On the lampshade was a pale yellow Post-it note that said, in thick marker, TOGETHER.

No doubt it was from Elan.

I climbed into Mom's bed on the other side. Trying to fill up the dent in the mattress where Dad had once snored beside her. I'd done this so many nights as a kid, and even as a teen. Renting girls-on-a-wacky-road-trip movies or howling at *SNL* next to her. We loved to tackle the pile of Sunday crossword puzzles side by side like this too. Mom never told me I was too old or annoying. She scratched my back and sang me Yiddish lullabies until I surrendered to sleep. And if by chance she started to doze while I was still bright-eyed, I poked her in the ribs so she'd stay awake with me.

She was my mom and Gus's mom. That was her primary focus for my entire life. And it wasn't until this moment, watching her drinking in long, steady breaths, that I saw her as anything more than that. For the first time, I could see how frail and resilient, scared and triumphant she was all at once.

For the first time, I could see how *human* my mom was.

"Noooo!" I heard from down the hall. "How could you do this to me? I look like a freak!" Gus squealed in between giggles.

"Sssssh," was the only response I could make out. Followed by high-pitched laughter.

I slipped off Mom's bed and shut her door behind me, following the noises to the bathroom.

"You have to give it some more time," a booming voice commanded. "Just *stay still*."

"Hello?" I said, tapping on the door with just one finger. I didn't know exactly what I was interrupting, but my eyes were already watering from the sharp stench of bleach.

Tata flung open the door and announced, "It's my fault. He wanted to do highlights."

"Highlights?"

"You're not allowed to laugh," Gus told me, even though I couldn't see him behind Tata's wide frame. She was wearing a bright red shirt that said *F the Patriarchy* in gold letters.

"Oh . . . kay."

With a sweep of her arm, Tata revealed my little brother, now decked out in a floral-print shower cap and a plastic Superman cape. He was picking bobby pins out from the nape of his neck.

"No no no no no no no," Tata yelled. She swatted his hands away and refastened the cap. "Stop that, ya big jerk."

"*You* stop that, ya big jerk," Gus replied, swatting her back. They got into this little slappy fight and Gus let loose with one of his hyena-like giggles again. I hadn't heard him laugh like that in such a long time. It did feel pretty spectacular to see his eyes flashing with giddy mischief. But I also had a job to do—which was protect Mom's convalescence and keep it quiet up here.

"Gus. *Please?*" I said. "Can you just keep it down because Mom really needs her rest."

"Gotcha." Tata gave me a thumbs-up and a wink. I wanted to tell her we weren't buds, but honestly, I was jealous of how much fun they were having and how Tata's sunny grin somehow made my stupor even darker. I turned to leave.

"Wait. Hank!" said Gus. "Remember Gusaletta?"

"Um, yeah." He hadn't spoken about his alter ego in so long. I felt like he was taking out a precious relic to show us. I didn't want to say the wrong thing and break his trust. "I loved Gus-aletta," I said. "I miss her. Or him. Or . . ."

"See?" Gus laughed. Tata was chuckling now too. "I told you. I've always been at least partly fabulous."

"I didn't say you weren't," Tata told him. "I just said you needed to embrace your fabulousness more." She turned to me for backup. "Am I right?"

"Sure," I answered. "Be fabulous."

Gus beamed. "And what was your name?" he asked me. "Madame Snorkelbutt?"

"I dunno."

"No, Archduke!" Gus yelped. "Archduke Snorkelbutt! And you wore Mom's mirrored goggles and those crazy Hawaiian shorts of Dad's. They came up to your armpits!"

Tata was full-on cracking up now.

"My dad was a big man," I said. "And he liked bright colors." It felt like I should defend him in some way.

"So I heard," Tata said. "Sounds awesome."

I wanted to be mad at Gus for sharing those memories with a total stranger. But then again, they were his memories too. And Tata actually looked like the one person who could appreciate those long-ago moments almost as much as we could. I felt my eyes filling up again and the back of my neck prickling. Because I had no one special to share those memories with, and I had no one to trust my alter ego with, and I had no one who could understand all that I was losing.

I really had to get out of this bathroom before I fragmented into a million sobbing pieces.

Gus grabbed me as I turned to go though. He drew me into a hug and whispered, "That took balls."

It was hot and there was so much ammonia and hair dye in there, but I wanted to stay in that embrace for the rest of the century.

"Thanks," I squeaked.

As I closed the door behind me, I heard Tata singing softly:

*"Clean up, clean up, everybody clean up
I help you and you help me!"*

It was the song Gus and I sang when we were little.

_Hold my hand, please.

_Always know I love you truly.

_No one has your patience, brilliance, or piano skizills.

_Not to mention your awesome hair.

_After this is all done I don't know who I'll be exactly, but I

_Hope I can be a great friend to you.

HANNAH

CHAPTER 20
prelude in c

I WAS OUTSIDE THE TOOBEYS' HOUSE THE FOLLOWING WEDNESDAY afternoon when I got the call from Travis.

"I just wanted to tell you that Zoe's intake process is done," he reported. "And I . . . I . . ." He drew in a jagged breath and then stuttered into silence. I really didn't want him to start crying on the phone.

"Thank you so much for telling me," I broke in.

"No, thank *you*," he replied.

"Sure. Okay."

I still had a mountain of unanswered questions—like had he decided on the clinic in New York City that looked like a spa with bubbling fountains and all-white furniture or the one outside of Philadelphia with pictures of girls holding hands in circles? Had

Alli ever come out of her narcissistic cocoon to help? Was there screaming, clawing, wailing? And how was Meowsers after his Ritalin overdose?

Actually, forget that. I really couldn't care less about that cat. Which maybe makes me a bad person. But it's the truth.

"I guess she hates us both now," said Travis.

"No no no," I protested. But I couldn't even convince myself. I didn't want to pretend that I had any insights or promises. There were too many things I just didn't know, especially about the future.

"Well, maybe," I added in a quieter voice. "Sorry."

"Sorry? No. What are *you* sorry for?" Travis asked.

"Right. I'm not sorry. I'm just sad for all the pain and difficulty and everything."

"You have been a great friend to my daughter."

"Ha! I don't know about that. I mean, I knew something was wrong and then I didn't say anything. And then I did say something, but it wasn't the right something. Or . . . I don't know."

Travis just let me ramble until I had nothing else to say. For a minute, I thought he'd hung up on me, but then I heard his breath, stilted and uneven.

"Hey, Hank?" he rumbled into the phone. "We're all doing the best we can, y'know?"

"Yeah," I heard myself squeak. There was no flirtatious wink or croony chorus to go with these words, but somehow I wanted to curl up and go to sleep inside the quiet acceptance Travis had just given me.

"Well." Travis cleared his throat. "I should get going. Just wanted to touch base."

"Thank you. Yes. And I have to get going too."

"Of course, of course."

"Well, just know, if you need anything. You have my number."

"Yeah, same here," I said. I wondered if Travis had anyone else to talk to about this. I vaguely remembered him having a younger brother and a strained relationship with his dad, but that was about it. The thought of me meeting with Zoe's dad in a café to chat about our feelings sounded highly illegal and unkosher though. Travis cleared his throat again and thanked me at least three more times before hanging up.

I didn't know if I'd ever hear from or see him again. Which shouldn't have meant diddly to me, but he had been a fixture in my life for so long. I hadn't realized until now that I was saying goodbye to so many faces besides Zoe's.

As I walked into the Toobeys', I heard *Arabesque No. 1* being played the way it was *supposed* to sound. The notes soaring and dipping as if on a lyrical trapeze. It was Mrs. Toobey on the piano bench. With accompaniment by Mr. Toobey, who hovered over her, humming. Clutching tightly on to the side of the piano, as if it were holding him up.

I didn't want to go into the room without being invited, but there was literally no place for me to sit in the living room. Mr. Toobey must have worked furiously over the course of the past week. There were at least a dozen new canvases leaning against different surfaces—a coffee table, a wooden chair, a walker. They weren't all bananas and bloodied soldiers either, which was a relief. These images were calmer—sunsets and mountain ridges. A lake fading into the horizon. A rowboat with two fuzzy figures leaning in toward each other—just like on my *Debussy* book jacket.

"Left your book here!" Mrs. Toobey shouted over the music without missing a note. "Come on over. We'll play it together."

"That's my Roslyn!" Mr. Toobey told me gleefully. He nodded his head and waved me over, but I wouldn't move. I waited in the doorway until the final chord progression floated out and disappeared. Watching Mrs. Toobey's weathered hands lift off the keys, levitating for a moment in the afterglow, and then dropping into her lap.

Mr. Toobey clapped and stomped his feet like a preschooler.

"I told you!" he yelled. "Bravo! Encore!"

Mrs. Toobey gave a quiet smile. Then she scooted herself away from the keyboard and stood up, waddling over to me.

"What's up?" she said, tipping her head back so we could meet eye to eye. Or eye to nostril. I tried not to gawk at her dark nose hairs.

"I'm just . . . I'm just having trouble." I faltered.

"You want to switch back to Saturdays instead? I kept your old time open," Mrs. Toobey said.

"No. I mean, no, thank you. I mean, I think I have to take a break. At least for now. It's too much."

"What's too much?"

"All of it. It's all just too much. I have all this homework and all these tests and pretty soon I'll be doing college applications too and now my best friend's in a clinic. Although I can't call her my best friend anymore because she hates me. And then my mom broke her ankle and I just . . ."

I knew my voice was grating and Mom's fracture had nothing to do with me, but I couldn't stop myself.

"Did you hear my Roslyn play yet?" Mr. Toobey asked us both.

"Yes," Mrs. Toobey and I answered in unison.

Then she turned back to me. Nodding solemnly while she chewed the inside of her cheek. She did not seem mad, just concerned. She took both my hands and sealed them between hers. As if she were holding me together. Maybe she was.

"First of all," she said, "thank you for telling me some of your feelings and I can appreciate that you have a lot going on right now. That must be very challenging. However—" She paused here and padded over to one of the windowsills shrouded in spider plants. There was a wooden cabinet underneath, the knobs bound together by a thick rubber band that she yanked off. As the doors popped open, a pile of music books slid out. She picked out what she needed and shoved the rest back in, then bounded back over to me with her selections. Her caftan was swishing so fast against her thighs, I thought she might catch fire.

"I do not accept your resignation," she declared.

I opened my mouth to protest, but she dumped the chosen books on top of one of her Steinways and ushered me toward the bench.

"Sit," she commanded. Then squeezed her ample tush in next to mine.

"Now, the closest thing to hip-hop I could find was this Billy Joel medley from a few years ago," she said, handing me a pamphlet of sheet music. "I can also order you something more hip-hoppy if you give me a more dynamic description—"

"Yeah, I don't need that anymore."

"But I want you to be playing music that *excites* you," she told me. "Can you show me an example, maybe on your iPhone 5000?"

I wondered what she'd say if I showed her the Pussycat video. I shook my head to clear away that thought.

"It was just—"

Her eyes blinked and fluttered. I watched the flecks of rhinestones in the corners of her cat-eye glasses, catching every last ray of sun from this day and scattering them across her wooden floor. I wanted to be this woman so badly. She was clear, strident, and determined. She devoted her life to sharing these sacred vibrations, often composed hundreds of years ago.

"To be honest, it was never my idea to begin with," I admitted.

She cocked her head to one side, trying to understand.

"I don't know what a hip-hop ballad is either," I added.

"Well, then!" Mrs. Toobey took that information in and leapt up from the bench on a mission. She started scrutinizing all the music she'd taken out. Licking the tip of her stubby pointer finger and riffling through the pages.

"Let's tackle something loud. Whaddaya say?" She didn't actually need me to agree. Most of Mrs. Toobey's questions were rhetorical. "Now I do think you have a great articulation of Chopin, and you have those lovely long fingers. Ooh, no, I know what!"

She kept opening up new tomes, snapping the spines or taking miniature busts of Beethoven and Mozart to keep the pages open.

"Listen," she told me. "I'm going to play a few of these for you, and when I get to something you like, you just yell. Got it?"

"Got it."

For the next half hour, Mrs. Toobey reeled through concertos and études. Cracking open new books and new sounds and minor chords that I never knew existed before. Sometimes she leaned into the keys and mined the faintest tones. Other times she sprang off the wooden bench and landed on the notes, splaying her fingers so wide I thought they'd pop out of their sockets. Mr. Toobey stayed glued to his spot by her side the whole time, singing along and swaying. Often reminding me that his Roslyn was going to Juilliard.

The piece I chose was *Prelude in C-sharp Minor* by a Russian composer named Rachmaninoff. It was complicated and stormy. With chords that used all ten of my fingers at once.

"Aha!" Mrs. Toobey said with a wide grin. She even pumped her fist in victory. "I knew you'd like that one."

"But is that crazy?" I asked. "Will it take me forever to learn?"

"And so what if it does?" she replied. "You in some kind of rush?"

"I guess not," I said. "Not that I know of."

There were no other places where I needed to be and no more fires to put out. Which broke my heart but also gave me so much more room to breathe and listen.

And, hopefully, get louder.

Hank!

Yes, this is the saddest invitation in the history of tears.

Boring, pitiful, pathetic, stupid, with a side of burdensome.

But here goes.

Next weekend we're having a Circle of Support meeting and everyone here is allowed to invite one or two people to come.

I was wondering if . . . _drumroll, please_ . . . you would be that one person for me.

Would you could you maybe sorta kinda?

I think it's an hour drive. And the meeting itself takes an hour.

I'm not even completely sure why I'm asking.

If you can't do it, that's fine. Or if you don't want to, that's okay too.

Either way, I just wanted you to know you're the only one I really want to invite.

Yours till the banana splits!

Xoxo, Z

Oh yeah, the details are on that other card.

YOU'RE INVITED!

WHERE: THE CEDAR KNOLLS
REHABILITATION CENTER
(AND PENITENTIARY)

WHEN: SUNDAY, DECEMBER 3, AT 1 P.M.

WHY: WHAT ELSE DO YOU HAVE TO DO?
(BESIDES EVERYTHING)

BLACK TIE IS OPTIONAL.

REFRESHMENTS WILL BE
SERVED BUT THEY WILL NOT
BE REFRESHING.

SPOILER ALERT: THERE WILL BE NO BOUNCY
HOUSE.

CHAPTER 21
the flight of the mourning doves

WHEN I CAME HOME FROM PIANO, IT WAS LOAMY AND COOL. THE SUN holding on by just a few pinkish threads. Mom was weeding out the wilted marigolds and planting tulip bulbs in our front yard. As soon as she heard me pull into the driveway, she scrambled up onto her crutches as if she'd just won the MegaBucks lottery, bounding toward the car.

"H to the A to the N to the K!" she cheered, waggling her hips from side to side and doing some weird ripply move with her neck that must've been cool a few decades ago.

"Hey," I said, getting out of the car. "Are you sure that's doctor approved?"

"Ha!" Mom scoffed, giving me a peck on the cheek. "Follow-up appointment isn't till tomorrow. In the meantime though, wanna see something amazing?" Without waiting for an answer, she gave my wrist a squeeze and then catapulted herself toward a runty-looking bush at the side of our house.

"Voilà!" Mom cried. "Le Hanukkah bush!"

It was a little fir tree sapling that my kindergarten teacher sent home with me on winter break. Apparently I'd told her that I was Jewish, so she could give it to someone else, but she'd insisted. And so we'd planted it and called it a Hanukkah bush. I used to feed it lots of fertilizer and check on its soil every day, but I'd tapered off a few years ago. It was still looking more like a straggly ball of foliage than a tree.

"Check it out," Mom said proudly. "It's an early Hanukkah miracle!"

She stuck her booted foot out in front of her and plopped down on her butt. Then she pointed to a small nest tucked into the branches. There was a crescent of shell left on the ground that she picked up to hand to me. It was as thin as paper but held so many pearly swirls of color.

I had forgotten that Mom was tracking the birds' progress over the summer. She'd determined from their calls that they were mourning doves. They staked out the bush late in July and gathered all their nesting fibers only to get sideswiped by a series of harsh August storms. Mom had come out each day after the winds had calmed and left out bowls of sunflower seeds and fresh water. Now the nest looked as orderly and intact as a nest could be, according to my untrained eye. And Mom was beaming.

"I even saw one of the little guys practicing his moves this morning," she told me. "Before they took off."

"Nice job," I said.

"Bah, it was all them," she answered. "I mean, I've been out here for hours watching them primp and pluck each other. There's so much to do when you're a bird. And then the sad thing is I read they only last a year or so. And they're migrating most of that time unless they live in the South."

"Wow, I guess you really are going buggy being home, huh? How much time do you need to be homebound?"

"Ha!" Mom climbed back up and blew the hair out of her face. "Actually, I chose to take the week off. I think it's exactly what I needed. What *we* needed."

I spun my head around so quickly I could hear my neck crack. There was no sign of Elan's moped or Subaru in the driveway. No wafting hints of his next seitan-garlic spectacular on the grill.

Mom intercepted my gaze. And I guess my thoughts too. "I mean *you* and *me*," she clarified. "It's been a while, huh? I mean, I have an entire pile of Sunday crosswords that are untouched on my night table."

"Yeah, well, things have been a little busy," I muttered.

"No excuse." Mom's voice was just sharp enough that I thought she could be legitimately mad. Only when I looked up and found her eyes, they were glimmering. "I guess I can't blame it *all* on you," she added with a grin.

"Yeah, that's not fair," I whimpered. "We used to do the crossword on Saturday nights and then you started . . ."

Mom waited to see if I'd fill in that blank. I couldn't though. I didn't want to say Elan's name and point to him like some assassin of everything we used to have.

"We stopped doing the crossword together way before Elan came along," Mom said. Once again sniffing out my pitiful musings. "If you recall, we were actually on my bed one Saturday night when Zoe started texting and IM'ing about some party in James HeartThrob's basement that you *had* to attend."

"HeartThrob?!" I couldn't help laughing at that. Mainly because James Hartwick III was the complete opposite of a heartthrob.

Mom continued. "And then it turned into a weekly thing. Which I don't mind. I think it's great. But I do want to set the record straight. That *you* were the one who started with the Saturday-night plans."

Mom didn't look upset. She just looked smaller than a few minutes ago. Maybe it was because she was propping herself up on those crutches and I could tell her arms were getting tired. More likely though, it was because she was all alone. She had been flying solo for so long now. Kissing our boo-boos and balancing the checkbook and going to sleep in that abandoned bed when that was never the life she'd imagined. And I had never really seen this so starkly before. Or acknowledged it ever.

"It's okay," Mom repeated. "It's really good, actually. We both need to get out and socialize. Gus too."

Mom reached out to cup both of my shoulders with her cool, sturdy hands. Her fingernails were blunt and lined with crescents of mud. I thought about how Alli's and Zoe's nails were always painted some shade of glossy gray or shimmering pink. How I'd longed to get matching ones without really knowing why. Without even appreciating the hands Mom had passed on to me.

"Can you tell me how you're feeling about all of this?"

All of this.

I didn't think there were enough adjectives in the English language to describe how lost and confused and free and furious I felt.

"How about—let's get a snack first, huh?" Mom suggested.

I followed her to the back porch, which was one of those projects my dad had started lifetimes ago, just after my parents moved to the 'burbs. It was only big enough to hold a small card table and a couple of chairs, and he'd used the wrong kind of paint, so it constantly peeled little curlicues of white into the grass below. Today, however, the porch looked like a quaint tea party was expected any minute. Mom just happened to have turned on the twinkly holiday lights that Gus and I strung from the roof to a pole in the grass. She'd also laid out her blue polka-dotted kettle, two mugs, and a sleeve of Girl Scout Thin Mint cookies that must have been hidden in the back of a drawer.

"Are you waiting for someone?" I asked.

"Yes, silly. You." Mom lightly swatted my butt with a gardening glove and then crutched past me up the wooden step with weeds sprouting through its cracks. "And I'm not going to wait any longer because my armpits are screaming from these things." She dropped into a chair and threw her crutches clattering to the ground. "Why don't they mention in the handbook of stupid injuries that you need pits of steel?"

She poured us both some tea and I could tell from sniffing the warm steam that it was my favorite: mint-chamomile. Also, even the crumbliest of those prehistoric cookies was delicious once I stuffed them into my mouth. We sat there, munching and sipping in a soft silence for a while, before Mom ventured to ask me again, "So?"

"So . . . ," I started. But I was nowhere nearer to having a real answer. "So, I mean, I don't know what I can really say about Zoe except it feels ridiculously sad and lonely. And I can't believe how many hours—or years really—I wasted trying to be like her. And then trying to be *not* like her. Or trying to be enough like her and also enough not like her that I could fit into her world. I mean seriously, some days I just stood in front of my closet and thought, *I wish I knew what she was wearing so I could blend into her color scheme.* How pathetic is that? And I don't know *why* even. I mean, she was a great friend. For a while. But I just got so *lost* in her."

Mom nodded and chewed the edge of another cookie.

"And . . . I don't know who I am without her."

Mom tucked a tuft of my hair behind my ear. Which usually I hated because it just made the curly chaos more uneven, but now I didn't protest.

"Can I tell you who I see?" she asked. I shrugged—not trusting my voice anymore.

"I see a beautiful, generous, kind, intelligent, bright soul who wants to do the right thing."

I blinked back as many tears as I could, then looked at my lap so they knew where to land.

"Sometimes you get too attached to one person, and you've always been this way. Dad and I both worried about that tendency in you."

"Really?" I gulped. "Why didn't you tell me that before? I mean, what did Dad say?" Even the mention of my dad made me feel possessive and grabby.

"I don't know exactly," Mom said. "I mean, it was a while ago. But I do know that he was concerned. As was I."

"*Think*," I demanded. "What did he say?" It was an outrageous request and I knew it. I was just so jealous that Mom got to hold on to all these memories. That she had gotten to whisper to him at night and snuggle with him in the predawn hours. That she had this whole history with Dad before I was even born— living in a studio apartment in Brooklyn and eating only rice and beans for a year to save money. Getting stranded in a two-door Honda on the side of the road somewhere near Memphis together. These were the tales that Mom got to pass down when and if she wanted to, and I had to wait thirstily for any drips or details.

"Okay," Mom said carefully. "I think he said something to the effect of, 'She gets very attached to people, doesn't she?'"

"What else?" I pressed.

Mom shook her head. "I don't know, sweetie."

"He didn't say anything else?"

"If he did, I don't remember."

"Why not?!" I yelled. Mom's lips tightened and she blinked hard. "Sorry," I said in a limp apology.

"No, *I'm* sorry," she said. "I didn't mean to upset you more. I just never know how much of the past you want to hear and how much I can actually recall . . ."

"I want to hear it all," I insisted. "Even if it's stupid or boring to you. I want to hear it."

"Okeydokey." I couldn't tell if she was pleased or nervous or a smorgasbord of both emotions. She drew in a long inhale and then let out an exhale. Wiping her brow and smearing mud across her nose.

"Well, you know how we met, right?" she began.

"In a coffee shop?"

"Right. Your dad was actually there with another girl. I think her name was January. She was a knockout."

"But wasn't she rude to you and then Dad dropped her off at the bus and came back to apologize and get your number?"

Mom smiled. "See? You remember this better than I do."

"Okay, so then he dumped January and found you and then what?"

Mom told me how he wooed her with a fresh bouquet of tulips every other day and sappy poetry that he admitted he needed a thesaurus to write. They fell in love. They fell in debt too. Mom was still in grad school for English literature. Dad was paying off a mountain of college loans but had no idea how to save. He lived large—renting fancy cars just to take Mom to the beach for the day, ordering one of everything off the menu when they went out. He was twice her size at least, and one time he gave her a piggyback ride all the way across the Brooklyn Bridge.

I knew all these tales, but I smiled and nodded anyway.

"He was incredible. A force of nature," Mom told me.

"Go on," I said. "Please."

Mom tried to dig back through the archives now—describing their first trip to meet her parents and Dad trying to impress them by speaking Yiddish but accidentally calling Grandma Doris a dick. I laughed even though I knew the punch line. Then she described moving into a tiny apartment together in Bay Ridge, Brooklyn, both scrambling to make rent. Dad worked a construction job for some guy upstate who had a mansion and only wore silver tracksuits. Mom stayed at the café and tried desperately to write her Great American Novel.

"And then, of course, you know how he wanted to propose to me at the top of the Empire State Building, but it was closed for renovation, and then he took me to a fancy restaurant that wouldn't accept personal checks."

"Ha!"

"There I was, all gussied up for some mysterious fancy date he was taking me on, and we wound up—"

"Eating hot dogs on the fire escape," I finished for her.

Yes, I'd memorized that anecdote too.

"I don't know that there's much more to tell you." Mom

sighed. "I loved your father very much, Hank. And he was crazy about you. He would do anything for his little girl."

"Wait—that reminds me!" I blurted. "Did you hear that whole debate about the train?"

"What train?" Mom asked. I knew Gus would be pissed at me for bringing it up again, but I refused to let that go.

"Elan said he used to take the 8:03 from Meadowlake to Penn Station and that he knew Dad from that train."

Mom's face brightened. "Yeah, isn't that a funny coinkidink?"

"No, it's not," I shot back. "It's impossible. Dad always peeled off at the corner when we were walking to school so he could catch the 7:29."

"Oh, right," Mom said slowly. "The 7:29," she repeated in a daze.

"Am I right?" I pounced. Then I answered for myself. "I'm right! I know I am because I asked Daddy to walk us all the way to school and he said he couldn't. Because he was taking the 7:29."

Mom squeezed my hands hard. She pressed them to her lips and I saw the edges of her eyes glittering.

"You are right, Hannah, dear," she said. "You have a fantastic memory and you are exactly correct. Your dad did take the 7:29 train a few times."

"A *few* times?"

She locked eyes with mine. "Most of the time though, he headed to the train station just a little bit early, so he could stop

279

at the deli and grab a bacon-egg-and-cheese sandwich. Before getting on the 8:03."

"No!" I snapped, pulling my hands away.

"It's not a bad thing," Mom said.

"Yes, it is!" I moaned. "He would never give up walking us to school just so he could get a *sandwich*!" I stamped my feet indignantly. Feeling so betrayed on behalf of the little girl who just wanted her daddy to walk her to the playground.

"He loved you so much," Mom cooed. "You were his little girl. You always will be," she promised. I still had to wail though. My eyes leaking full, furious tears.

"It's just not fair!" I bleated. "Nobody else I know has this kind of hole. I mean, Zoe treats her dad like shit and he's just—I mean, at least he's *alive*."

"I know," Mom said. She coaxed me onto her lap and I mashed my nose into her shoulder. "I swear, when your father died . . ." I could hear Mom choking back her own tears now. "Well, you know—it was the worst time of my life. I was completely alone."

I sat up and scowled. "Wait. Completely alone? Me and Gus were there." She raised her eyebrows at me. "Gus and *I*," I self-corrected with teeth clenched.

"Right," Mom said slowly. "I'm sorry I worded it like that. What I meant was, I *felt* completely alone. As a parent. And frankly, as a woman, with desires and needs."

"Whoa whoa whoa, wait a second." I scooted back into my

own chair. "I don't really need to know all *this*." I instinctually went to cover my ears, only Mom took my hands in hers again.

"I know it's hard. But I think it's important," she told me. "I want you to understand where I'm coming from too, you know."

"Oh-kay . . ." I didn't know if she was going to give me a sex-ed talk or if we were still talking about grief. Either of those two options made me a little queasy.

But Mom had a completely different agenda.

"Hank, when I started seeing Elan, it wasn't to replace your father in any way," she said.

"I know that," I snipped.

"Do you, though?"

Which was a fair question. I did size up his every move in comparison to my dad's larger-than-life legacy.

"I want you to know that I thought long and hard about how this would affect you," she continued. "And Gus. And I knew it wouldn't be easy, but Elan is kind, he's funny, he cleans the gutters . . ."

She waited for me to offer up a smile of recognition. I think I made it halfway to a grin.

"And most important, he really adores my kids," Mom concluded.

"He *adores* us?"

Mom nodded.

"Huh," I said. Because I didn't have any more outrage or heartache to hurl. Mom had felt all of that too—probably more so than me. She had found a way to move forward, despite the pain. Or maybe because of it.

This was Mom's biggest sin. While I was furiously trying to revive our past, she had put one foot in front of the next. And she'd discovered some momentum.

"Please don't make me go camping with you guys though, okay?" I said.

Mom laughed. "Yeah, I'm not exactly keen on camping any more right now either," she answered.

"And can I ask a question?" I said.

"Anything."

"Does he do the crossword with you?"

"Never," Mom said. "And I have no plans to ask him. That's just for you and me."

She handed me the last Thin Mint and I snapped it in half. Or at least that was my intention. Really, we each got about a quarter and the rest crumbled out of my hands.

I'm thinking a mourning dove enjoyed them for dessert.

Dear Zoe,

Wow. How many times have I started a letter that way?

Answer: too many to count.

Yeah, I even named my diary Zoe when we did that project in Ms. Cotter's sixth-grade class about Anne Frank. Remember that? We had to pretend the world was shattering all around us and write down what it felt like to be cramped in a hidden annex. And I thought, if I'm going to write anything really meaningful, I'd better name it Zoe.

[insert pathetic emoji here]

There were so many things I didn't know how to tell you face-to-face. It just felt easier to write them down, I guess. I actually have a stack of letters and diaries addressed to you in the back of my sock drawer. In case you have a spare year and feel like laughing.

I love you, Zoe. I always have. A little too much, some might say. You swooped into my life like some fairy sprite and plucked me out of my sad, dull existence. You made me excited about dancing and singing and popcorn and life.

I wanted to be you so badly.

Too badly.

And now—slowly—I am trying to figure out who I am without you.

In answer to your questions:

- Yoshi's did have a small fire—smelled like burned toast for weeks—but the damage was minimal.
- Gus is really flourishing. He's in choir and has this awesome bestie and is definitely a better dresser than I am. I'm super-happy for him.
- I started a hard piece on the piano. It's Russian and it sounds like church bells.
- I don't care what you look like. I never have. It's your energy that's always been magnetic to me.
- And you asked about Elan—thank you for that. He's actually moving into our place in January, and somehow, I'm okay with it. It feels calm. It makes my mom happy. Though I refuse to eat his tempeh balls.
- Balls.

Also, Amelia Hartwick wants you to know that she lost her virginity to someone on the Fairbrook lacrosse team. Phew!

So, thank you for the invite to your Circle of Support next week. I really appreciate that. I won't be there though. That's the same day that I'm going to the Young Maestros of Essex & Bergen Counties auditions. I'm playing this crazy-hard piece so if I make it through the first page it will be a minor miracle. I'm committed though. And excited.

That's all for now. Cuz now's all we have, right?

XOXO, Hank

RESOURCES

If you or anyone you know is hurting, please reach out to someone who can help. Here are just a few great organizations with mental health professionals who are much wiser than me. ☺

NAMI: The National Alliance on Mental Health is the largest grassroots mental health organization dedicated to building better lives for people affected by mental illness.
nami.org

NATIONAL SUICIDE PREVENTION LIFELINE: A 24-7, free and confidential support network for people in distress. 1-800-273-8255
suicidepreventionlifeline.org

NEDA: The National Eating Disorders Association is the largest nonprofit organization invested in supporting those affected by eating disorders. 1-800-931-2237
nationaleatingdisorders.org

TEEN LINE: This is a community-based organization helping troubled teens address their problems. Call 310-855-4673 or text TEEN to 839863.

teenlineonline.org

TO WRITE LOVE ON HER ARMS: This is a nonprofit movement dedicated to presenting hope and finding help for individuals struggling with depression, self-injury, addiction, and suicide.

twloha.com

ANAD: The National Association of Anorexia Nervosa and Associated Disorders is a nonprofit organization that offers support, awareness, advocacy, referral, education, and prevention.

anad.org

ACKNOWLEDGMENTS

Some Words of Thanks...

There are so many people to thank. First and foremost, you, my friend. Yes, you. The one holding this book. Because chances are, if you've read all the way to here, you have experienced in your own life some piece of Hank or Zoe's story. And we're each just doing the best we can, right?

Thank you to my amazing agent, Mollie Glick at CAA, for always pushing me to tell deeper truths. Thank you to my awesome editor, Joy Peskin at Farrar Straus Giroux, for making me dare. Thank you to Nicholas Henderson, Elizabeth Lee, Joy Fowlkes, Julie Flanagan, Hayley Jozwiak, and Chandra Wohleber.

Thank you to my faithful readers and friends—Katie, Brian, Tori, Jenny, Marcy, Roger, Kimmi, Anna, Tara, Cynthia, Marvi, Stacey, Sandra, Joselin. Thank you to the powerful women who have been with me from kindergarten—Gabra, Sara, and Sam. And Indy, who is already more woman than I'll ever be. Thank you to Mrs. Tobey and the lady in the gym. Thank you to the incredible staff at Highland Park Eating Disorders Clinic, especially Ducky. Thank you to Melanie for walking across the Brooklyn Bridge and serving me grilled cheese, whether I could eat it or not. Thank you to Alysia Reiner and Sarah Gerard for their brutal and beautiful honesty. Thank you to Pema Chödrön and Thich Nhat Hanh and Boppy and CK. Thank you to Peggy for her incredible patience and lentil soup.

Thank you to Ari and the Teenage FBI for letting me pepper them with questions.

Thank you to Sue Shapiro for her tireless motivation. Thank you to Jecca Eve, Betsy B., EmSims, and Sam A. for keeping me honest. Thank you to Tara and Sharon for beating me up. Thank you to TS. You know who you are, I hope.

Thank you to my fantastic husband, Jason, and the intervention surprise party he orchestrated. And thank you to our three extraordinary children—Sonya, Zev, and Samson—who remind me that this life is fragile and magnificent and our scars make us stronger.

Thank you.